# CYTHI

## By Joseph H

CW00866883

# I

It was, probably, Lee Randon realized, the last time he would play golf that year. He concluded this standing on a shorn hill about which the country was spread in sere diminishing tones to the grey horizon. Below, a stream held a cold glimmer in a meadow of brown, frost-killed grass; and the wind, the bitter flaws where Lee stood, was thinly scattered with soft crystals of snow. He was alone, no one would play with him so late in the season, and there had been no boy present to carry his clubs. Yes, this was the last time he'd try it until spring: Peyton Morris, who had married Lee's niece and was at least fourteen years his junior, had been justified in a refusal which, at its expression, had made Lee cross.

At worse than forty-five, he had told Morris curtly, he was more active than the young men hardly out of the universities. To this Peyton had replied that undoubtedly Lee had more energy than he; personally he felt as old as—as Egypt. Ridiculous, Lee decided, trying to make up his mind whether he might continue playing or return, beaten by November, to the clubhouse. In the end, with numb fingers, he picked up his ball, and walked slowly back over the empty course. The wind, now, was behind him, and increasingly comfortable he grew reflective:

The comparison of Peyton Morris's age with his, recalling the fact, to be precise, of his forty-seven years, created a vague questioning dissatisfaction. Suddenly he saw himself—a comfortable body in a comfortable existence, a happy existence, he added sharply—objectively; and the stout figure in knickerbockers, rough stockings, a yellow buckskin jacket and checked cap pulled over a face which, he felt, was brightly red, surprised and a little annoyed him. In the abrupt appearance of this image it seemed that there had been no transitional years between his slender youth and the present. He had an absurd momentary impression that an act of malicious magic had in a second transformed him into a shape decidedly too heavy for grace. His breathing, where the ground turned upward, was even slightly labored.

It was, Lee thought with all the intensity of an original discovery, devilish unpleasant to grow old; to die progressively on one's feet, he elaborated the fact. That was what happened to a man—his liver thickened, his teeth went, his veins became brittle pipes of lime. Worse than all that, his potency, the spirit and heat of living, met without any renewal its inescapable winter. This might, did, occur while his being was rebellious with vain hope. Today, in spite of the slight clogging of his breath, his body's loss of flexibility, his imagination was as vigorous, as curious, as ever ... take that nonsense about the doll, which, in a recalled classical allusion, he had privately named Cytherea. Peyton Morris would never have entered into that!

Lee Randon, on one of his infrequent trips to New York, had seen it in a confectioner's window on Fifth Avenue, and instantly it had captivated his attention, brought him to a halt. The doll, beautifully dressed in the belled skirt of the eighteen-forties, wore plum-colored silk with a bodice and wide short sleeves of pale yellow and, crossed on the breast, a strip of black Spanish lace that fell to the hem of the skirt. It wasn't, of course, the clothes that attracted him—he only grew conscious of them perhaps a month later—but the wilful charm, the enigmatic fascination, of the still face. The eyes were long and half closed under finely arched brows, there was a minute patch at the right corner of a pale scarlet, smiling mouth; a pointed chin marked an elusive oval beneath black hair drawn down upon a long slim neck, hair to which was pinned an odd headdress of old gilt with, at the back, pendent ornamental strands of gold-glass beads.

Insistently conventional, selectly ordinary, in appearance, the stick with a pig-skin handle hanging from his left arm, he had studied the doll with a deepening interest. Never in life, he told himself, had he seen a woman with such a magnetic and disturbing charm. Fixed in intent regard he became conscious that, strangely, rather than small the figure seemed diminished by a distance which yet left every feature clear. With this he grew satirical at himself; and, moving resolutely down the Avenue, treated his absorption with ridicule. But the vision of the face, the smile, the narrowed eyes, persisted in his mind; the truth was that they troubled him; and within three blocks he had turned. The second view intensified rather than lessened his feeling, and he walked quickly into the shop odorous with burned sugar. The doll was removed from the window—it had come from Paris, he learned—and, after a single covert glance, he bought it, for, he needlessly informed the girl wrapping it in an unwieldy light package, his daughter.

To his secret satisfaction, Helena, who was twelve, hadn't been strongly prepossessed; and the doll—though Lee Randon no longer thought of it as merely that—left downstairs, had been finally placed on the white over-mantel of the fireplace by the dining-room door.

There, when he was alone, he very often stopped to gaze at the figure; and, during such a moment of speculative abstraction, he had, from the memories of early reading, called her Cytherea. That, Lee remembered vaguely, was the Cytheranian name of the mysterious goddess of love, Venus, of the principle, the passion, of life stirring in plants and men. But in the shape above him it had been strangely modified from an apparently original purpose, made infinitely difficult if not impossible of understanding. His Cytherea bore the traces, the results, of old and lost and polished civilizations; there was about her even a breath of immemorial China. It mingled with a suggestion of Venice, the eighteenth century Venice of the princes of Naxos—how curiously she brought back tags of discarded reading!—and of the rococo Viennese court. This much he grasped; but the secret of her fascination, of what, at heart, she represented, what in her had happened to love, entirely escaped him.

Lee was interested in this, he reassured his normal intelligence, because really it bore upon him, upon the whole of his married life with Fanny. He wasn't, merely, the victim of a vagrant obsession, the tyranny of a threatening fixed idea. No, the question advanced without answer by Cytherea was not confined to her, it had very decidedly entered into him, and touched, practically, everyone he knew, everyone, that was, who had a trace of imagination. Existence had been enormously upset, in a manner at once incalculable and clear, by the late war. Why, for example, the present spirit of restlessness should particularly affect the relation of men and women he couldn't begin to grasp. Not, he added immediately, again, that it had clouded or shaken his happiness.

It had only given him the desire, the safe necessity, to comprehend the powerful emotion that held Fanny and him secure against any accident to their love. To their love! The repetition, against his contrary intention, took on the accent of a challenge. However, he proceeded mentally, it wasn't the unassailable fact that was challenged, but the indefinable word love. Admiration, affection, passion, were clear in their meanings—but love! His brow contracted in a frown spreading in a shadowy doubt over his face when he saw that he had almost reached the clubhouse; its long steep-pitched bulk lay directly across the path of dusk, approaching from the east; and a ruddy flicker in the glass doors on the veranda showed that a fire had been lighted. To his left, down over the dead sod and beyond a road, he could see the broad low façade of his house with its terraced lawn and aged stripped maples. There, too, a window was bright on the first floor: probably Fanny was hearing the children's lessons.

That cheerful interior he completely visualized: Fanny, in the nicest possible attire, sitting in the curly-maple rocking-chair, her slippered feet—she had a premonition of rheumatism—elevated on the collapsible stool she carried about with her; and Helena and Gregory hanging on her knees. Gregory, of course, had tomorrow's task easily in hand, with another star for a day's good conduct in school; but Helena, shining in the gold and flush of her radiant inattention, would know nothing. Helena, Lee Randon acknowledged, spelled atrociously. If it weren't for the clubs and his spiked shoes he'd turn and go home directly, himself supervise the children's efforts at education. But Fanny did it much better than he; Helena and Gregory were closer to her; while they volunteered endless personal and trivial admissions to her, he had to ask them, detail by detail, what they were doing.

After he had changed his shoes and secured the latticed steel door of his locker he went up to the main room of the clubhouse, where, on the long divan before the open fire, he found Peyton Morris lounging with Anette Sherwin by a low tea table. The hot water, they informed Lee comfortably, was cold, inviting him by implication to ring for more; and then they returned to the conversation he had interrupted. Anette said:

"I asked her from Friday till Monday, over the dance, you see; but she wired she couldn't be sure. They are going to begin rehearsing at any minute, and then shoot—it is shoot, isn't it?—the picture. What did she tell you at the Plaza?"

"The same thing," Peyton replied moodily. "I only saw her for a scrappy dinner; she couldn't even wait for coffee, but rushed up to a conference with her director."

They were, Lee knew, talking about Mina Raff, a friend of Anette's earlier summers by the sea who was beginning to be highly successful in the more serious moving pictures. He had met her a number of years ago, in Eastlake, but he retained no clear impression of her; and, admitting that he hadn't gone to see her in a picture, wondered aloud at her sudden fame. Peyton Morris glanced at him, frowning; he seemed at the point of vigorous speech, then said nothing.

"Mina is lovely now, Lee," Anette spoke in his place; "you will realize that at once. She's like a—a wistful April moon, or corn silk."

"I like black hair," Randon asserted.

"That's amusing, when you think Fanny's is quite brown," Anette replied. "Whom have you been meeting with black hair? There's none I can remember in Eastlake."

"There isn't anybody in particular," Lee reassured her; "it is just an idea of mine." He had a vision of intense black hair swept about an enigmatic still smile, of an old gilt headdress. "Mina Raff must have developed if she gets half the pay advertised."

"She'll get twice that when this contract expires," Peyton put in; "and that will be increased again. No one on the screen can touch her." He made these declarations in a manner both shadowed and aggressive. Lee observed that he held a cigarette in one hand and a match in the other with no effort at conjunction.

"Mina simply tells you everything," Anette continued. "If she comes you must do your best. It's perfectly marvelous, with so much else, that she even considers it. I couldn't budge her when she was practically free."

"How is Claire?" Randon abruptly demanded.

"She's all right," her husband returned; "a little offhand, but no more than usual. I want her to go to the West Indies and take Ira but she won't listen. Why anyone who doesn't have to stay through these rotten winters I can't imagine." A flaming log brought out his handsomely proportioned face, the clear grey eyes, the light carefully brushed hair and stubborn chin. Peyton was a striking if slightly sullen appearing youth—yet he must be on the mark of thirty—and it was undeniable that he was well thought of generally. At his university, Princeton, he had belonged to a most select club; his family, his prospects, even his present—junior partner in a young but successful firm of bond brokers—were beyond reproach. Yet Lee Randon was aware that he had never completely liked Peyton.

His exterior was too hard, too obviously certain, to allow any penetration of the inevitable human and personal irregularities beneath. It might be possible that he was all of a piece of the conventional stereotyped proprieties; but Lee couldn't imagine Claire marrying or holding to a man so empty, or, rather, so dully solid. Claire he admired without reservation—a girl who had become a wife, a mother, with no loss of her vivid character. Her attitude toward Ira, now four years old—wholly different from Fanny's manner with her children—was lightly humorous; publicly she treated her obligations as jokes; but actually, Lee knew, she was indefatigable.

This was a type of high spirits, of highly bred courage, to which he was entirely delivered. Fanny was a perfect mother, a remarkably fine wife, but she bore an evident sense of her responsibilities. She wasn't so good-looking as Claire, who at times was almost beautiful; but Fanny had a very decided kind of attractiveness which Lee Randon wished she would more bring out. She was a little too serious. He didn't actually want her to drink and swear in public, that wouldn't become her; but something of that sort, he felt, might help her. At times, when she had had more than her customary cocktail and a half, he saw in her a promise of what he desired.

God knew he wasn't criticizing Fanny, he hastened to reassure even himself: how could he, in the face of all she had brought him—the freedom of money and undeviating devotion and their two splendid children? His house was as absolute in its restrained luxury of taste as was the unfailing attention to his comfort. It was purely for her own happiness that he wanted her to be, well—a little gayer. She was already developing a tendency to sit serenely on the veranda of the club through the dances, to encourage others rather than take an active part herself.

Expanding in the glow of the fire and hot strong tea he forgot all about his uncomfortable premonitions of age. Now it seemed to him that he had never been younger in the sense of being merely alive; after the tonic of the cold his nerves were strung like steel, his blood was in a full tide. Lee was aware of a marked sense of pleasure at the closeness to him of Anette; settling back, she willingly, voluntarily, leaned her firm elastic body against him; her legs, as evident in woolen stockings as his own, were thrust frankly out toward the flames.

"I'll meet her," he heard Peyton say, and realized that they were still talking about Mina Raff. She wouldn't attract him, Lee Randon, in the least, he was sure of that ... no wistful April moon. What, then, did engage him? He was unable to say, he didn't know. It was something intangible, a charm without definite form; and his thoughts returned to Cytherea—if he could grasp the secret of her fascination he would be able to settle a great many disturbing feelings and needs. Yes, what she mutely expressed was what, beneath his comprehension, he had come to long for. He had never recognized it as the property of any woman nor satisfied it in himself.

Here, certainly, his loyalty, his affection for Fanny, weren't damaged; he was, he thought, beyond assault there. It was only that, together with his fidelity to his wife, an increasing uneasiness possessed him, an unabated separate interest in life, in women. He was searching for something essential, he couldn't discover what; but, dismissing the problem of how he'd act if he found it, the profound conviction remained that when his hopeful quest was over then indeed he'd die, finished, drained. Lee Randon secretly cherished, jealously guarded, that restless, vital reaching for the indefinable perfection of his hidden desire. For a flash it was almost perceptible in Anette, her head half-buried in the darkness of the divan behind the rise and fall of her breasts in a close sweater of Jaeger wool.

She stirred, smiled at him absently, and, with Peyton's assistance, rose. The long room, unlighted except for the fire, was lost in obscurity; the blackness against the window-panes was absolute. Outside, however, Lee found a lingering glint of day; the snow had stopped, but the wind had increased and was blowing over the open expanse of the course in the high gaunt key of winter. His house, across the road, showed regular cheerful rectangles of orange illumination: he always returned to it with a feeling of relief and pleasant anticipation, but he was very far from sharing Fanny's passionate attachment to their home. Away—on past trips to the Michigan iron ore fields and now on shorter journeys to eastern financial centers—he never thought of it, he was absorbed by business.

But in that he wasn't alone, it was true of the majority of successful men he knew over forty; they saw their wives, their homes, they thought of their families, only in the intervals of their tyrannical occupations. He, in reality, was rather better there than most, for he occasionally stayed out at Eastlake to play golf; he was locally interested, active, in the small town of Fanny's birth. Other men—

He made a calculation of how much time a practising lawyer saw his wife: certainly he was out of the house before nine—Lee knew lawyers who were in their offices at seven-thirty—and he was hardly back until after five. Nine hours absent daily through the week; and it was probable that he was in bed by eleven, up at seven—seven hours' sleep; of the eight hours left in twenty-four half if not two-thirds of the Sundays and some part of the others were devoted to a recreation; and this took no account of the briefcases brought home, the thought and contributary preoccupations.

More than that, his mind, his hopes and planning, were constantly directed toward his legal concerns; the wife of such a man filled about the position of his golf or billiards. Lee Randon had never analyzed this before, and the result amazed him. With younger men, of course, it was different; they had more time and interest for their homes, their wives and children. Everything constantly shifted, changed, perished; all, that was, but the unintelligible spurring need beyond any accomplishment.

In him it was almost as though there were—or, perhaps, had been—two distinct, opposed processes of thought, two different personalities, a fact still admirably illustrated by his private interest in the doll, in Cytherea. Much younger he had been fond of music, of opera and then symphony concerts, and his university years had been devoted to a wide indiscriminate reading: sitting until morning with college men of poetic tendencies, he had discussed the intricacies of conduct in the light of beauty rather than prudence. This followed him shyly into the world, the offices of the Magnolia Iron Works; where, he had told himself optimistically, he was but finding a temporary competence. What, when he should be free to follow his inclination, he'd do, Lee never particularized; it was in the clouds nebulous and bright, and accompanied by music. His dream left him imperceptibly, its vagueness killed partly by the superior reality of pig iron and ore and partly because he never had anyone with whom to talk it over; he could find no sympathy to keep it alive.

That it wasn't very robust was evident; and yet, throughout his youth, it had been his main source of incentive. No one, in the Magnolia works, knew the difference between the Glucks, Alma and Christopher, nor read anything but the most current of magazines. At intervals Lee had found a woman who responded to the inner side of him, and together they swept into an aesthetic emotional debauch; but they came inevitably, in the surrounding ugliness of thought and ascribed motives, to humiliating and ugly ends; and he drifted with increasing rapidity to his present financial and material sanity.

What remained of the other was hardly more than a rare accelerated heart-beat at a chord of music like the memory of a lost happiness, or at the sea shimmering with morning. He never spoke of it now, not even to Fanny; although it was possible that he might be doing her an understanding an injustice. Fanny, generally, was a woman in whom the best of sense triumphed; Fanny was practical. It was she who saw that the furnace pipes were inspected, the chimney flues cleaned before winter; and who had the tomato frames properly laid away in the stable. Problems of drainage, of controversies with the neighbors, were instinctively brought to her, and she met and disposed of them with an unfailing vigorous good judgment.

A remarkable companion, he told himself; he had been a fortunate man. She was at once conventional and an individual: Fanny never, for example, wore the underclothes of colored crepe de chines, the elaborate trifles, Lee saw in the shop windows, nightgowns of sheer exposure and candy-like ribbons; hers were always of fine white cambric, scalloped, perhaps, or with chaste embroidery, but nothing more. Neither did she use perfumes of any sort, there was no array of ornamental bottles on her dressing-table, no sachet among her handkerchiefs, her cambric was not laid in scented flannel. Her dressing, a little severe, perhaps—she liked tailored suits with crisp linen waists and blue serge with no more than a touch of color—was otherwise faultless in choice and order; and, it might be that she was wholly wise: Fanny was thin and, for a woman, tall, with square erectly held shoulders. Her face was thin, too, almost bony, and that magnified, emphasized, the open bright blueness of her eyes; all her spirit, her integrity and beauty, were gathered in them; her hair was pale and quite scanty.

Yes, Fanny's eyes were her principal attraction, they were forever startling, contrasted with the rest, not only remarkable in shade but, as well, in light; in her quick unreasoning tempers, the only perceptible flaw of her character, they sparkled with brilliancy. The tempers, Lee decided, descending the narrow stony road from the club-house to his gate, were an unavoidable part of her special qualities: her quick decisiveness, her sharp recognitions of right and her obdurate condemnation of wrong—these distinctions were never obscured in Fanny—necessitated a finality of judgment open to anger at any contrary position. Aside from that she was as secure, as predictable, as any heavenly orbit; her love for him, beginning before marriage, had quietly and constantly increased; her usual mood was moulded to his need; nothing had ever contested the supremacy of his place with her.

Lee swung open the white wicket that broke the middle of his border hedge and went up the path over the broad lawn; the house, an admirable copy of locally colonial dwellings, was a yellow stucco, with a porch on his left and the dining-room at the extreme right. Beyond the porch was the square of the formal garden, indistinguishable at this season, and the garage, the driveway, were hidden at the back. He mounted the broad steps of field stone at the terrace, but, in place of going directly in under the main portico, turned aside to the porch, past the dim bare forms of the old maples. Just as he had anticipated, the glass door showed him Fanny sitting in the maple slatted-back rocking-chair; Gregory, in blue, was present, but Helena not to be seen.

His wife's hands were lying idly in her lap, and she was gazing into nothingness with an expression he had never before noticed, there was a faint troubled doubt on her brow, a questioning expression about her eyes. As he stood momentarily quiet he saw her hands slowly clasp until he felt that they were rigid, and her mouth became pinched; her face seemed actually hard. Gregory spoke to her, with his fat fingers on her sleeve, but she made no reply, paid no attention to him. Lee could hear Gregory's demanding voice; and then, gathering herself, Fanny sighed deeply and smiled at her boy. She was wearing her pearls, her rings sparkled in glittering prisms; and, as he opened the door, Lee Randon wondered if he had forgotten an engagement to go out for dinner?

4

He asked at once if this were so, but found that they were staying at home. She regarded him still, he realized, a little withdrawn in the abstraction he had surprised. This, because it was so uncommon, disturbed him, and he demanded what was worrying her.

"Nothing, really. What made you suppose I was bothered?" Her reply was instinctive; and then, after a pause, she continued, more insecurely, "I was only thinking about some things.... Lee," she inquired, "you love me very much, don't you?"

"Why, of course," he spoke almost impatiently.

"That is all I have, you see," she admitted; "and that was what was in my mind. The other women I know are so different; they seem to have so many more interests than I, and to care less for them than I do for my one. It is exactly as though I belonged before the war and they came afterwards. It is true—I am old-fashioned. Well, I don't care if you don't! But, just the same, it's a problem; I don't want to be out of the times or narrow; and yet I can't, I don't know how, and I honestly don't want to, change.

"It wouldn't be any better if I smoked more cigarettes or drank more gin, that would be silly." Lee was startled by the similarity of her words to his unformed thought. "No one likes fun better than I do, but the fun now is so different," her voice had the sound of a wail, "it's nothing but legs and getting kissed by anybody but your husband. I don't want other men to kiss me, Lee, only you. And I want you to be glad about that, to care for it more than anything else. You do, don't you?"

Again she hesitated, and again he assured her, in a species of annoyance, of his feeling.

"It's because I adore you," Fanny insisted; "it may be awfully foolish and ark-like to say, but you're all I want, absolutely." Her manner grew indignant. "Some women at tea today laughed at me. They did nothing but describe how they held their husbands' affections; actually that, as though it were difficult, necessary; the details were sickening, and reminded me of that old joke about leaving off your wedding ring. It was all too horrid! And, underneath, they were bitter and vindictive, yes—they were uneasy, afraid of something, of somebody, and treated every good-looking woman as a dangerous enemy. I couldn't live like that, I'd rather die: I told them they didn't trust the men they were married to."

"What did they say to that?" Lee asked, standing in the door.

"Agreed with me. Alice Lucian said I was damned well right she didn't trust hers. She loved him, too, but she didn't propose to take any liberties with the sanctity of her bed. They all thought Claire was a fool to let Peyton see Mina Raff like that in New York—the way to avoid trouble was to make sure it couldn't begin. Has Peyton said anything to you about Mina Raff? She is perfectly stunning, of course, and an actress."

"Not to me," Lee told her; then he recalled the prolonged attention to Mina Raff on the divan at the Club. "What if he is crazy about her?" he observed indifferently; "it can't come to anything. It won't hurt Claire if Peyton sits out a few dances with a public idol."

"I shouldn't think so either, but the others were so positive. I just told them how happy we are together and how devoted you are—fifteen marvelous years, Lee. It was plain that they envied us." She rose and came close to him, her widely-opened candid blue eyes level with his gaze. "Not the slightest atom must ever come between us," she said; "I couldn't stand it, I've been spoiled. I won't have to, will I, Lee? Lee, kiss me."

He met the clinging thin passionate purity of her mouth. "No, certainly not, never," he muttered, extraordinarily stirred. He asserted to himself that he would make no such fatal mistake. The other, the errant fancy, was no more than a vagrant unimportant impulse. "Don't let these women, who cat around, upset you; probably they are thinking not so much about their husbands as they are of themselves. I've seen that Alice Lucian parked out in a limousine during a dance, and she was going right to it."

"It is foolish of me," Fanny agreed, "and not complimentary to our love. I have kept you so long over nothing that you will be late for dinner. I don't care!" Her manner bore a foreign trace of abandon in its radiant happiness; and, with spread fingers on his back, she propelled him toward the stairs. But, in their room, he failed to change his clothes: he sat lost in a concentration of thought, of summoned determination.

The interior, with dotted white Swiss curtains at the large windows, both an anomaly and an improvement on the architectural origin, was furnished largely in dull rubbed mahogany, the beds had high slender fluted posts, snowy ruffled canopies and counterpanes stitched in a primitive design. He possessed an inlaid chest of drawers across from the graceful low-boy used by Fanny as a dressing-table; there was a bed stand with brass-tipped feet, a Duncan Fyfe, she declared; split hickory chairs painted a dark claret color; small hooked rugs on the waxed floor; and, against the mirror on his chest of drawers, a big photograph of Fanny and the two children in the window-seat of the living room.

A dinner shirt lay in readiness on the bed, the red morocco boxes that held his moonstone cuff links and studs were evident, but he ignored those provisions for his ease. There was a strange, a different and unaccountable, uneasiness, a marked discomfort, at his heart. The burden of it was that he had a very great deal of which, it might well be, he wasn't worthy. In Fanny, he told himself, as against everything else discoverable, he had the utmost priceless security life could offer. Outside the brightness and warmth and charm of their house the November night was slashed by a black homeless wind.

Her sureness, undeniably, was founded on the inalterable strength of her convictions; against that sustaining power, it occurred to him, the correctness of her beliefs might be relatively unimportant. Could any more be required of a faith than its ability, like a life preserver on water, to hold an individual safe from sinking? Strangely enough, the one or two greatly powerful men with whom he had come in contact were like Fanny, prejudiced, closed against all opinions contrary to their own, impatient of doubt and self-questioning.

Fanny, Lee Randon recognized, was indefatigable in her efforts to form him in her own unassailable mould; she insisted in the most trivial, and often tiresome, ways, that he should reach and maintain her standards. He had been in return, more often than not, rebellious, humorously or with a suspicion of annoyance; but now, suddenly, it seemed to him that just that, the limitation of Fanny's determined attitude, was, perhaps, the most desirable thing possible. If it were possible of acquisition! Such a certainty wasn't his naturally—those two diverse strains in him again; but one, he added, had been practically obliterated. The first step in such a course of practical wisdom would be to put Cytherea out of his life, dislodge her finally from his thoughts, and the over-mantel downstairs. This, diplomatically with the doll, he could, of course, do now, whenever he chose. With that, and whatever it represented, accomplished, Lee had a premonition, his life would be secure, placid.

The disturbance caused by Fanny's searching tenderness subsided a little; and, as it dwindled, the other restlessness, the sense, yes—of wasted possibilities and years, once more grew evident. By God, if Fanny insisted on being, at any cost, herself, it would be unreasonable in her not to recognize the same need in him. But Lee was obliged to add the old and familiar and increasingly heavy provision: any individuality of being, of desire, must not be allowed to impair the validity of their common existence, their marriage. Fanny had an advantage over him there, for all her aspirations turned inward to their love, their home and children; and his ... but if he knew their goal he could have beaten life.


Footfalls approaching over the hall—the maid to tell him dinner was served—brought him sharply to his feet, and he hurried down to where Fanny, who liked to do such things, had finished lighting the candles on the table. In reply to the glance of interrogation at his inappropriate clothes he explained that, trivially occupied, he had been unaware of the flight of time. Throughout dinner Fanny and he said little; their children had a supper at six o'clock, and at seven were sent to bed; so there were commonly but two at the other table. He had an occasional glimpse of his wife, behind a high centerpiece of late chrysanthemums, the color of bright copper pennies and hardly larger; and he was struck, as he was so often, by Fanny's youthful appearance; but that wasn't, he decided, so much because of her actual person—although since her marriage she had shown practically no change—as from a spirit of rigorous purity; she was, in spite of everything, Lee realized, completely virginal in mind.

The way she sat and walked, with her elbows close to her body and her high square shoulders carried forward, gave her an air of eagerness, of youthful hurry. Perhaps she grew more easily tired now than formerly; her face then seemed thinner than ever, the temples sunken and cheek-bones evident, and her eyes startling in their size and blueness and prominence. She kept, too, the almost shrinking delicacy of a girl's mind: Fanny never repeated stories not sufficiently saved from the gross by their humor. Her private severity with women who did, he felt, was too extreme. The truth was that she regarded the mechanism of nature with distaste; Fanny was never lost, never abandoned, in passion—Lee Randon had wondered if she regarded that as more than a duty, the discharge of a moral, if not actually a religious, obligation. It was certain that she was clothed in a sense of bodily shame, of instinctive extreme modesty, which no situation or degree of feeling could destroy.

He understood, however, that he could not have Fanny as she was, immeasurably fine, without accepting all the implications of her character—other qualities, which he might desire, would as well bring their defects. Lee didn't for a second want a wife like Anette. His admiration for Fanny was, fundamentally, enormous. He was glad that there was nothing hidden in his life which could seriously disturb her; nothing, that was, irrevocable. Which had he been—wise or fortunate, or only trivial? Perhaps, everything considered, merely fortunate; and he wondered how she would have met an infidelity of his? He put his question in the past tense because now, Lee congratulated himself, all the danger was passed: forty-seven, with responsibilities that increased every month in importance, and swiftly growing children; the hair above his ears was patched with grey.

"I don't like that centerpiece," Fanny observed, "I can't see you. Still, it's as well, I suppose, since you didn't change. You look so much better in dark clothes, Lee, thinner."

"You shouldn't make me so comfortable."

"You'd see to that, anyhow; men always do. Honestly, Alice Lucian was a scream this afternoon, she said that she hated and distrusted all men; yet I'm sure no one could be more considerate or dependable than Warner. Now, if she had a husband like George Willard—"

"What would you do," Lee asked, "if I spent my spare time with the very young ones?"

"I'd have a doctor see you," she replied coolly. "What in the world put that in your head? Haven't you everything here a man could want? That's exactly what they were talking about; it's so—so idiotic. Those younger girls ought to be smacked and put to bed, with their one-piece swimming-suits and shimmying. They give a very misleading impression."

He lost the course of her speech in considering how little of themselves women, old and young, showed each other. If Fanny meant, if she for a moment thought, where the girls they were discussing came in, that there was smoke without fire.... It was all devilish strange, the present day, disturbing. The young men, since the war, had grown sober, and the older men resembled George Willard. The exploding of so much powder, the release of such naked passions, had over-thrown the balance of conduct and pressure. How fortunate, he thought again, he was in having Fanny.

They moved into the enclosure by the fire-place, where Cytherea was remote in shadow against the chimney, and through the hall to the living room for coffee. His wife placed the portable stool under her feet, and silence enveloped them. At intervals the clear treble of the children's voices was audible from above, and once Fanny called up for them to be quiet. The room was large, it filled that end of the lower floor, and Lee's gaze idly rested on the smoke of his cigar, veiling the grand piano in the far corner. There were no overhead lights, the plugs for the lamps were set in the baseboard, and the radiance was pleasantly diffused, warm and subdued: the dull immaculately white paint of the bookshelves on his left, silver frames on a table, harmonious fabrics and spots of color, consciously and sub-consciously spread a restful pattern. In reply to his comment Fanny acknowledged that she had seen the snow; she hated winter, she proceeded, and thought that if it turned out as bad as last year they might get away to Cuba and see Daniel.

Daniel was Lee's brother, four years his junior, an administrador of a sugar estancia in the Province of Camagüey; a man who, absorbed in his crops and his adopted Spanish-tropical civilization, rarely returned to the United States. This projected trip to Cuba they had discussed for many Novembers; every year Fanny and he promised each other that, early in February, they would actually go; and preparatory letters were exchanged with Daniel Randon; but it always came to nothing. Either it was impossible for Fanny to leave the children, the house, or the servants, or Lee's affairs were in need of close supervision.

Suddenly it annoyed him to discuss again, uselessly, Camagüey; it had become only a vain pretence, a sustained mirage, of escape from disagreeable days. While it was hot in Cuba, Daniel maintained, the trade wind coming with evening made the nights cool; it was far more comfortable, summer and winter, at La Quinta than in Eastlake. Cuba, he made it seem, Havana and the colonias of cane, the coast and the interior, was a place with none of the drawbacks of a northern land or society; there were, certainly, conventions—the Spanish were a very punctilious people—but they operated in a conveniently definite, Daniel might almost say a sensible masculine, manner. He had not gone into any further detail, but had sunk into his celebrated immobility of expression. Lee, therefore, had drawn his own, natural, conclusions; he had come to regard Cuba in the same light as that of the early Castilian adventurers—an El Dorado, but of freedom rather than gold.

A perverse restlessness settled upon him, and he put down his coffee cup abruptly; the contentment in his surroundings vanished. Lee wanted to be somewhere else, see something different, not so—so tranquil, so complacently delivered to the uneventful. Fanny, he told himself resentfully, would be satisfied to sit exactly where she was for a year. She met his fleet scrutiny with a faint smile. Her face wouldn't be greatly changed by old age, by death. She was like that, inside and out. Whirling ungracious fancies passed through his brain. He shook his head, and Fanny instantly demanded, "What is it, Lee, what is worrying you?" Nothing, he replied, but she continued to study him until, giving it up, she turned to the approaching dance; there would be a dinner at the Club before it, and forty people from out of town had accepted. They must all have a perfect time, she declared. Gregory could be heard laughing, and, with a sense of relief, of escape, he volunteered to go up and see what kept the children roused. He would only make them worse, Fanny observed, he was as fidgety as Helena; but her tone carried to him her compelling affection.

The darkened room where Helena and Gregory slept held a cold glimmering whiteness; and the light he switched on showed a most sanitary bareness and two severe iron beds. There was a moment's stillness as he entered, the scrutiny of two rosy faces framed in blanket and sheet—there were no pillows—and then there was a delighted vociferous recognition of his presence.

"You must sit on my bed," Helena insisted.

"No, mine!" Gregory cried; and, as he settled by his daughter, "For every minute you're there, father, you must sit here. Guess what I have with me." Lee Randon had no idea, and Gregory produced a willow switch. "That's for anybody who isn't good."

There was a wriggle down under the blanket, and Lee leaned forward; "Are those your feet?" he demanded; "do you go that far down, are you that tall?"

"Gracious, that's nothing," Helena cut in; "just see where I go." He discovered that her active toes were almost under the end bar of the bed. The covers were moulded by her firm body. In a few years, he thought with a constricted throat, Helena would be grown up, flung into the complex troubles of maturity. However, he knew, life wouldn't greatly upset her—she had a calmness more stolid than Fanny's together with his own sharpened sensibilities: it was probable that she would marry soon.

7

Gregory was different; while Helena, in small ways, was unamenable, he was as good as the gold stars he continually got for admirable conduct. He had a deliberate, careful mind and, already, a sense of responsibilities. He spoke slowly, giving the impression that the selection of words was a heavy business; where Helena's speech came in careless rushes. Gregory, too, Lee Randon told himself, would not be at a loss later. The two children actually demanded very little from him now beyond the love they took for granted and its obvious return. But, for his part, did he give them much, indeed, any more? Was there, Lee wondered, a deficiency in his sense of parenthood?

He knew men all of whose labor was for their children; they slaved to have comfortable sums against their children's futures; they schemed and talked, often fatuously, for and about their sons and, in lesser degree, daughters. They were, in short, wholly absorbed, no more than parents; at the advent of a family they lost individuality, ambition, initiative; nature trapped them, blotted them out; it used them for its great purpose and then cast them aside, just as corporations used men for a single task and dropped them when their productiveness was over.

But he wasn't like that, it might well be unfortunately. His personality, his peculiar needs, had survived marriage; the vague longings of youth had not been entirely killed. They were still potent and still nameless; they had refused to be gathered into a definition as exact as ambition. Lee had moved to Gregory's bed, and was holding one of the small warm hands, inattentive to the eager clamor of voices. Perhaps his ambition had vanished when he had left the first plan of his future for the more tangible second: there wasn't much in the material industry of iron founding, nor in his present wider activities, to satisfy the imagination.

Taking the place of that, he had an uncommon amount of energy, vitality, a force of some kind or other. Whatever he undertook he followed with a full vigorous sweep; he was successful in convincing a large proportion of the people with whom he dealt that their ends were the same as his; and here, as well, chance, fate, had been with Lee—no one, practically, had lost through a belief in him.

His situation today, he wholly and gladly admitted, had resulted from the money Fanny brought him. Until his marriage he had been confined to the Magnolia Iron Works; of which, it was conceivable, he would in time be manager, maybe, much later, part owner. But, with fresh resources, he tried fresh fields, investments, purchases, every one of which prospered. He owned or operated or controlled an extraordinary diversity of industries—a bottling works for nonalcoholic beverages, a small structural steel plant, the Eastlake daily paper— a property that returned forty per cent on his capital—a box works, purchased before the war, with an output that had leaped, almost over night, from thousands to millions, a well-known cigarette—

His energies, forever turning from routine paths and stereotyped preoccupations, took him vividly into countless phases of existence. He had accumulated nearly a million dollars and Fanny's affairs had benefited greatly; his administration of her money had been rigid: but—for whatever it was worth—his wife had, in liberating him from the company of the super-hot cupolas, made it all possible.

A fist, now, was softly pounding him; and Gregory's voice threatened tears. "What is it?" Lee Randon asked. "You will have to excuse me, I was thinking."

The narrative which followed, the confused history of a two and a half dollar gold-piece finally taken from Gregory by his mother, was broken into by Helena's irrepressible contempt at his youthfulness.

"He thinks the money is gone," she explained, "because Mother put it in the bank for him. I told him when he got it there would be a lot more, but he just wouldn't listen to me. No matter what anybody said it was no good."

"Well," Gregory inquired, "how much more?"

"I don't know, silly; but packs."

"Seventy-seven dollars?"

"That depends on how long you leave it in the bank," Lee instructed him. "If you didn't ask for it for twenty years—"

"But I want it next Thursday," Gregory hotly interrupted; "won't it be any bigger then?"

"He does nothing but ask and ask questions," Helena added. Lee patted Gregory's cheek:

"Don't let Helena discourage you. If I don't put the light out your mother will make me go to bed."

There were breathless delighted giggles at the thought of that absurdity. He leaned over his son. "Kiss me!" Helena cried. "Now kiss me," Gregory echoed. "Kiss me back again—"

The light went out with a sharp click, and the room was once more a glimmering darkness, blanched and cold. The ruddy faces of the children, their bright hair, even their voices, were subdued. Fanny, apparently, hadn't moved; the light at her shoulder was reflected in the cut steel buckles of her slippers; she had slight but graceful ankles. He recognized this, drawing a sheaf of reports from his brief-case; but, after a perfunctory glance, he dropped them beside him on the floor.

"Really, Lee, your condition is getting dreadful," Fanny observed; "you are too nervous for words. Go in and look at that doll you brought from New York. She ought to teach you repose even if I can't." A swift concern shadowed her eyes. "Are you doing too much, do you think? It isn't necessary, you know. We have plenty. I don't understand why you will go so hard at all those fool concerns of yours. There might be a mortgage on us, from the way you work."

8

The latter part of her speech he forgot in the calling of his attention to Cytherea. Fanny had said that the doll might tranquilize him. The opposite was more probable—Cytherea, what could be more disturbing? Fanny hadn't noticed her smile, the long half-closed eyes, the expression of malicious tenderness, if such a thing were possible, the pale seductiveness of her wrists and hands, the finger nails stained with vermilion. He tried to imagine a woman like that, warm, no—burning, with life. It seemed to Lee the doll became animated in a whisper of cool silk, but he couldn't invent a place, a society, into which she fitted. Not Eastlake, certainly, nor New York ... perhaps Cuba. What a vanity of nonsense his thoughts had led him back into: Cytherea, a thing of wax, was on the over-mantel beyond the hall; Cuba beyond the sea.

The smoke of another cigar, precisely in the manner of the one before, hung between him and the piano. His wife settled contentedly in the curly maple rocker, her rings flashing in the swift drawing of threads from a square of linen.

Early in the morning Lee Randon drove himself, in a Ford sedan, to a station on the main line of a railway which bore him into the city and his office. It was nine miles from Eastlake to the station, where he left the car for his return; and, under ordinary circumstances, he accomplished the distance in twenty minutes. The road was good and lay through open rolling country, grazing and farmed land; he knew its every aspect thoroughly, each hill and turning and old stone house, in the pale green of early spring with the flushed petals of the apple blossoms falling on the dark ploughed ground; yellow with grain; a sweeping stubble with the corn shocked in which rabbit hunters, brown like the sheaves, called to their dogs.

Now it was sombre and, in the morning and evening, wrapped in blue mist; the air had the thick damp coldness usually precipitated in snow; the cattle, gathered about the fodder spread in the fields, were huddled against the rising winds. The smoke of a chimney was flattened on a low roof; and Lee, who had sometimes wished that he were a part of the measured countryside life, had a sudden feeling of revolt from such binding circumstances. He wasn't surprised, this morning, that it was difficult to get men to work in the comparative loneliness of the farms, or that farmers' sons went continually to the cities.

When they couldn't get there they crowded into their borough towns, into Eastlake, at every opportunity, attracted by the gaiety, the lights, the stir, the contact with humanity. Before prohibition they had drunk at the hotel bars, and driven home, with discordant laughter and the urged clatter of hoofs, to the silence of star-lit fields. The buggies had gone; High Street, on Saturday night, was filled with automobiles; there was practically no drunkenness; but there was no lessening in the restless seeking stream of men, the curiosity of the women with folded hands and tightly folded lips.

They all wanted a mitigation of a life which, fundamentally, did not fill them; they had an absorbing labor, love and home and children, the church, yet they were unsatisfied. They were discontented with the primary facts of existence, the serious phases, and wanted, above everything, tinsel and laughter. If a girl passing on the street smiled boldly at such youths they were fired with triumph and happiness; they nudged each other violently and made brazen declarations which, faced by the girls, escaped in disconcerted laughter. Their language—and this, too, was a revolt—was like the sweepings of the cow barns.

Life, it occurred to Lee Randon, in this connection, was amazingly muddled; and he wondered what would happen if the restraint, since it was no better than sham, should be swept away, and men acknowledged what they so largely were? A fresh standard, a new set of values, would have to be established. But before that could be accomplished an underlying motive must be discovered. That he searched for in himself; suppose he were absolutely free, not tomorrow, that evening, but now—

Would he go to the office, to the affairs of the Zenith cigarette, and, once there, would he come home again—the four thirty-seven train and the Ford in the shed by the station? Lee couldn't answer this finally. A road led over the hills on the right, beyond a horizon of trees. He knew it for only a short distance; where ultimately it led he had no idea. But it was an enticing way, and he had an idiotic impulse to turn aside, follow it, and never come back any more. Actually he almost cut in, and he had to swing the car sharply to the left.

If he had been in trouble or debt, if his life had been a failure, he would have understood his impulse; but as it was, with Fanny and Helena and Gregory, all his flourishing affairs—why, it was insanity! However, what absorbed him in his present state of mind, of inquiry, was its honesty; nothing could be served by conventional protests and nice sentiments. Lee had long wanted to escape from life, from the accumulating limiting circumstances. Or was it death he tried to avoid?

What became clearest was that, of all the things which had happened to him, he would not, at the beginning, have deliberately chosen any. One, it seemed, bred by the other, had overtaken him, fastened upon him, while he was asleep. Lee knew a man who, because of his light strength and mastery of horses, had spent a prolonged youth riding in gentlemen's steeplechases for the great Virginia stables; a career of racing silk and odds and danger, of highly ornamental women and champagne, of paddocks and formal halls and surreptitious little ante-rooms. That he envied; and, recalling his safe ignominious usefulness during the war, he envied the young half-drunk aviators sweeping in reckless arcs above the fortified German cities.

9

Or was it, again, only youth that he lamented, conscious of its slipping supinely from his grasp? Yet, if that were all, why was he rebellious about the present, the future, rather than the past? Lee Randon wasn't looking back in a self-indulgent melancholy. Nor was he an isolated, peculiar being; yes, all the men he knew had, more or less, his own feeling; he could think of none, even half intelligent, who was happy. Each had Lee's aspect of having been forced into a consummation he would not have selected, of something temporary, hurried, apologetic.

He thought more specially of men celebrated in great industries, who had accumulated power beyond measure, millions almost beyond count—what extravagantly mad outlets they turned to! The captains of steel, of finance, were old, spent, before they were fifty, broken by machinery and strain in mid-life, by a responsibility in which they were like pig iron in an open hearth furnace. What man would choose to crumble, to find his brain paralysed, at forty-five or six? Such labor was a form of desperation, of drowning, forgetting, an affair at best an implied failure.

That was the strength, the anodyne, of drink, of cocktails, that they spread a glittering transformation about crass reality; people danced at stated times, in hot crowded rooms, because life was pedestrian; they were sick of walking in an ugly meaningless clamor and wanted to move to music, to wear pearl studs and fragile slippers and floating chiffons. "The whole damned business is a mess," he said aloud. Then, reaching the city, he threw himself with a familiar vigor into the activities he had challenged.

Returning over the familiar road, in his small closed car, he was quieter mentally, critical of his useless dissatisfaction; he was making needless trouble for himself. Small things filled his thoughts, among them the question of how much gin would be consumed by the cocktail party Fanny and he were having before the dinner dance at the Country Club. Peyton and Claire Morris, Anette and, if she came, Mina Raff, with two men, and the Lucians. Perhaps twelve in all; two quarts. The Country Club dances, principally made up of people who had known each other long and intimately, decidedly needed an impetus; society was rather dreadful without rum. Anette was an attractive girl; she had beautiful legs; but they were hardly better than Fanny's; why in the name of God was he captivated by Anette's casual ankles and indifferent to his wife's?

Women's legs—they were even no longer hidden—were only a reasonable anatomical provision exactly shared by men. Why, he particularized, did he prefer them in silk stockings rather than bare, and in black more than bright colors? Anette's had never failed to excite his imagination, but Alice Lucian's, graceful enough, were without interest for him. How stupid was the spectacle of women in tights! Short bathing skirts left him cold, but the unexpected, the casual, the vagaries of fashion and the wind, were unfailingly potential. Humiliating, he thought, a curiosity that should be left with the fresh experience of youth; but it wasn't—comic opera with its choruses and the burlesque stage were principally the extravagances of middle age.

The orange juice and square bottles of clear gin, the array of glasses and ice-filled pewter pitcher in which Lee mixed his drinks, were standing conveniently on a table in the small reception room. Fanny, in a lavender dress with a very full skirt decorated with erratically placed pale yellow flowers, had everything in readiness. "Mina Raff came," she announced, as he descended the stairs. "Anette telephoned. To be quite frank I didn't much care whether she did or didn't. She used to be too stiff, too selfish, I thought; and I never liked Anette."

"Nothing but prejudice, that," he replied decidedly. "Anette has a very good head. You have just heard stories from envious women." He was careful to say nothing about her legs. "I haven't found her the least bit out of the way; and she thinks a lot of you."

"Bosh," Fanny said inattentively; "I know what she thinks of me. I am surprised, Lee, that you do so well, because really you are nothing but an impressionable old fool." She touched him affectionately on the cheek, "But I can take care of you and Anette too."

He didn't in the slightest wish to be taken care of in the manner she indicated; yet there was nothing he could answer; and, at the sound of a motor on the drive, he turned toward the entrance at the back. It was the Lucians; and as he greeted them the whole small company swept into the house. Claire, with her narrow dark vivid face, wore diagonals of black and grey, with a long trailing girdle of soft blues and pinks. She came up at once to Lee and kissed him with a warm friendliness. "Have you seen Mina Raff?" she asked; "she's wonderful."

As Claire spoke Lee Randon saw the woman who was becoming such a noted personality. She was slim, neither tall nor short—Peyton Morris was removing a voluminous white cloak with dull red stripes and a high collar of fox. He had been wrong in his remembrance of her, for her loveliness was beyond challenge. Yes, a wistful April moon described her very well: Mina Raff was ashen blonde, her face was a very pure oval, and her large eyes, the delicate slightly drooping mouth, held an expression of devastating sweetness.

She came forward promptly, and yet with a little touching air of hesitation, and accused him, in a serious low voice, of having forgotten her. That, he returned, was ridiculous, an impossibility. Pictures of her were in all the magazines. Close by her he recognized that the sweetness was far from sugary; there were indications of a determination that reached stubbornness; already there were faint lines—skilfully covered—at the corners of her eyes, and she was palpably, physically, weary. It was that, he decided, which gave her the wistful charm. That and something more. She was considered, he knew, and by the judges best qualified, to have a very sure and perfect talent; and he had no doubt that that possession stamped and qualified her.

He was obliged to attend to the cocktails; and, at his back, a gay chatter of voices rose. He had fleeting impressions of very different people: a strange man in naval uniform with the insignia of a commander; Anette in a scanty sheath of satin from which an airy skirt spread to the left like a fan; Alice Lucian sitting on the steps with George Willard: Frank Carver remote and lost in his bitter thoughts; Elsie Wayland with the gold halo of an income almost a dollar a minute.

Mina Raff, with Peyton Morris at her shoulder, smiled at him. "What an adorable house," she pronounced; "I wish I could have it near the studio." She waved Peyton away unceremoniously, "Come, everybody has had enough drinks, and show it to me." They passed through the hall, and into the quiet of the space beyond, lighted by a single unobtrusive lamp. "What a satisfactory fireplace!" she exclaimed in her faint key, as though, Lee thought, her silent acting were depriving her of voice. She sank onto the cushioned bench against the partition. "How did they feel, do you suppose—the people, the men and women, who belonged to such things?" As Lee watched her it seemed that she grew more remote, shadowy, like a memory of long vanished beauty made before his eyes from the shifting firelight and immaterial shadows. Mina Raff lost her reality in an unreal charm that compressed his heart. The atmosphere around her stirred with re-created dead emotions. Then:

"Ah!" she cried softly, unexpectedly, "what a wonderful doll." She rose, with a graceful gesture of her hands up to where Cytherea rested. "Where did you get her? But that doesn't matter: do you suppose, would it be possible for me, could I buy her?"

"I'm sorry," Lee answered promptly; "we can't do without her. She belongs to Helena," he lied.

"But not to a child," Mina Raff protested, with what, in her, was animation and color; "it has a wicked, irresistible beauty." She gazed with a sudden flash of penetration at Lee Randon. "Are you sure it's your daughter's?" she asked, once more repressed, negative. "Are you quite certain it is not yours and you are in love with it?"

He laughed uncomfortably. "You seem to think I'm insane—"

"No," she replied, "but you might, perhaps, be about that." Her voice was as impersonal as an oracle's. "You would be better off without her in your house; she might easily ruin it. No common infidelity could be half as dangerous. How blind women are—your wife would keep that about and yet divorce you for kissing a servant. What did you call her?"

"Cytherea."

"I don't know what that means."

He told her, and she studied him in a brief masked appraisal. "Do you know," she went on, "that I get four hundred letters a week from men; they are put everywhere, sometimes in my bed; and last week a man killed himself because I wouldn't see him. You'd think that he had all a man wanted from life; yet, in his library, with his secretary waiting for him, he.... Why?" she demanded, questioning him with her subdued magic.

"Have you ever cared for any of them?" he asked indirectly.

"I'm not sure," she replied, with an evident honesty; "I am trying to make up my mind now. But I hope not, it will bring so much trouble. I do all I can to avoid that; I really hate to hurt people. If it happens, though, what can you do? Which is worse—to damage others or yourself? Of course, underneath I am entirely selfish; I have to be; I always was. Art is the most exhausting thing that is. But I don't know a great deal about it; other people, who act rather badly, can explain so fully."

From where Lee sat he could see Cytherea; the unsteady light fell on the gilt headdress, the black hair and the pale disturbing smile. She seemed to have paused in a slow graceful walk, waiting, with that wisdom at once satirical and tender, for him. Together, slowly, deliberately, they would move away from the known, the commonplace, the bound, into the unknown—dark gardens and white marble and the murmur of an ultramarine sea. He was rudely disturbed by the entrance of Anette and Peyton Morris. "We're so sorry," Anette said in an exaggerated air of apology; "come on away, Peyton." But the latter told Lee that Fanny was looking for him. "We are ready to go over to the Club; it's ten minutes past eight."

Mina Raff gazed up at the doll. "I have an idea the devil made you," she declared.

"You are to go with us, Mina," Peyton told her; "if you will get your cloak—" The two women left, and Morris demanded:

"What was that damned rot about the doll?"

"Miss Raff wanted it."

"Well, why not?"

Lee Randon turned away coldly. "Little girls can't have everything they put their eyes on." Morris muttered, and Lee asked, "What's that?" The other failed to reply, but his remark had sounded remarkably like, "She can." Going, Lee looked back involuntarily: he hadn't, after all, imagined Cytherea's quality, Mina Raff had recognized it, too; the dance had lost its attraction for him.

The automobiles started in a concentration of accelerated gasoline explosions, their headlights sweeping across the house and plunging into the farther night. Fanny gathered her wrap closely about her throat. "I'm cold," she asserted; "it was so nice at home, with the children, and plans—I intend to take out that yellow rambler and try a climbing American beauty rose there. What a lovely dress of Anette's; it must be the one she's been talking about so much, that Miss Zillinger made; really good for Eastlake. What was that man's name who was in the navy, and did you notice his rank? The officers of the navy are a lot better looking than army men. And Mina Raff, after all did you find her interesting?"

"Quite. She struck me as very intelligent." He had no wish to repeat the conversation about Cytherea. It was queer, that; the more he considered it the more significant it appeared to be. "Did it seem to you," he asked, "that Peyton was very attentive?"

"I didn't have time to notice. Do you think it's true about her getting all that money? It looks almost wicked to me, with so many people needing just a little. But anybody could see that she thinks only of herself; I don't mean she isn't charitable, but in—in other ways."

They were late, and the main floor was being emptied of a small crowd moving into the dining-room. There the long table of the club dinner reached from end wall to wall; and, with the scraping of chairs, a confusion of voices, the places were filled. Lee found himself between Bemis Fox, a younger girl familiar enough at the dances but whose presence had only just been recognized, and Mrs. Craddock, in Eastlake for the winter. Anette was across the board, and her lips formed the query, "The first dance?"

Lee Randon nodded; he was measurably fond of her; he usually enjoyed a party at which he found Anette. That she liked him was very evident; not desperately, but enough to dispose of most restraint; she repeated to Lee what stories, formal and informal, men told her, and she asked his advice about situations always intimate and interesting.

The flood of voices, sustained on cocktails, rose and fell, there were challenges down the length of the table and quickly exchanged confidences. Bemis, publicly ingenuous, laid a light eager hand on his arm, and Mrs. Craddock answered a question in a decided manner. The dinner, Lee saw, was wholly characteristic of the club and its members: they had all, practically, known each other for years, since childhood; meeting casually on the street, in the discharge of a common living, their greetings and conversation were based on mutual long familiarity and recognized facts; but here, at such dances, they put on, together with the appropriate dress, a totally other aspect.

An artificial and exotic air enveloped whatever they did and said—hardy perennials, Lee thought, in terms Fanny's rather than his, they were determined to transform themselves into the delicate and rare flowers of a conservatory. Women to whom giggling was an anomaly giggled persistently; others, the perfect forms of housewife and virtue, seemed intent on creating the opposite engaging impression; they were all seriously, desperately, addressed to a necessity of being as different from their actual useful fates as possible.

The men, with the exception of the very young and the perpetually young, were, Lee Randon knew, more annoyed than anything else; there was hardly one of them who, with opportunity, would not have avoided the dinner as a damned nuisance; scarcely a man would have put his stamp of approval on that kind of entertainment. It was the women who engineered it, the entire society of America, who had invented all the popular forms of pleasure; it was their show, for the magnifying of their charms and the spectacle of their gay satins and scented lace; and the men came, paid, with a good humor, a patience, not without its resemblance to imbecility. Women, Lee continued, constantly complained about living in a world made by men for men; but the truth of that was very limited: in the details, the details which, enormously multiplied, filled life, women were omnipotent. No man could withstand the steady friction, the inexhaustible wearing, of feminine prejudice; forever rolled in the resistless stream of women's ambition, their men became round and smooth and admirable, like pebbles. This, he saw, in Fanny's loving care, was happening to him: she had spun him into the center of a silken web—

"You are not very polite," Mrs. Craddock said.

"Are you a mind-reader," he replied, "or haven't I heard you?"

"It doesn't matter," she explained, "but you were so far away."

He told her something of what had been in his thoughts, and she rewarded him with a swift speculative interest. "I hadn't realized you were so critical about your guinea hen," she acknowledged. "Well, if what you say is true, what can you do about it?"

"Nothing," Lee returned non-committally; "I am comfortable." This, he instantly decided, sounded unfair to Fanny, and he substituted happy. Mrs. Craddock obviously was not interested in the change. "I get as tired of this as you do," she asserted abruptly; "it's like being on a merry-go-round someone else started and can't stop. You have no idea how we get to hate the tunes."

"But you mustn't forget the chance of catching a gold ring," he reminded her.

"It's brass," Mrs. Craddock asserted.

The orchestra began in the other room and, though dinner was not over, there were breaks in the table, couples dancing beyond. Anette rose, and Lee Randon, taking her into his arms, swept out from the doorway. "What was she talking about?" Anette demanded. "You," he replied experimentally. "I like her; experience has brought her some wisdom; and she knows men, too."

12

"God knows she ought to," Anette's face was close to his, and he caught the flash of malice in her eyes. Conscious of the flavor of an acceptable flattery he didn't let this disturb him. "What a marvelous dance," she proceeded; "there must be twenty men over. But I like it better when the porch isn't inclosed, and you can sit on the bunkers."

How was it that she contrived to make nearly everything she said stir his imagination? Anette had the art of investing the most trivial comments with a suggestion of license. It was a stimulating quality, but dangerous for her—she was past thirty with no sign of marriage on the horizon. He wondered if she really had thrown her slipper over the hedge? It wasn't important, Lee decided, if she had. How ludicrous it was to judge all women, weigh their character, by the single standard of chastity. But this much must be admitted, when that convention of morality was broken it had no more significance than the fragments of a coconut shell. The dance came to an end and they returned to their vanilla mousse, coffee and cigarettes.

Some of the men were leaning over the table, drunk and noisy; a woman's laugh was shrill, senseless. Senseless! That, for Lee Randon, described the whole proceeding. He had looked forward to the dance with a happy anticipation, and, now that it was here, even before he had come, he was out of key with it. The efforts of the people about him to forget themselves were stiff and unconvincing; their attitudes were no more than masks held before their faces; there wasn't a genuine daring emotion, the courage of an admitted thrill, to be found. And then, as if to mock his understanding, he saw Peyton Morris with such a desperately white face bent over Mina Raff that he had an impulse to reprove him for his shameless exposure.

Instead, he cut in on their dancing and carried her to the other end of the floor. "I don't know why you did that," she complained; "you don't like me. But you can dance, and with Peyton it's a little like rushing down a football field. There! Shall we drop the encore and go outside? My wrap is on a chair in the corner."

"I don't go to parties," she explained; "I am only here on Anette's account. That was Oscar Hammerstein's idea—he wouldn't let his actresses even ride in a public car; he said that mystery was a part of their value, and that people wouldn't pay to see them if they were always on the streets. Beside, I am tired all the time; you can't possibly know how hard I work; a hundred times harder than you, for instance."

"I've been told that about moving pictures."

"The glare of the silver-foil reflectors is unbearable," she looked up, with a pointed and famous effect. "But you don't like me?"

"I do; aside from that, though, I'm not sure; probably because you are so remote and cold."

"Thank God!" she replied. "You haven't stopped to think where I'd be if I weren't. And yet, no one, in their work, is supposed to be more emotional. It's funny, and I don't pretend to understand. The trouble with me is that I have no life of my own: ever since I was sixteen I've done what directors told me, for the public; it is time I had some private feelings."

"It must be a nuisance," he agreed.

Another dance began, but neither of them stirred; from where Lee sat the long doors were panels of shifting colors and movement. The music beat, fluctuated, in erratic bars. A deep unhappiness possessed him, an appalling loneliness that sometimes descended on him in crowds. Even Fanny, the thought of his children, could not banish it. Above the drum he thought he could hear the sibilant dissatisfaction of the throng striving for an eternity of youth. The glass about the porch, blotted with night, was icy cold, but it was hot within; the steam pipes were heated to their full capacity, and the women's painted and powdered faces were streaked—their assumption of vitality and color was running from them.

"Hideous," Mina Raff said with a small grimace. She had the strange ability of catching his unexpressed thoughts and putting them into words. "Women," she went on, "spend all their money and half their lives trying to look well, and you'd suppose they would learn something, but they don't."

"What do women dress for?" he demanded; "is it to make themselves seductive to men or to have other women admire and envy them?"

"Both," she answered, "but mostly it's a sort of competition with men for the prize. I'll tell you something about us if you like—we are not made of sugar and spice and other pleasant bits, but only of two: prostitute and mother. Not, of course, separately, or in equal parts; some of us have more of one, others more of the other. That girl across the table from you is all prostitute, the married woman you were talking to is both, quite evenly divided; your wife is a mother, even with her remarkable eyes." She stopped his obvious inquiry:

"I am an artist, and no one has yet discovered what that is. Do you remember the straw you used to get with a glass of soda water? You see, often I think I'm like that, a thing for bright colors to pour through. It's very discouraging. There is Peyton, and he'll want to dance." She rose, slipping out of her cloak.

Lee Randon saw Fanny not far away, and he dropped into a chair beside her. "Well," he asked, "how is it going?"

"It seems all right," she told him, with one of her engaging smiles. "I was surprised that you talked so long to Mina Raff; I had the idea you didn't like her." Women, he reflected, were uncanny. "Three women are just plastered up in the dressing-room," she continued; "Sophie Tane ruined her dress completely, and Crystal Willard has been sobbing for an hour. Lee, there are horrid bruises on her arm—do you think he is brutal?"

He told her not to bother about the Willards, and then rose to get a chair for Claire Morris. "Peyton is simply fascinated," Claire asserted lightly. "This Mina ought to have something handsome for giving him such a splendid time. She is a lovely wench, Lee."

"You have it over her like a tent, Claire," he insisted; "you're lovely and human both."

"Thank you, darling; I'm human, fast enough, now that the drink is dying. I believe for the first time in my life I am ready to leave a dance before the last flourish of the music. Fanny, we are getting older; it's hideous but so. We're getting on, but our young men are gayer every day."

Fanny Randon's smile, her expression, were secure.

This made Lee restive, and, patting her hand, he left to dance with Alice Lucian. "When this is over," she informed him, "we'll get Anette and George, and go out to my car. There is a Thermos bottle of cocktails hidden under the seat." The girl who had sat at Lee's right was dancing with a tall fair-haired boy in a corner. Entirely oblivious of the rest of the room, they were advancing two matched steps and then retreating, their eyes tightly shut and cheeks together. A man fell in the middle of the floor, catching his partner's skirt and tearing it from the waistband. Everywhere the mad effort at escape!

Lee Randon lost his impression of the triviality of the occasion: they all seemed desperately searching for that something he had lost and which was overwhelmingly important to him; and all the while the music stuttered and mocked and confused a tragic need. Or it was like a momentary release from deadly confinement, a respite that, by its rare intoxication, drove the participants into forms of incredulous cramped abandon. Positively, he thought, they were grasping at light, at color, at the commonplace sounds of a few instruments, as though they were incalculable treasures. Alice, when she danced, held her head back with eyes half closed; and suddenly, with her mouth a little parted, she, too, had a look of Cytherea, a flash of the withheld beauty which filled him with restlessness.

It startled him, and, sub-consciously, his arm tightened about her. She responded immediately, with an accelerated breath, and the resemblance was gone. Greatly to his relief, a man cut in on them, and once more he found himself dancing with Anette. She asked him, in a murmurous warmth, if he liked her, at all. And, with a new and surprising, a distasteful, sense of lying, he replied that he did, tremendously. No, a feeling in him, automatic and strange, responded—not Anette! He wanted to leave her, to leave everyone here, and go. For what? At the same time he realized that he would stay, and go out, drink, in the Lucians' car. He had a haunting impression, familiar to him in the past weeks, that he was betraying an essential quality of his being.

Yet along with this his other consciousness, his interest in Anette, lingered; it existed in him tangibly, a thing of the flesh, not to be denied. She was all prostitute, Mina Raff had said, using the word in a general sense rather than particularly, without an obvious condemning morality. Indeed, it might easily be converted into a term of praise, for what, necessarily, it described was the incentive that forever drove men out to difficult accomplishment, to anything rather than ease. Good or bad, bad or good—which, such magic or maternity, was which?

"What are you thinking about?"

"It would take years to tell you."

"I wish ... you might; but I didn't mean to say that, to let you know—"

"You didn't let me know anything," he broke into her period impatiently. "If we get on together isn't that enough? It's really not necessary to hide ourselves behind a lot of pretentious words. And what we feel tonight hasn't a thing to do with tomorrow; probably then we'll be entirely different; how can it matter?"

"It does, though, because you might hate me tomorrow for being myself tonight. What you think of me has to be big enough to guard against that. You hurt me, Lee, very much, talking in that way."


Alice Lucian, with George Willard, passed them and nodded significantly toward the entrance. "You will need a cloak," Lee told Anette; "it's blowing colder and colder." She vanished up the stairs, to the dressing-rooms, while Lee stood waiting with Willard. He didn't especially like the latter, a man with an exuberant loud friendliness, a good nature, that served as a cover for a facilely predatory sensuality.

He was continually taking hold of feminine arms, bending close over dinner dresses; and he used—with a show of humorous frankness—his long knowledge of the girls of Eastlake as a reason for kissing them on every possible occasion.

Anette and Alice appeared, with their wraps turned to exhibit the silk linings, bright like their dresses; and, at a favorable moment, they slipped out into the malice of the wind beating on them from the darkness. Anette was pressed tightly against Lee, Alice and George Willard were vaguely ahead; and, after a short breathless distance, they were in the protection of the shed. The Lucians' automobile had an elaborate enclosed body: shutting the doors they were completely comfortable, unobserved and warm. "No," Alice directed, "don't put on the light; I can find it. There! We'll have to use the cap for a glass." The aluminum top of the bottle was filled and refilled; the frigid gin and orange juice brought Lee Randon a glow of careless well-being, irresponsibility.

The others had gone to the front seat, where they were squeezed into a remarkably small space. Anette sat leaning forward, her chin propped in her left hand and the right lightly resting on Lee's knee. A loose board in the shed kept up an exasperating clatter. A match flared and Willard lighted a cigarette. It was curious about Alice—only in the last year, and for no reason Lee could discover, had she done things such as this. Perhaps, with no children, and the money Warner had accumulated comparatively lately, she hadn't enough to do. Of course, Warner, a splendid individual, could not be called entertaining; he was totally absorbed in his business, often away at the wood-pulp mill, in the Laurentian Mountains, in which he had a large interest.

Warner Lucian had nearly all the principal virtues—integrity, generosity, courage, and he was as single in mind as Willard was dubious; but, in spite of so much, it was clear that he had begun to weary Alice. She was publicly indifferent to him, careless of his wishes; she had even complained to Lee about her husband's good conduct, explaining that if he would only have what she termed an affair he would be more human.

"I am still very cross at you." Anette spoke out of a gloom in which her face was barely distinguishable. "You took all the niceness out of our friendship and made it seem horrid; just as though you had pulled off my clothes; I—I haven't the same feeling about you."

His effort at honesty, at discovering the mystery of profound disturbing needs, had been vain. Gathering Anette in his arms Lee kissed her. She rested there for a moment; then, with her hands against his chest, pushed him away. "I can't, now," she told him; "somehow it's all spoiled. It seemed as though you were studying me disapprovingly. I'm not just bad, you know."

"I don't think you are bad at all," he replied irritably; "you brought that into it. Why, in the name of heaven, should I?"

"Fanny doesn't like me," she said at a tangent.

"Who put that in your head?"

"Fanny. She's hardly civil."

"If you mean she's jealous, she isn't."

"You hardly need to add that. Of course, I realize Fanny Randon couldn't be jealous of me. Good Lord, no! Why should she be? No one would give me a thought."

Anette, wholly irrational, was furious. Damn women, anyway! It was impossible to get along with them, since they hadn't a grain of reason. He was superior to her temper, indifferent to it, because he was indifferent to her. Suddenly the charm she had had for him was gone, the seductiveness dissolved, leaving only Anette, a fairly good-looking girl he had known for a great while. His warm response to her was dead; whatever she had aroused and satisfied, or left in suspense, no longer contented him. The memory of his interest in her, the thought he had expended, was now a cause of surprise, incomprehensible. Lee wanted to return to the club house and Fanny.

There was an obscure indication of Alice's hands raised in the rearrangement of her hair. George Willard half turned, facing the rear of the car. "I can't see much," he said, "but it is evident that you two have been fighting. Why don't you live in peace and happiness? The trouble's all with Lee, too, you don't have to tell me that, Anette; he is too cursed cantankerous; and it would serve him right if you'd come up here with us."

Anette opened the door and an icy draft swept about their knees. "Not yet," Willard begged; "we won't be missed."

"You may stay as long as you want," Anette replied, "but I am going back." Positively her voice bore a trace of tears. What, what was it all about? It was Alice who decided that they should return together: "The bottle's empty, my hair net is fixed for the third time, and we had better. You get out, George, please. No, I told you."

Lee Randon welcomed the solid rushing of the wind; it swept in full blast across the open of the golf course and made walking precarious. Anette was lost, forgotten. If the chill air could only take the fever, the desire, out of his mind and blood! He wished that he might be absorbed into the night, the storm, become one with its anonymous force, one with the trees he heard laboring on their trunks. Instead of the safety of being a part of nature he felt that, without directions, he had been arbitrarily set down on earth, left to wander blindly with no knowledge of his destination or its means of accomplishment.

Fragments of a dance measure were audible, and he returned to the pounding music, the heat, the perceptibly chlorinated perfumes and determined activity. He went at once in search of his wife; she had apparently not moved from the chair in which he had left her. Meeting her slightly frowning, questioning expression he told her simply, without premeditation or reserve, that he had been out in an automobile. Fanny was obviously not prepared for his candor, and she studied him with the question held on her lifted face. Then banishing that she proceeded to scold him:

"You know how I hate you to do such things, and it seems precisely as though my wish were nothing. It isn't because I am afraid of how you'll act, Lee; but I will not let you make a fool of yourself. And that, exactly, is what happens. I don't want women like Anette to have anything on you, or to think you'll come whenever they call you. I can't make out what it is in your character that's so—so weak. There simply isn't any other name for

15

it. I don't doubt you, Lee," she repeated, in a different, fuller voice, "I know you love me; and I am just as certain you have never lied to me. I'm sure you haven't, in spite of what the girls say about men."

He was cut by an unbearably sharp, a knife-like, regret that he had ever, with Fanny, departed from the utmost truth. Lee Randon had a sudden vision, born of that feeling returning from the shed, of the illimitable tranquility, the release from all triviality, of an honesty beyond equivocation or assault. Fanny, in her way, possessed it; but that, he saw, was made vulnerable, open to disaster, through her love for him. It was necessary, for complete safety, to be entirely insulated from the humanity of emotions. That condition he instinctively put from his thoughts as being as undesirable as it was beyond realization. Lee, with all his vitality, drew away from a conception, a figure, with the cold immobility of death. After all, he reassured himself, he had never essentially lied to Fanny; he had merely suppressed some unnecessary details in order to make their existence smoother. The welcome collapse of his small affair with Anette proved the wisdom of avoiding the exaggeration and difficulty of explanations.

"Lee," Fanny said, changing the direction of their thoughts, "I don't want to bother you, but I am uneasy about Claire and Peyton. He hasn't left Mina Raff a minute this evening. And he has such an unhappy expression, not at all as though he were enjoying himself."

"I noticed that," Lee agreed; "but it will do him no good with Mina—she's a cold potato, career's the only thing in her head." Then he remembered what Mina Raff had told him about her individuality, her personal desire; and he repeated it to his wife.

"I don't think Claire is entirely wise," she went on; "but you can't tell her a thing. She listens as sweetly as possible and then says that she won't interfere with Peyton. Well, someone else will. Claire has too much reserve, she is too well-bred and quietly superior. You wait and see if I am not right; life is very vulgar, and it will take advantage of her."

"I wonder if you are? Well, as you say, we shall see. If Mina Raff fixes her mind on him there will be a lot to watch."

"You must speak to him."

"Now there," Lee expostulated, "you make me sick. How—will you tell me—can I speak to Peyton until he first says something? And when that happens, as easily as not it may be a cable from Peru. You want to interfere too much, Fanny, and insist that everybody follow your idea of right."

She retired into a silence of wisdom that merely looked down on him. Her face was troubled, her lips tightly compressed. "What time is it?" she asked sharply; "the ribbon of my watch is worn out. Oh, we can go home with decency. It makes me rather sick here."

He went below, for his hat and coat, and found the room beyond the lockers, built as an informal café before the era of prohibition, occupied by a number of men transferring the balance of fulness from a row of bottles to themselves.

He accepted a drink, more for the purpose of considering Peyton Morris, moodily abstracted by the table, than for itself. It seemed to Lee that the young man had actually aged since the cocktail party at his house, earlier in the evening. Peyton's mouth was hard and sullen; his brow was corrugated. "We're going home," Lee told him; "and it seemed to me that an hour ago Claire was tired."

"She didn't tell me," Peyton responded punctiliously; "and certainly if she's low we'll go too." He rose promptly, and, with his outer garb, accompanied Lee Randon. His step was uncertain, and Lee put a hand under his elbow. "Liquored?" he asked casually.

"Not in my brain," Peyton Morris returned: "it seems like I could never get drunk again; but my dam' feet are all over the place. Thanks for hanging on to me: I have an idea you are going to drop me pretty quickly."

"I don't want to question you," Randon said, "or in any way force a confidence, but, Peyton, in addition to the relationship, I am exceptionally fond of Claire; and, since helping you is practically the same thing as helping her—"

"I wish to Christ I had been sunk in the North Sea," Morris broke in bitterly.

They were up the stairs and standing on the emptied floor of an intermission. Fanny, prepared to leave, was gazing about for him. "You've been an age," she cried to Lee; "and, Peyton, Claire is at last looking for you; although she'd kill me for saying it. You had better go outside a minute, first, and clear your head."

He came very near to her, slightly swaying. "Fanny, you are a darling, but you are hard; you are hard as the Commandments."

"That is not very kind, Peyton," she protested; "but I have some common sense."

"Haven't you any uncommon sense?" he begged. "That's what I want. A little just now might save everything."

"You must try to find out," she informed him; "I think I have been successful with Lee; anyhow he ought to say so."

"I do," Lee Randon asserted quickly. "Fanny is wonderful. If I'm of no use go to her."

"You don't know," Peyton muttered; "you can have no idea."

"What in the world was he talking about?" she asked Lee in the automobile.

"Peyton is in love with Mina Raff," he admitted shortly, in a pressure of conflicting emotions.

"Lee!" she exclaimed; "are you sure? Did he say so? That is simply frightful."

"I imagine it's worse than you realize."

"Do you mean—"

"Nothing actual yet," he interrupted her impatiently; "perhaps nothing you would bother about. But you'd be wrong. It's all in his thoughts—some damned spoiled ideal, and as dangerous as possible."

"Poor Claire," she said.

"Of course, that's the thing to say," he agreed. "The man is always a criminal in such situations."

"You are not trying to defend him?" she asked quietly.

"Maybe I am; I don't know. After all, we are jumping at conclusions; Peyton was drunk. But, for heaven's sake, if either of them comes to you don't just be moral. Try to understand what may have happened. If you lecture them they will leave you like a shot."

Fanny was driving, and she moved one hand from the wheel to his cheek. "It isn't us, anyhow, Lee; and that is really all I care for. We are closer than others, different. I don't know what I'd do if you should die first— I couldn't move, I couldn't go on."

"You would have the children," he reminded her.

"They are nothing compared with you." It was the only time she had made such an admission, and it moved him profoundly. It at once surcharged him with gratitude and an obscure disturbance.

"You mustn't pin so much to me," he protested; "you ought to think of a hundred other things."

"I would if I could; I often try, but it is impossible. It is terrible to care for a man the way I do for you; and that's why I am so glad you are what you are: silly at times, ridiculously impressionable, but not at all like George Willard, or Peyton Morris."

He had an overwhelming impulse to explain himself in the most searching unsparing detail to Fanny, the strange conviction that in doing it he would anticipate, perhaps escape, grave trouble. Lee Randon realized, however, that he would have to begin with the doll, Cytherea; and the difficulty, the preposterousness, of trying to make that clear to his wife, discouraged and kept him silent. No woman, and least of any the one to whom he was married, could be trusted to understand his feeling, his dissatisfaction in satisfaction, the restlessness at the heart of his peace.

Fanny went up at once, but he lingered, with a cigar, in the living room. A clock struck one. A photograph of Claire with her bridesmaids, Peyton and his ushers, on a lawn, in the wide flowered hats of summer and identical boutonnières, stood on a table against the wall; and beyond was an early girlish picture of Fanny, in clothes already absurdly out of mode. She had a pure hovering smile; the aspect of innocence time had been powerless to change was accentuated; and her hands managed to convey an impression of appeal. He had been, in the phrase now current, crazy about her; he was still, he told himself strictly. Well, he was ... yet he had kissed Anette; not for the first time, either; but, he recognized, for the last. He was free of that! A space, a phase, of his life was definitely behind him. A pervading regret mingled with the relief of his escape from what he had finally seen as a petty sensuality. The little might, in the sequence, be safer, better, than the great. But he vigorously cast off that ignominious idea. A sense of curious pause, stillness, enveloped Lee and surprised him, startled him really, into sitting forward and attentive. The wind had dropped, vanished into the night and sky: the silence without was as utter as though Lee Randon were at the center of a vacuum.

## II

On Saturday morning Lee telephoned to his office, found nothing that required his immediate attention there and, the brief-case again in evidence, stayed at Eastlake. Fanny, too, with her hair severely plain and an air of practical accomplishment, was occupied with her day book. She kept this faithfully; but Lee couldn't decide whether the obvious labor or her pleasure in the accomplishment were uppermost. She addressed the day book with a frowning concentration, supplementary additions and subtractions on stray fragments of paper, which at times brought him with an offer of assistance to her shoulder. But this she resolutely declined—she must, she insisted, maintain her obligation along with his. However, Fanny, like all other women, he thought, was entirely ignorant of the principle of which money was no more than a symbol: she saw it not as an obligation, or implied power, but as an actuality, pouring from a central inexhaustible place of bright ringing gold and crisp currency.

However, Fanny had always been accustomed to the ease of its possession, familiar with it; and that had stamped her with its superiority of finish. How necessary, he continued, money was to women; or, rather, to the women who engaged his imagination; and women were usually the first consideration, the jewelled rewards, of wealth. As he visualized, dwelt on, them, their magnetic grace of feeling and body was uppermost: sturdy utilitarian women in the kitchen, red-faced maids dusting his stairs, heavily breasted nurses, mothers, wives at their petty accounts—he ended abruptly a mental period escaping from the bounds of propriety. What he meant, all that he meant, was that beauty should be the main consideration. Lee applied himself to far different values; and, before he had finished, lunch was ready.

"I have been thinking half the morning about Claire and Peyton," Fanny told him; "I do feel that we exaggerated the situation last night; it all seemed more immediate, bigger, than it will turn out. Heavens, as you said, they can't do anything, nothing can happen."

He was still inclined to believe that. "There is a tremendous lot of talk and no result; yes—no one really does a thing. They want to, and that's all it comes to."

Fanny cast a glance of repressed attention at him across a lower center-piece. "If you could be whatever you wanted, what and where, what would you choose?" she asked.

"Here, with you and the children," his voice replied without hesitation. The youth of her expression was happily stained by a flush. He meant it, Lee told himself sharply. But about Peyton—

"Of course, he was drunk last night, and he said nothing conclusive; he was only wretchedly unhappy—wished he had been killed in the war and all the romantic rest."

"It is too much for me," Fanny decided generally; "but I am glad that I was young when I was; being alive was quite simple then. I am comparatively young, Lee, 'way under forty—well, two years—but you can't realize how things have changed in such a short while. The women we knew didn't even smoke then. Wasn't it only five or six years ago they were first allowed to in nice cafés? And, not simply that, men didn't, either, when they were with us. We used to go to Cape May; they called the dances hops; and do you, oh, do you, remember the bathing suits?"

"I am not so certain about any great change," he objected. "I seem to recall—"

"Horrid people will always be horrid!" she exclaimed. "I knew one or two very fast girls; but they were different about it from now, it was only whispered around and condemned, and it's shouted out today. I wish I had known you sooner; I would have done a lot better than your mother. I'd like to have had you, Lee, as a little boy; but I suppose you're enough that yet."

His opposition to Fanny's maternal manner, directed at him, was stronger than customary; she seemed to accept in herself every responsibility for him; as though, whenever his actions were unfortunate, it had been due to her imperfect control. With practically no experience of life, guarded from its threatening aspects, her attitude was that, not without patience, she brought him with relative safety through a maze in which otherwise he'd be lost. This was evident now in what he felt to be the complacency of her voice and expression; and a perverse impulse grew in him to combat and shatter her blind satisfaction. Lee subdued this, in the merest decency; but the effort left him thoroughly irritated. He found, finally, an outlet for his annoyance in the restlessness of Helena; and he ordered her from the table.

This show of paternal discipline Fanny met with lowered eyes and a silence that endured until Gregory had walked sedately from the room; then she reminded Lee that he must never, absolutely never, correct his children when he was in an ill temper.

"That's nonsense," he returned shortly; "you ought to see that because it's impossible. Even theoretically I don't agree with you—a child can understand a punishment in which there is some warmth. You are dealing with a little animal and not a reasonable being." To this Fanny replied that her children were not animals.

"Really, Fanny, you don't know what you are talking about," he asserted; "we are all, men and women and children and giraffes, animals. You might look that up in the dictionary."

"I haven't any need to," she observed, with a calmness that further tried him. "If the dictionary says that it isn't a very good one. And if you are trying to tell me that Helena and Gregory are no better than giraffes you're sillier than usual."

"That isn't in the least what I said," Lee retorted, with widely separated words. "I wasn't speaking of the comparative but of the absolute. It is a fact that we are animals, more responsible and with greater powers than the others, but animals, animals."

"Then what is an animal?" Fanny demanded.

"A mammal."

A marked expression of distaste invaded her. "It has a nasty sound," she admitted with her instinctive recoiling from life. "I don't see how we got on this subject anyhow, it's too much like sex. It seems you are able to discuss nothing else."

"It is only nasty in your mind," he declared.

"That's exactly like you, you all over, to blame things on me. It's convenient, I must say, but not fair nor true: it was you who got in a wicked temper and sent Helena, who was feeling miserable, away."

"You always say the children are sick when they misbehave."

"I wish I could be as sure of you as I was of that," she answered quickly; "for instance, when you go out in automobiles at the dances with women."

"Now, we are beginning," he told her with emphasis; "we never had an argument that didn't degenerate into this; and I'm sick of it."

"I thought I was the one who was sick of it," Fanny complained; "I wonder that I don't just let you go."

"I wish you would," he said, rising; "I give you my word, I'd rather be damned comfortably than have this endless trouble." In a position of unassailable quiet behind his papers he told himself that the scene with Fanny had been particularly vain because, underneath, he agreed with her opinion about the casual expression of small emotions; he no longer wanted it any more than she did. Yes, at last they were one there. And yet he felt further from her even than before—whatever his marriage hadn't satisfied, that he had stilled in minor ways, was now without check. The truth was that it had increased, become more serious, insistent.

The tangible facts, the letters and memoranda, before him, retreated and came back to his consciousness. Tobacco worms had been boring through his cigars, and destroyed a third of the box. Helena passed, affecting a grievance out of any proportion to its cause in him. Outside, the country was flooded with a deceptive golden radiance; and he remembered, suddenly, that Alice Lucian had told him to bring Fanny to the Club and a tea that afternoon, which she was giving for Mina Raff. He repeated this to his wife, in a conciliatory regret at his forgetfulness; and she replied that if he cared to go she would come over later for him in the car. Lee, standing at a window, thought he wouldn't; but, adding that Peyton would be there, he decided that, in view of the possible developments, his presence might be wise.

The early gloom gathered familiarly in the long main room of the clubhouse; the fire cast out fanwise and undependable flickering light upon the relaxed figures; it shone on tea cups, sparkled in rich translucent preserves, and glimmered through a glass sugar bowl. It was all, practically, Lee Randon reflected, as it had been before and would be again. How few things, out of a worldful, the ordinary individual saw,—that was—to comprehend, to experience: a limited number of interiors, certain roads and streets, fields and views. He made his way through life blinded to the customary and unaware of the strange; summer was hot and winter, usually, cold; the spring became green under rain; winds blew and the leaves fell in fall—of how much more was he conscious?

It was the same with regard to people; he, Lee Randon, knew a great many, or rather, he could repeat their names, recognize their superficial features at sight. But to say that he actually knew them—that was nonsense! Why, he was almost totally ignorant of himself. How much could he explain of Fanny's late state of mind? She had done all that was possible to make it clear to him; with little result. Fanny was an extraordinarily honest person; or, damn it, she seemed to be. He had a reputation for truthfulness; but how much of what was in his mind would he admit to his wife? The discrepancy between what he appeared and what he felt himself to be, what he thought and what published, was enormous, astounding.

There, as well, was Peyton Morris; Lee would have sworn that he understood him thoroughly—a character as simple, as obvious as Fanny's. But here was Morris seated with Mina Raff on the stairs to the upper floor, beyond the radius of the fire; and, though they were not ten feet away, he could not hear a word of what they were saying. At intervals there was an indistinct murmur, nothing more. Claire, at Lee Randon's side, was sitting with her chin high and a gaze concentrated on the twisting flames: talking generally had fallen into a pause.

The door from without opened, Fanny entered, and there was a momentary revival of animation. "Is Lee here?" she demanded; "but I know he is. The fire is just as attractive at home, yet, even with nothing to do, he'll hardly wait to give it a poke. Where's Peyton?"

"On the stairs," someone answered casually.

There was a movement, and Mina Raff approached. "It's so hot here," she asserted.

"It is warmer out," Fanny informed her; "I wonder what the weather is in New York?"

"I can't say, I'm sure; but I shall discover tomorrow morning. I have to be back as early as possible. Then—work, work, work."

"Mina has been made a star," Peyton Morris announced. But he stopped awkwardly, apparently conscious of the warmth, the largeness, in his voice. Fanny whispered to Lee that it was quite too outrageous. In return, he asked, "What?" and, indignant, she drew away from him.

The conversation died again. Lee Randon could see Mina Raff's profile, held darkly against the glow; her lips and chin were firm. "Where," Anette asked her, "shall you stay when you get back—at Savina Grove's?" No, Mina replied, her hours would be too long and uncertain to allow that; probably she would be at the Plaza. Lee had heard the Groves' name mentioned before in connection with Mina Raff; and he made an effort to recall the reason. The Groves—it was the William Loyd Groves—were rather important people, financially and socially; and one of them, yes, that was it, was related to Mina, but which he didn't know.

More came back to him: Mina Raff's parents had died when she was a young girl, and the Groves had rescued her from the undistinguished evils of improvidence; she had lived with them until, against their intensest objections, she had gone into moving pictures. Probably the Groves' opposition had lasted until Mina's success; or, in other words, their support had been withheld from her through the period when it had been most needed.

Yes, the girl had a determined mouth. If he, Lee Randon, had followed his first inclinations—were they in the way of literature?—how different his life would have been. Mina Raff had been stronger, more selfish, than her environment: selfishness and success were synonymous. Yet, as a human quality, it was more hated, more reviled, than any other. Its opposite was held as the perfect, the heavenly, ethics of conduct. To be sacrificed, that was the accepted essence of Christ; fineness came through relinquishment. He didn't believe it, he told himself fiercely; something deep, integral, in him revolted absolutely.

19

Mina Raff had been wholly justified; the very people who had thrown all their weight against her admitted it fully. It was only when such a self-belief was without compensating result, value, that it was wrong. But who could say what any outcome would be? Some people took the chance and others didn't; he had not. Then the question came up of whether he had not failed as it was? No one would agree with him that it might be failure; he hadn't called it that. Suddenly, vehemently, he wished that he could grow old at once, in a second; anything to quiet the restlessness at his heart.

Lee had a conviction that he ought to decide the case of the individual against the world, the feeling that it was of the greatest importance to him; but for centuries men had considered, without answer, just that. The thing to do was to live, not to think; for it was possible that those who thought, weighed causes and results, hardly lived at all in the sense he meant. All the people he knew were cautious before they were anything else; they existed primarily for their stomachs. The widely advertised beauty of self sacrifice was golden only when it adorned like a halo the heads of others. That was natural, inevitable to the struggle for survival; it didn't answer Lee's question, which, he felt, was of the spirit rather than the body.

"It's getting late," Fanny said briskly. There was a general movement, sighs and the settling of skirts. The lights were switched on, and the fire, that had been a source of magic, became nothing more than ugly grey charring logs with a few thin tongues of flame. Lee, with his wife, stopped to say good-bye to Mina Raff; Fanny's manner was bright, conventional; as palpably insincere to the other woman, Lee was certain, as it was to him. He said:

"I hope your new picture will go well."

"Thank you," she responded, her slight hand lingeringly holding his; "perhaps you will like me better on the screen than in reality."

"Could you tell me which was which?"

She hesitated. "Three months ago, yes, but not now; I'm not sure of myself."

"That was positively indecent," Fanny observed afterward; "she is as bold as brass. I hope I am not as big a fool as Claire."

"Claire and you are very different," he told her; "I have an idea that she is doing whatever is possible. But then we don't know what we are talking about: it's fairly evident that Peyton and Mina Raff are interested in each other, they may be in love; and, if they are, what does that mean? It isn't your feeling for the children or mine for you; they are both love; yet what is it?"

"It is God in us," Fanny said gravely; "and keeps us all, Helena and Gregory and you and me, safely together."

She seldom spoke to him of religion, but it dwelt closely, vitally, within her, and not as an inherited abstraction or correct social observation, but definitely personal in its intercommunication. Lee Randon had none at all; and in her rare references to it he could only preserve an awkward silence. That had always been a bar between his family and himself, particularly with the children: he was obliged to maintain an endless hypocrisy about the miracles, the dogmas and affairs, of Sunday school and the church. As a child he had been so filled with a literal Presbyterian imagery that, when a degree of reason discarded figures of speech seen as concrete actualities, nothing had been left. With the lapse of a purely pictorial heaven and hell, the loss of eternal white choirs and caldrons of the unrepentant, only earth remained.

He could recall in gloomy detail his early impression of Paradise: it was a sombre plain floating cloud-like in air, with, doubling through it, an unspeakable sluggish river of blood; God, bearded and frowning in the severity of chronic judgment, dominated from an architectural throne a throng of the saved in straight garments and sandalled feet; and, in the foreground, a lamb with a halo and an uplifted cross was intent on the baptism of individuals issuing unaccountably white from the thickly crimson flood.

Yet his children, in a modified Episcopalian form, were being taught the same thing: the Mosaic God; Christ Jesus who took unto Himself the sin of the world; the rugged disciple, St. Peter and the loving disciple, St. John. The sky, they learned, was the habitation of light-winged angels. The ark was still reported on its memorable voyage, with its providential pairs of animals gathered from every zone, but there was a growing reticence about Jonah. The persistence of such credulity, Lee thought, was depressing; just as the churches, leaning on the broken support of a charity they were held to dispense, were a commentary on the poverty of the minds and spirits of men.

Yes, the necessity of charging Helena and Gregory with such assurances, their rigid bending into mental forms, large and small, in which he had no confidence, put Lee outside the solidity of his family. In the instruction, the influences, widely held paramount in the welding of polite Christian characters, Fanny was indefatigable—the piece of silver firmly clasped in the hand for collection, the courtesy when addressed by elders, the convention that nature, birds, were sentimentally beneficent. When Gregory brought out these convictions, lessons, in his indescribably fresh eager tones, Lee listened with a helpless disapproval.

Everything, it seemed to Lee Randon, increased the position of self-delusion at the expense of what he felt to be reality. His doubts, for example, were real; with no will, no effort on his part, they invaded his mind ceaselessly. Cytherea's disturbing charm was real, as definite as Fanny's quiet actuality. However, he wasn't interested in an abstract arraignment of life, but intent only on the truth about himself. Lee wanted to discharge fully his duty to existence—in the more inglorious phrase, he didn't want to make a fool of himself—and yet it was growing more difficult all the while to distinguish folly from sense.

This affair, if it did exist, of Peyton's with Mina Raff wasn't so easily determined as Fanny insisted. Perhaps, like his own, Peyton Morris' life had been restricted by artificial barriers thrown about the rebellious integrity of his fundamental being. Few children could stand out against the combined forces of the older world; but it was conceivable that, later, like a chrysalis, they might burst the hard, superimposed skin and emerge triumphant.

That damned problem of self-sacrifice!

How much claim had men upon each other? What did children gain who sacrificed their lives for their parents? It was supposed to bring them nobility; but, at the same time, didn't it develop in the parents the utmost callous selfishness; didn't the latter, as their needs were exclusively consulted, grow more exacting, unreasonable? Was not love itself the most unreasonable and exacting thing imaginable?

Once surrendered to it, the tyranny of a beloved subject was absolute: Lee told himself that the emotion he was considering—the most sacred of earthly ties—ignominiously resembled the properties of fly paper. He turned abruptly from that graceless thought: it was a great deal warmer, and a mist, curiously tangible in the night, was rising through the bare branches of the maple trees.

"I am going to talk to Claire," Fanny said firmly.

"It would do both of you no good," he informed her; "besides, you'll have to take so much for granted."

"Claire will tell me."

"I wonder?" They were in their room, preparing for bed; Fanny, with her hair spread in a thin brown tide over the chaste shoulders of her nightgown, was incredibly like a girl. The mechanical sweep of her hand with a brush kept a brief sleeve falling back from the thinness of her arm. How delicately methodical she was—an indispensable quality in the repeated trying contacts, the lost privacy, of marriage. So much depended upon the very elusiveness which the security of possession, habit, destroyed.

"This love," he continued his speculations aloud, "isn't at all understood—we are ignorant about it in spite of endless experience and reports and poetry. Take us," he had one of his dangerous impulses of complete honesty, "before we were married, while we were engaged, we had an impracticable romantic attraction for each other. I know that I thought of you all the time, day and night; and, just because you existed, the whole world was full of prismatic colors; it was as though an orchestra were playing continually and I were floating on the finest music. You were like a figure in heaven that drew me up to you.

"Well, that lasted quite a while into our marriage; at first I had an even greater emotion. Then, as Helena and Gregory were born, it changed." Midway in the brushing of her hair Fanny was motionless and intent. "I don't say it decreased, Fanny, that it lost any of its importance; but it did change; and in you as well as me. It wasn't as prismatic, as musical, and there's no use contradicting me. I can explain it best for myself by saying that my feeling for you became largely tenderness."

"Oh!" Fanny exclaimed, in a little lifting gasp; "oh, and that tenderness," her cheeks were bright with sudden color, "why, it is no more than pity."

"That isn't just," he replied; "unless you want to speak of pity at its very best. No, that won't do: my affection for you is made of all our experiences, our lives and emotions, together. We are tied by a thousand strings—common disappointments and joy and sickness and hope and pain and heaven knows what else. We're held by habit, too, and convenience and the opinion of society. Certainly it is no smaller than the first," he argued, but more to himself than to Fanny; "that was nothing but a state of mind, of spirit; you can't live on music."

"Don't you think you have said enough for one night?" she asked, in a calm voice belied by the angry sparkle of her eyes, the faint irrepressible trembling of her lips. "Do you think I want to hear that it is only convention and our neighbors that keep you with me? You have no right to insist that your horridness is true of me, either. I—I could hear music, if you would let me." She sank on the little cushioned bench before her dressing table, where her youthfulness took on a piercing aspect of misery. Fanny's declaration, not far from tears, that she was just as she had always been was admirably upheld by her appealing presence.

The tenderness he had admitted, reduced by a perceptive impatience and the sense of having been wholly, wilfully, misunderstood, carried him over to her. He took Fanny, with her face strained away from him, into his arms. "Don't be an idiot," he begged softly; "you ought to be used to my talking by now. Let me go on, it can't come to anything—" She stiffened in his embrace:

"What do you mean by that?"

"Nothing, nothing," he answered shortly, releasing her; "where is all that certainty you assured me of? If you go on like this I shall never be able to tell you my thoughts, discuss problems with you; and it seems to me that's very necessary."

"It has been lately," she spoke in a metallic voice; "nothing satisfies you any more; and I suppose I should have been prepared to have you say things to me, too. But I'm not; you might even find that I am not the idiot you suspect."

"I was giving you a chance to prove that," he pointed out.

"Now you have discovered the fatal truth you can save yourself more trouble in the future." She emphatically switched off a light beside her, leaving him standing in a sole unsparing illumination. Yet in her extreme resentment she was, he recognized, rubbing Vaseline into her finger nails, her final nightly rite. Then there was silence where once he had kissed her with a reluctance to lose her in even the short oblivion of sleep.

Throughout Monday, at his office, Lee Randon thought at uncomfortable intervals of the late incipient scenes with Fanny. They had quarrels—who hadn't?—but they had usually ended in Fanny shedding some tears that warmly recemented their deep affections. This latter time, however, she had not wept—at the point of dissolving into the old surrender she had turned away from him, both in reality and metaphorically, and fallen asleep in an unexpected cold reserve. He was sorry, for it brought into their relationship a definite new quality of difference. He was aware of the thorough inconsistency of his attitude toward their marriage; again two opposed forces were present in him—one, Fanny, as, bound to her, he knew and cherished; and the other—the devil take the other!

He was organizing a new company, and, figuring impatiently, he pressed the button for Mrs. Wald, his secretary. She appeared at once and quietly, her notebook and pencil ready, took a place at his side. "Run this out, please, Mrs. Wald," and an involved financial transaction followed. What he wanted to ascertain was, with a preferred stock bearing eight per cent at a stated capitalization, and the gift of a bonus of common, share for share, how much pie would remain to be cut up between a Mr. Hadly, Sanford, and himself? The woman worked rapidly, in long columns of minute neat figures. "About thirty-four thousand dollars, each, Mr. Randon," she announced almost directly. "Is that close enough; or do you want it to the fraction?"

"Good enough; send Miss Mathews in."

Almost anyone on his staff, Lee reflected, knew more about the processes of his business than he did; he supplied the energy, the responsibility of the decisions, more than the brains of his organization; and it perfected the details. The stenographer, Miss Mathews, was very elaborately blonde, very personable; and, dictating to her, Lee Randon remembered the advice given him by a large wielder of labor and finance. "Lee," he had said, touching him with the emphasis of a finger, "never play around with an employee or a client."

He, John Lenning Partins, had been a man of eccentric humors, and—like all individuals who supported heavy mental burdens, inordinately taxed their brains—he had his hours, unknown to the investing public, of erratic, but the word was erotic, conduct. On more than one occasion he had peremptorily telegraphed for Lee to join him at some unexpected place, for a party. Once, following a ball at the Grand Opera House, in Paris, they had motored in a taxi-cab, with charming company, to Calais. During that short stay in France John Partins had spent, flung variously away, four hundred thousand dollars.

The industrious, the clerks, efficient women like Mrs. Wald, the middle-aged lawyers in his office, were rewarded...by a pension. It was all very strange, upside down: what rot that was about the infinite capacity for taking pains! He supposed it wouldn't do to make this public, the tritest maxims were safer for the majority; but it was too bad; it spread the eternal hypocrisies of living. He asked Miss Mathews:

"You're not thinking of getting married, are you? Because if you do I'll have your young man deported; I simply won't let go of you."

"I don't see any signs of it, Mr. Randon," she replied, half serious and half smiling; "my mother thinks it's awful, but I'm not in any hurry. There are men I know, who might like me; they show me a very good time; but somehow I am not anxious. I guess in a way it's the other married girls I see: either they housework at home, and I couldn't be bothered with that; or they are in an office and, somehow, that seems wrong, too. I want so much," she admitted; "and with what clothes cost now it's terrible."

"Moralists and social investigators would call you a bad girl," he told her; "but I agree with you; get your pretty hats and suits, and smart shoes, as long as you are able. You're not a bit better in a kitchen than you are here, taking dictation from me; and I am not sure you would be more valuable at home with a child or two. You are a very unusual stenographer, rapid and accurate, and you have a good mind in addition to your figure. Why should you lose all that at once, give it up, for the accidents of cholera infantum and a man, as likely as not, with a consumptive lung?"

"But what about love, Mr. Randon? That's what throws me off. Some say it's the only thing in life."

"I'm damned if I know," he admitted, leaning back from his wide flat-topped desk. "I hear the same thing, and I am rather inclined to believe it. But I have an idea that it is very different from what most people insist; I don't think it is very useful around the house; it has more to do with the pretty hat than with the dishpan. If you fall in love go after the thing itself, then; don't hesitate about tomorrow or yesterday; and, above all else, don't ask yourself if it will last; that's immaterial."

"You make it sound wild enough," she commented, rising.

"The wilder the better," he insisted; "if it is not delirious it's nothing."

The road and countryside over which he returned in the motor sedan, partly frozen, were streaked by rills of muddy surface water; the sky, which appeared definitely to rest on the surrounding hills, was grey with a faint suffusion of yellow at the western horizon. It was all as dreary, as sodden, as possible. Eastlake, appearing beyond a shoulder of bare woods, showed a monotonous scattering of wet black roofs, raw brick chimneys, at the end of a long paved highway glistening with steel tracks.

Lee Randon was weary, depressed: nothing in his life, in any existence, offered the least recompense for the misfortune of having been born. He left his car at the entrance of his dwelling; Christopher, the gardener, came sloshing over the sod to take it into the garage; and, within, he found the dinner-table set for three. "It's Claire," his wife informed him; "she called up not half an hour ago to ask if she could come. Peyton was away over night, she said, and she wanted to see us." He went on up to his room, inattentive even to Claire's possible troubles.

He dressed slowly, automatically, and descended to the fire-lit space that held Cytherea in her mocking, her becoming, aloofness. In the brightly illuminated room beyond the hall Helena and Gregory were playing parchesi—Gregory firmly grasped the cup from which he intently rolled the dice; Helena shook the fair hair from her eyes and, it immediately developed, moved a pink marker farther than proper.

"You only got seven!" Gregory exclaimed; "and you took it nine right on that safety."

"What if I did?" she returned undisturbed. "I guess a girl can make a mistake without having somebody yell at her. Your manners aren't very good."

"Yes, they are, too," he asserted, aggrieved; "I have to tell you if you move to a safety where you don't belong." He shook the dice from the cup. "Now, see there—that just brings me to your man, and I can send him home."

"I don't care," Helena informed him; "it's a young sort of game, anyhow. Now I'm wearing waists and buttoned skirts I'd just as leaves write a letter to Margaret West with no boys in it at all."

She left the parchesi board, and crossed the room to the piano, where she stood turning over sheets of music with a successful appearance of critical interest. Gregory, silently struggling with the injustice of this, gazed up with a shadowed brow at Lee. "I was going to beat her," he said, "I was almost home, and she went away. She just got up like nothing was happening." Helena put in, "Neither there was." Lee Randon took her place. "You can beat me instead," he proposed. His interest in the game, he felt, was as false as Helena's pretended musical preoccupation; but he rolled the dice and shifted the counters, under Gregory's undeviating scrutiny, with the conviction that parchesi was not conspicuously different from the other more resounding movements of the world and its affairs. Gregory easily vanquished him, and Lee rose with a curt, unwarranted nod of dismissal.

Freezing cocktails in the pewter pitcher, in the repetition of minor duties which, Lee Randon thought, now constituted four-fifths of his life, he told himself that Claire Morris had never looked better: she was wearing a dress of a soft negative blue material, high about her throat, with glimpses of bright embroidery that brought out her darkly vivid personality. Claire had a slim low-breasted figure, gracefully broad shoulders; and her face, it might be because of its definite, almost sharp, outline, held the stamp of decided opinions. Claire's appearance, he recognized, her bearing, gave an impression of arrogance which, however, was only superficially true—she could be very disagreeable in situations, with people, that she found inferior, brutally casual and unsympathetic; but more privately, intimately, she was remarkably simple-hearted, free from reserve. She was related to Lee through her father, a good blood, he told himself; but her mother had brought her a concentration of what particular vigorous aristocracy—an unlimited habit of luxury without the responsibility of acknowledged place—the land afforded.

The drinks had been consumed, the soup disposed of, when Claire said abruptly, "Peyton is going to leave me."

Although, in a way, Lee had been prepared for such an announcement, the actuality upset him extremely. Fanny gasped, and then nodded warningly toward the waitress, leaving the dining-room; at any conceivable disaster, he reflected, Fanny would consider the proprieties.

"When did he tell you?" Fanny demanded.

"He didn't," Claire replied; "I told him. It was a great relief to both of us."

"Say what you like outside," Lee put in vigorously; "but at least with us be honest."

"I am, quite," she assured him; "naturally I don't want Peyton to go—I happen to love him. And there's Ira. But it was an impossible position; it couldn't go on, Peyton was absolutely wretched, we both were; and so I ended it. I laid out all his best silk pajamas so that he'd look smart—"

"How can you?" Fanny cried; "oh, how can you? It is too wicked, all too horrible, for words. I don't think you are advanced or superior, Claire, you failed him and yourself both. It's perfectly amazing to me, after the men you have met, that you don't know them. You must keep them going in the right direction; you can't let them stop, or look around, once; I only learned that lately, but it is so. They haven't an idea of what they want, and they try everything. Then if you let a man go he is the first to blame you; it's like winking at murder."

"How could I keep him when he didn't want to stay?" Claire asked wearily; "I am not too moral, but I couldn't quite manage that. Then what you say might do for some men, but not Peyton. You see, he has always been very pure; all his friends at Princeton were like that; they were proud of it and very severe on the other. And afterwards, when he went into the city, it was the same; Peyton would get drunk any number of times with any number of men, but, as he said, he was off women. The stage door, it seems, is very old-fashioned now.

"When we were engaged, and he told me that he was really pure, I was simply mad with happiness. I thought it was such a marvelous thing for a girl to find. I still think that; and yet, I don't know. If he were different, had had more experience, perhaps this wouldn't have hit him so hard. He would have kissed his Mina on the porch, outside the dance, and come home."

"As for that Raff woman—" Fanny stopped, at a loss for a term to express her disgust.

"Why not?" Claire asked. "She wanted Peyton and went after him; he isn't for her art, I believe, but for herself. I haven't talked to her; I can't make up my mind about that. Probably it would do no good. Peyton is splendidly healthy; it won't be necessary to tell her anything about draughts and stomach bands."

"Claire, you're utterly, tragically wrong," Fanny wailed. "I wish I could shake sense into you. Up to a point this is your fault; you are behaving in a criminally foolish way."

"What do you think Claire should do?" Lee asked his wife.

She turned to him, a flood of speech on her lips; but, suddenly, she suppressed it; the expression, the lines, of concern were banished from her face. "There is so much," she replied equably; "they haven't discussed it enough; why, it ought to take a year, two, before they reached such a decision. Peyton can't know his mind, nor Claire hers. And Ira, that darling innocent little child."

"Damn Ira!" Claire Morris exclaimed.

"You mustn't," Fanny asserted; "you're not yourself. Mina Raff should be burned alive, something terrible done to her." Fanny's voice had the hard cold edge of fanatical conviction. "If she had come into my house making trouble.... But that couldn't have happened; I'd have known at once."

"You are more feminine than I am," Claire told her. "I see this in a very detached manner, as if it didn't concern me. I suppose I can't realize that it has happened to us. It has! But if you are right, Fanny, and it's necessary to treat a man like a green hunter, then this was bound to occur. I couldn't do anything so—so humiliating; he could bolt sooner or later. I did the best I knew how: I was amusing as possible and always looked well enough. I never bothered Peyton about himself and encouraged him to keep as much of his freedom as possible.

"I don't believe in the other," she said to Fanny Randon in a sharp accession of rebellion; "it is degrading, and I won't live that way, I won't put up with it. If he wants to go, to be with Mina Raff, how in God's name can I stop it? I won't have him in my bed with another woman in his heart; I made that clear to you. And I can't have him hot and cold—now all Mina and then the sanctity of his home. I've never had a house of that kind; it was christened, like a ship, with champagne.

"I have never cared for domestic things. I'd rather wear a dinner-gown than an apron; I'd a damn sight rather spin a roulette wheel than rock a cradle. And, perhaps, Peyton wanted a housewife; though heaven knows he hasn't turned to one. It's her blonde, no bland, charm and destructive air of innocence. I've admitted and understood too much; but I couldn't help it—my mother and grandmother, all that lot, were the same way, and went after things themselves. The men hated sham and sentimentality; they asked, and gave, nothing."

Fanny, it was evident, was growing impatient at what was not without its challenge of her character and expressed convictions. "I do agree with you, Claire, that we are not alike," she admitted. Her voice bore a perceptible note of complacency, of superior strength and position. "Just last week I was telling Lee that I belonged before the war—things were so different then, and, apparently, it's only in my house they haven't changed. We are frightfully behind the times, and you'd be surprised at how glad we are. It was your mother's father, wasn't it, who fell in love with the Spanish woman while he was in the Embassy at Seville? My family weren't people of public connections, although a great-aunt married Senator Carlinton; but they had the highest principles."

"They were lucky," Claire Morris replied indifferently; "I am beginning to think it isn't what you have so much as what happens to it. Anyhow, Peyton is going away with Mina Raff, and I am sorry for him; he's so young and so certain; but this has shaken him. Peyton's a snob, really, like the rest of his friends, and Mina's crowd won't have that for a moment: he can't go through her world judging men by their slang and by whom they knew at college. I envy him, it will be a tremendously interesting experience." If her eyes were particularly brilliant it was because they were surrounded by an extreme darkness. Her voice, commonly no more than a little rough in its deliberate forthrightness, was high and metallic. She gave Lee the heroic impression that no most mighty tempest would ever see her robbed of her erect defiance. It was at once her weakness and strength that she could be broken but not bent.

After dinner Claire, who was staying with the Randons until tomorrow, played picquet with Lee; and his wife, her shapely feet elevated above the possible airs of the floor, continued to draw threads from the handkerchiefs she was making for Christmas. Claire played very well and, at five cents a point, he had to watch the game. On a specially big hand she piqued and repiqued. "That," she declared, "will pay you for caputting me." The jargon of their preoccupation, "A point of six; yes, to the ace; paid; and a quatorze, kings," was the only sound until Fanny rose, decidedly. "I am going to bed." She hesitated at the door. "I hope you'll be comfortable, Claire: I had some club soda and rye put in your room, since you like it so well. Don't be too late, please, Lee; it makes you tired starting so early in the morning."

"You'll have to forgive me," Claire said, when Fanny had gone; "but I don't—I never did—like women."

"Do you think any more of men, now?"

"Heavens, yes. I wish I could find someone to blame for what has happened, Peyton specially, but I can't, not to save my life. It seems so hopelessly inevitable. I don't want you to suppose I'm not unhappy, Lee; or that I care only a little for Peyton. I love him very much; I needed him, and my love, more than I can explain. As Fanny as good as told me, I am a wild bird; anything, almost, with what is behind me, may happen. It was just the irony of chance that this affair caught Peyton, the immaculate, instead of me. I was awfully glad that I had an anchor that seemed so strong; in my own faulty way I adored everything I had; I wanted to be tranquil, and it had a look of security."

"It isn't over, Claire," Lee asserted. "I haven't seen that young fool yet."

"Please don't bother him; and it's too much to drag out the moralities on my account."

"Moralities!" he echoed indignantly, "who said a word about them? I'm not interested in morals. Lord, Claire, how little you know me. And as for bothering him, he'll have to put up with that. He has invited a certain amount of it."

They forgot the game and faced each other across the disordered cards. "If I won't argue with him," she insisted, "you can't. But we needn't discuss it—he won't listen to you, Peyton's all gone. I never saw such a complete wreck."

"He can't avoid it," Lee went on; "I'll have to do it if it is only for myself; I am most infernally curious about the whole works. I want to find out what it's about."

"If you mean love, he can't tell you; he hasn't had enough experience to express it. You might do better with me."

"No, I want it from the man; a woman's feeling, even yours, would do me no good. You see, this has always been explored, accounted for, condemned, written about, from the feminine side. Where the man is considered it is always in the most damnable light. If, in the novels, a man leaves his home he is a rascal of the darkest sort, and his end is a remorse no one would care to invite. That may be, but I am not prepared to say. No, dear Claire, I am not considering it in preparation for anything; I want to know; that's all."

"The books are stuff, of course," she agreed. "The grandfather of mine who was killed in Madrid—it wasn't Seville—must have had a gorgeous time: a love affair with one of the most beautiful women alive. It lasted five months before it was found out and ended; and his wife and he had been sick of living together. After it was over she was pleased at being connected with such a celebrated scandal; it made her better looking by reflected loveliness. She was rather second class, I believe, and particularly fancied the duchess part."

"It wouldn't be like that in the current novels, or even in the better: either your grandparent or the duchess would be a villainous person, and the other a victim. I'm inclined to think that most of the ideas about life and conduct are lifted from cheap fiction. They have the look of it. But that realization wouldn't help us, with the world entirely on the other side."

"No, it isn't," Claire objected; "and it's getting less so all around us. Perhaps men haven't changed much, yet; but you don't hear the women talk as I do. I don't like them, as I said; they are too damned skulking for me; but they are gathering a lot more sense in a short while."

"I don't agree with you there," he replied; "you are getting your own infinitesimal world confused with the real overwhelming majority; you haven't an idea how it feels and, in particular, of what it thinks of you, smoking and gambling and damning your fate. It may be largely envy—personally I am convinced it is—but they have you ticketed straight for hell just the same."

"It doesn't interest me." Claire increasingly showed the strain, the unhappiness, through which she was parsing. Nor did it him, he ended lamely, except in the abstract. This at once had the elements of a lie and the unelaborate truth; he couldn't see how his curiosity applied to him, and yet he was intent on its solving. The fixed mobile smile of Cytherea flashed into his thoughts. His perpetual restlessness struck through him.

His attitude toward the Morrises was largely dictated by his fondness for Claire. He had determined what, exactly, he would say to Peyton. Yet, as a fact, he returned to his former assertion to Fanny, the boy would make it difficult, if not impossible, to discuss such intimate relationships. And as Claire had pointed out, the very openness of Peyton's life would make him exceptionally far to reach; he was particularly youthful in his hardness, his confidence in his acts and friends and beliefs; yet all that couldn't help but be upset now.

"Fanny will think I have designs on you," Claire remarked; "go up when you like. I am not a bit sleepy."

Lee had no intention of going to bed then, and told her so. It seemed to him that, perhaps, with Claire, he might discover something that would set his questioning at rest. Vain delusion. He asked what her plans were:

"I'll stay in Eastlake for the winter, and, in March, go to Italy, to give Peyton his divorce—Florence; I lived a while at Arcetri; it's very lovely."

He had a momentary experimental vision of a small yellow villa among the olives of the Florentine hills, of crumbling pink walls with emerald green lizards along the stones, of myrtles and remarkable lilies-of-the-valley. Twenty years ago it would have drawn him irresistibly; but not now; he wanted—where his wants were articulate—a far different thing. It had nothing to do with Italy, or any other country; his intentness had been withdrawn from the surfaces of life, however charming; they had plunged into the profounder mysteries of being. Lee had gained nothing if not a certain freedom from exterior circumstance; his implied revolt against trivialities, if it did no other good, had at least liberated him from the furniture of existence. However, it had begun to appear that this was not an unmixed blessing; he had the uncomfortable sensation of having put out, on a limitless sea, in a very little boat too late to arrive at any far hidden desirable coast.

Claire shivered, and, discovering that she was cold, he insisted on her going upstairs. "To my pure sheets," she said, with a touch of her familiar daring. Left alone, Lee was depressed by the hour; the room, his house, seemed strange, meaningless, to him. There was a menace in the unnatural stillness; Fanny's unfinished handkerchief, her stool, were without the warmth of familiar association. It might have been a place into which he had wandered by accident, where he didn't belong, wouldn't stay. It was inconceivable that, above him, his wife and children were sleeping; the ceiling, the supine heavy bodies, seemed to sag until they rested on his shoulders; he was, like Atlas, holding the whole house up. It was with acute difficulty that he shook off the illusion, the weight. From outside came the thin howling of a dog, and it, too, seemed to hold a remote and desperate interrogation.


He slept badly, in short broken stretches, with the Morrises constantly in his mind; and what, in the slightest dislocation of reality, was dream and what waking he couldn't determine; at times his vision seemed to hold both—a door, the irrevocable door, swung open, the end impended, but he was unable to see the faces of the man and woman; when he looked anxiously a blind spot intervened. The morning found him unrefreshed, impatient; and he was glad that his early breakfast was solitary; Lee didn't want then to see either Claire or Fanny, he was in no mood to discuss Peyton's seizure. That, it seemed to Lee Randon, was exactly what had happened to the younger man—Peyton had gone within the region of a contagious fever that had run through all his blood.

Yet, at dinner, to his surprise, Fanny said very little about what had entirely occupied their thoughts; she was quiet, reserved; her attitude was marked by a careful dignity. Her gaze, even more than commonly, rested on her husband. "I had a wretched night, too," she told him; "my head is like a kite. I've thought and thought until my brain aches, it is so full. But there are some things I decided; and if you don't agree with them I'm sorry; because, Lee, I am right, I am indeed."

"Of course you are," he replied; "but, possibly, only for yourself. I mean, for instance, that you can't be sure you're right for Claire."

"No, no, that's just the same as saying there isn't any right or wrong at all, and you know better. Yes, what I am certain about is duty; you must do that before everything else. Peyton's duty is to Claire and their child. It is as clear as this soup. Nothing else matters so much, or at all. Why, Lee, the world is made up of people doing their duty; what, I'd like to know, would become of it if they didn't? You don't seem to realize it, but there are loads of obligations I get dreadfully tired of, like the Social Service when it is my month to follow the accounts, and visits to Annie Hazard who has a cancer of the stomach and is dying, and thinking every day what to get you and the children and the servants to eat. Suppose, some morning, I didn't stir, but just rested in bed—what would happen? What did happen last winter when I had pleurisy? Why, the whole house went to pieces, and, when you weren't worrying about me, while I was getting well, you were the most uncomfortable man imaginable. I don't want you to think I am complaining, or that I don't love every minute and stick and stone of my home and life; I do. But you seem to forget about me ... that's because the house goes along so smoothly. It would be a good lesson if you had to live with some other woman for a while."

"I'm sure every word is so," he returned; "no one could have a better wife; you've spoiled me outrageously; I feel like that pig Christopher has in a pen out by the stable."

"You might think of something nicer to say," she protested. "You're not easy to live with, either," Fanny continued; "you hardly ever agree with what other people think; and you curse fearfully. I wish you wouldn't swear like that, Lee. I object to it very much in Claire; I can't help believing that she thinks it is smart or funny. And you encourage her. If Claire had been different—no, don't interrupt me—this would never have happened. You may say what you like about her good breeding: she's been too flippant. I felt that last night. Claire doesn't accept her obligations seriously enough. She's kept herself lovely looking, but that isn't the whole thing."

"What is the whole thing?" he demanded.

"I've told you, but you won't listen—duty."

"You put that above all the rest?"

Fanny hesitated. "I said my head hurt because I've thought so much. Love and duty, yes; I see them as the same. Duty without love would be hard, and there isn't any love without duty." Fanny evidently grew aware of her threatening incoherence. "It isn't necessary to tell you in so many words," she said defensively; "you are only being contrary."

"You have explained yourself beautifully," he hastened to assure her; "I am the person who is at sea."

"Why, Lee!" she exclaimed, surprised; "I don't know anyone who is so decided. That's what makes me raging, you're so dogmatic. There, that is a splendid word. Don't eat that apple, it isn't baked; I can see from here." She rang. "Varney," Fanny addressed the maid, "take Mr. Randon's apple out and see if there isn't another better done, please. I warned you about that; he can't eat them uncooked."

"Let me keep it," he protested; "it might have an excellent effect on my disposition."

"Don't interfere, Lee," she responded coldly: "yes, Varney. It's really idiotic of you," she turned to him; "you are not a boy any more, you're not even a young man, and you can't take liberties with your digestion. You are quite like Helena with her prayers—if she feels very well she's apt to forget them, but if she's sick she says them as hard as possible. I wish she were like Gregory."

"Gregory and you are cut out of the same gold cloth," Lee Randon pronounced.

"That was lovely of you, Lee." Fanny radiated happiness. "No one could say anything prettier to his old wife." Dinner was over, and, rising, she walked around the table and laid a confident arm on his shoulders. The knife-like tenderness which, principally, he had for her overwhelmed him; and he held Fanny against him in a silent and straining embrace. For that reason he was annoyed at himself when, sitting through an uneventful evening, his simile of the pig, enormously fat, sleepily contented, in its pen, returned to him. It wasn't that he found an actual analogy between the pig and life, individuals, on a higher plane, so much as that he was vaguely disturbed by the impression that there was an ultimate similitude between him, Lee Randon, and a fattened somnolence of existence.

After all, were his individual opinions and doubts expressed in a manner forceful enough to diversify him from a porcine apathy? The pig, secure against the inequalities of fate and weather, wallowed through life with a dull fullness of food as regular as the solar course. Christopher was his wife. Now that, Lee told himself, with a vision of the gardener's moustache, sadly drooping and stained with tobacco, his pale doubtful gaze, was inexcusable. He abruptly directed his thoughts to Peyton and Claire Morris; how exact Claire had been in the expression of her personality! What, he grasped, was different in her from other women was precisely that; together with an astonishing lack of sentimental bias, it operated with the cutting realism of a surgeon's blade. She had, as well, courage.

That was the result of her heritage; and he wondered if all strong traits were the action of superior blood strayed into expected and unexpected places? It was probable, but not susceptible of proof. The pig's blood was that of the best registered Berkshire. God damn the pig!

He asked Fanny if she had heard any further particulars of the proposed rearrangement of the Morrises' lives; when they were to separate; but she knew no more than he. "I hope he doesn't come here," she said vigorously: "I should refuse to speak to him or have him at my table. Outrageous! I can't make out why you take it so coolly. Mina Raff's a rotten immoral woman; it doesn't matter how it's arranged. Why," she gasped, "she can be no more than Peyton's mistress, no better than the women on the street."

"That is so," he agreed. But his following question of the accepted badness of mistresses and streetwalkers he wisely kept to himself. Were they darker than the shadow cast by the inelastic institution of matrimony? At one time prostitutes were greatly honored; but that had passed, he was convinced, forever; and this, on the whole, he concluded, was fortunate; for, perhaps, if prostitution were thoroughly discredited, marriage might, in some Elysian future, be swept of most of its rubbish. Houses of prostitution, mistresses, like charity, absorbed and dissipated a great deal of the dissatisfaction inseparable from the present misconceptions of love and society. The first move, obviously, in stopping war was the suppression of such ameliorating forces as the Red Cross; and, conversely, with complete unions, infidelity would languish and disappear.

He thought of this further in the darkened theatre to which, driven by his growing curiosity, he had gone to see Mina Raff in the leading part of a moving picture. It was a new version, in a new medium, of an old and perennial melodrama; but, too late for the opening scenes, the story for the moment was incomprehensible to him. However, it had to do with the misadventures of a simple country girl in what, obviously, was the conventional idea of a most sophisticated and urbane society. Lee waited, and not vainly, to see the feminine grub transformed, by brilliant clothes, into a butterfly easily surpassing all the select glittering creatures of the city; and he told himself that, personally, he vastly preferred Mina Raff in her plainest dress.

It was strange—seeing her there; while, in fact, she was in New York with far different things occupying her thoughts. Here she was no more than an illusion, a pattern, without substance, of projected light and shade; she had neither voice nor warmth nor color; only the most primitive minds could be carried away, lost, in the convention of her flat mobile effigy! Yet, after a little, he found that he as well was absorbed in the atmosphere of emotional verity she created. It was clear to him now that not the Mina Raff in New York, but this, was the important reality. In herself she was little compared to what she so miraculously did. Then—the final step in a surrender, however much he hated the word, to art—he forgot Mina Raff completely. He lost her partly in his own mental processes and partly in the unhappy girl she was portraying:

It was an uncomplicated story of betrayal, of a marriage that was no marriage, and the birth, in circumstances of wretched loneliness, of an illegitimate baby. The father annoyed Lee excessively; he was the anciently familiar inaccurate shape of conventionalized lust without an identifying human trait. Not for a second did Lee believe in his grease-pencilled incontinence and perfidy; but the child he seduced, incidents of the seduction charged with the beauty of pity, thronged Lee's mind with sensations and ideas. However, it was the world surrounding the central motive, the action, that most engaged him; hardly a trait of generosity dignified it; and, exaggeratedly as a universal meanness and self-righteous cruelty was shown, it scarcely departed, he felt, from the truth.

Why was it that virtue, continence, corroded the heart? Why did people who, through predilection, went to churches, regard those who didn't with such an insistent animosity? Why did the church itself seek to obliterate—as though they were a breathing menace—all who stood outside its doors? There was something terribly wrong in the reaction of life to religion, or in the religion that was applied to life. It began, in the symbolical person of Christ, with, at least, a measure of generosity; but that had been long lost. Now the bitterness of the religious rather resembled envy.

In the picture flickering on the screen the girl who had suffered the agonies of birth sat, with her baby on her young lap, in the forlorn room of a village boarding house. The baby was sick, a doctor had left shortly before, and one minute clenched hand rested on the mother's bare breast. Lee found himself gazing fixedly at the girl's face: trouble slowly clouded it, the trouble was invaded by fear, a terrible question. He realized that the hand was growing cold—the baby was dead.

Waves of suffering passed darkly over the mother, incredulity swiftly followed by a frozen knowledge; she tried with her lips, her mouth, to breath life into the flesh already meaningless, lost to her. Then the tragedy of existence drew her face into a mask universal and timeless, a staring tearless shocked regard as white and inhuman as plaster of Paris. Emotion choked at Lee's throat; and, in a sense of shame at having been so shaken, he admitted that Mina Raff had an extraordinary ability: he evaded the impressive reality by a return to the trivial fact. In the gloom there was only a scattering of applause, a failure of approbation caused either by an excess of emotion in the audience, or—this he thought more probable—a general uneasiness before a great moment of life. The crowded theatre was wholly relieved, itself again, in a succeeding passage of trivial clowning.

Hatred pursued the youthful informally maternal figure: that, eventually, she was saved by the love of an individual was small before the opposed mass—women surrounded her with vitriolic whispers, women turned her maliciously from house to house, a woman had betrayed her. Finally the tide of Christianity rose, burst, in a biblical father who drove her into a night of snow that was a triumph of the actual substituted for the cut paper of stage convention. That she would be rescued, no doubt was permitted; and Lee took no part in the storm of applause which greeted this act of satisfactory heroics.

The other spirit had appalled him: in his state of mental doubt—it might equally have been a condition of obscure hope—he had been rudely shoved toward pessimism; the converse of the announced purpose of the picture. The audience, for one thing, was so depressingly wrong in the placing of its merriment: it laughed delightedly at a gaunt feminine vindictiveness hurrying through the snow on an errand of destruction. The fact that the girl's maternity was transcendent in a generous and confident heart, made lovely by spiritual passion, escaped everyone. The phrase, spiritual passion, had occurred to him without forethought and he wondered if it were permissible, if it meant anything? It did decidedly to him; he told himself further that it was the fusion of the body and all the aspirations called spirit in one supreme act of feeling.

It had been his and Fanny's ... at first. Then the spirit, though it had lingered in other relationships, had deserted the consummation of passion. That hadn't grown perfunctory, but it became a thing more and more strictly of the flesh; with this it was less thrilling. There, he believed, they were not singular; or, anyhow, he wasn't; he saw what he was convinced was the same failure in the men past youth about him. But in Fanny there was, he recognized, that fierce if narrow singleness of impulse, of purity. His thoughts of other women were not innocent of provocative conjecture—Anette's sinuous body, now as dead to him as Alohabad, recurred to his mind—but in this Fanny was utterly loyal. Yes, she had, a thing impossible for any man he had known, a mental singleness of desire.

Was it that which had in her an affinity with the oppressors of the picture, which made her, mechanically, the vigorously enlisted enemy of the actual Mina Raff? It startled him a little to realize that Fanny—for all her marked superiority—was definitely arrayed with the righteous mob. She was sorry for those who failed in the discharge of duty to God and man, and she worked untiringly to reinstate them—in her good opinion. That was it, and it was no more! All such attempted salvation resolved itself into the mere effort to drag men up to the complacent plane of the incidental savior.

This recognition took a great deal of the vigor from his intended conversation with Peyton Morris: anything in the way of patronage, he reflected, would be as useless as it would be false. But he had no impulse to forego his purpose; he was engaged to help Claire who was too proud to help herself; yes, by heaven, and too right for the least humiliation. If Claire suffered, it must be because the world was too inferior for hope of any kind.

28

Lee was not unaware of the incongruity of his position, for he was equally ignoring the needs of two others, Peyton and Mina Raff. It was evident to him now, since he had seen her in a picture, that she was well worth the greatest consideration. She lay outside the stream of ordinary responsibilities. What held him steady was the belief that she and Peyton were not so important to each other as they thought; Claire needed him more badly than Mina. There was a possibility—no, it was probable—that Claire deserted would develop into an individual as empty and as vacantly sounding as a drum. She had said as much. Her heritage, together with its splendors of courage and charm, signally carried that menace.

So much, joined to what already was thronging his thoughts, brought Lee's mind to resemble the sheet of an enormous ledger covered with a jumble of figures apparently beyond any reduction to an answer. He was considering Claire and Mina Raff, Mina and Claire, at a hunt breakfast at Willing Spencer's in Nantbrook Valley, north of Eastlake, when, with a plate of food in one hand and a cup of coffee in the other, he collided with Peyton Morris, his face pinched and his eyes dull from a lack of rest. The Spencer house was sparely furnished, a square unimpressive dwelling principally adapted to the early summers of its energetic children; and Peyton and Lee Randon allowed themselves to be crowded into the bare angle formed by a high inner door.

"Claire told you," the younger said.

"Yes," Lee replied briefly. It wouldn't, after all, be difficult to talk to Peyton; he was obviously miserable from the necessity of suppressing what absorbed his entire consciousness.

"Well, I suppose you think there's nothing to be said for me," his voice was defiant; "and that I ought to be shot."

"Very much to the contrary," Lee asserted; "there is so much to say that it's difficult to know where to begin. With another situation practically the same, I might have agreed with you thoroughly; but, with Claire and what I have gathered of you, in this special one I can't."

"It isn't absolutely necessary," the other pointed out; "Mina and I will have a lot to ignore."

"The first thing you'll have to manage," Lee observed sharply, "is to grow up. You are not in a place to be helped by leather-headed satire and visions of solitary grandeur. My interest comes only from Claire and some personal curiosity; Mina Raff doesn't require anyone's assistance. Of you all, her position is clearest. I don't know if you can be brought to see it, but this is only incidental, a momentary indulgence, with her."

"What you don't seem to get," Peyton told him, with a brutally cold face, "is that I may smash you; now, where you are."

"That was possible," Lee agreed; "and you are right—I had overlooked it. I think that's passed, though; I'm going to keep on as if it were. Why, you young fool, you seem to have no conception, none in the world, of what you propose to do. In a week, in your frame of mind, you'd have a hundred fights; there would be time for nothing else but knocking out the men who insulted you. You'll collapse over Sunday if you are not absolutely and totally impervious to everything and everybody. The only way you can throw the world over is to ignore it; while you appear to have the idea that it should put a rose in your buttonhole."

"You don't have to tell me it's going to be stiff," Peyton Morris asserted gloomily. "I can take care of that. Claire and Ira are the hard part. Lee, if anyone a year ago had said that I was like this, that I was even capable of it, I'd have ruined him. God, what a thing to happen! I want you to understand that we, Mina and I, didn't have a particle to do with it—it just flatly occurred. I had seen her only three times when it was too late; and if you think I didn't try to break it, and myself, too—"

Lee nodded. "Certainly. Why not, since it's bound to knock you on the head? You've been very unfortunate: I can't imagine a man to whom this would come worse."

"If I can make Mina happy I don't care about myself."

"Of course, that is understood," Lee Randon returned impatiently; "it is nothing but sentimental rot, all the same. If you are not contented, easy in mind, how can she be happy? You have got to believe entirely in what you are doing, it must be right to you on every possible side; and you can't make that grade, Peyton; you are too conventional underneath."

"Sink your spurs in me," he said doggedly; "it's funny when you really think about it. Why, only a little while ago, if I had heard of a man doing this, I would have beaten him up just on general principles: running away from his wife and child, with another woman, an actress, that's what it is! I tell myself that, but the words haven't a trace of meaning or importance. Somehow, they don't seem to apply to me, to us; they can say what they like, but Mina isn't wicked. She—she loves me, Lee; and, suddenly, that swept everything else out of sight.

"But go back to me—you realize that I was rather in favor of what I was, what I had. Brandenhouse is a good school and my crowd ran it. We were pretty abrupt with boys who whored about; and, at Princeton, well, we thought we were it. We were, still, there; and I got a heavy idea of what I liked and was like. We were very damned honorable and the icing on the cake generally. That was good after I left college, too; but what's the use of going into it; I was in the same old Brandenhouse surrounding. The war split us wide open. Or I thought it did; but, Lee, by God, I don't believe it changed a thing. I got my touch of concussion early, Ira was born, and, and—"

"Disaster," Lee Randon pronounced shortly.

"Call it that if you choose; there isn't much use in calling it at all: it simply is."

"With someone else, yes; but with you, no, not finally; you haven't the character and disposition to get away with it. You don't, secretly, approve of yourself, Peyton; and that will be fatal. The truth is that, while you want this now, in a year, or two years, or five, you'll demand the other. You think it is going to be different from everything else in heaven and earth, you're convinced it's going to stay all in the sky; but it will be on the solid familiar ground. Understand again—it isn't your plan I'm attacking; but your ability; that and your real ignorance of Mina Raff.

"If you imagine for an instant that this love will be bigger than her work, if you suppose that, against her acting, it will last, you are an idiot for your pains. If I don't know the side of her you do, I have become fairly familiar with one you haven't dreamed of. She is a greater actress than people yet recognize, principally because of the general doubt about moving pictures; but that recognition will come, and, when it does, you will be swept out of sight.

"No, you haven't the slightest suspicion of what it is about; that side of her, and it's very nearly the whole woman, is a blank. She admitted to me that she couldn't understand it herself. But what she is doing is dragging into her genius what it needs. She loves you now, and tomorrow she'll love a Belgian violinist, a great engineer, a Spanish prince at San Sebastian. How will you take sitting in the salon and hearing them padding around over your head? It's no good your getting mad at me; I am not blaming Mina Raff; you are. I admire her tremendously.

"In the beginning I said she could watch out for herself, and I intimated that I was reasonably indifferent to what happened to you: it is Claire I am concerned about. Unfortunately for her, and without much reason, she loves you too. When Mina is done with you and you stray back, from, perhaps, South America, Claire won't be here. I don't mean that she will have gone away, or be dead in the familiar sense. I haven't any doubt but that she would live with you again—she is not small-minded and she's far more unconventional than you—what there was of her."

"If you or anyone else thinks that I don't admire Claire—" he stopped desperately. "We won't get far talking," Peyton added; "even if all you have said is a fact. You can't hit on much that I've missed. You might just as well curse me and let me go."

"Nothing of the sort," Lee Randon returned equably; "that's exactly what I have no intention of doing. In the interest of Claire I must try to open your eyes." The younger man said indignantly:

"You talk as though I were a day-old kitten. It's cursed impertinent: I don't seem to remember asking for so much advice."

Throughout their conversation they were both holding the plates of sausage and scrambled eggs, from which rose a pungent odor, inevitable to the occasion. And, in a silence which fell upon them, Lee realized the absurdity of their position behind the door. "We can't keep this up," he declared, and moved into the eddying throng, the intermingling ceaseless conversations. Almost at once Peyton Morris disappeared, and Lee found Fanny at his shoulder. Neither of them fox-hunted, although they hacked a great deal over the country roads and fields, and they had ridden to the Spencers' that morning. Fanny wore dark brown and a flattened hunting derby which, with her hair in a short braid tied by a stiff black ribbon, was particularly becoming. She was, he told himself, with her face positively animated, sparkling, from talk, unusually attractive. Fanny was like that—at times she was singularly engaging.

"What did he say?" she demanded, nodding in the direction in which Peyton had disappeared. "I have avoided him all morning."

"An uncommon lot for Peyton," Lee acknowledged. "I almost think he has been jarred out of his self-complacency. But, on the whole, that is not possible. It's temporary with him. At one time I thought—in the language of youth—he was going to crown me."

"The little beast!" she exclaimed viciously. "If he had I'd have made him sorry. I saw Claire a few minutes ago, and she asked me to tell you, if she missed you, that she had something for you to see. Wasn't it strange that she said nothing to me about it? I should think, in her scrape, she'd rather turn to a woman than to a man. But Claire isn't very feminine: I've always felt her hardness."

"Then that's why she didn't speak to you," Lee assented superficially. "I'll go over tonight, after dinner. They must be pretty nearly ready to drop the fox, and it's beginning to drizzle."

There was, soon after that, an exodus from the back of the house to the fields beyond. It was a very fair hunting country, rolling and clear of brush, with grouped woods on the surrounding hills and streams in the swales below. The clouds were broken and aqueous, and the grass held a silver veil of fine raindrops. Only an inconsiderable part of those present were following the hounds; the others, in a restricted variety of sporting garb—the men in knickerbockers and gaiters or riding breeches, the women breeched and severely coated or swathed in wide reddish tweed capes—stood, with a scattering of umbrellas and upturned collars, in a semi-circle on the soggy turf.

30

There was a baying of hounds from the direction of the stables, and the Master swung up on a bright chestnut horse with a braided tail. A huntsman appeared with a shuttered box, holding the fox, and an old brown and white hound bitch, wise with many years of hunting, to follow and establish and announce the scent. "If you are ready, Brace," the Master said to his huntsman, "you may drop." A stable boy held the hound, and, raising the shutter, Brace shook the fox out on the ground.

The animal—in view of the commotion about to pursue it—was surprisingly small, slim flanked; proportionately the tail seemed extravagant. "I hope the brush won't get wet," a man behind Lee spoke; "when it does they can't run." As it was, the fox, obviously, was reluctant to start; it crouched in the rough grass and glanced fleetly around with incredibly sharp black eyes. The men shouted and flung up their arms; but the animal was indifferent to their laudable efforts. The hunt, Lee Randon thought, had assumed an aspect of the ridiculous; the men and women on expensive excited horses, the pack yelping from beyond a road, the expectant on-lookers, were mocked by the immobility of the puzzled subject of the chase. Finally the fox obligingly moved a few steps; it hesitated again, and then trotted forward, slipping under a fence. Lee could follow it clearly across the next field and into the next; its progress was unhurried, deliberate, insolent.

"Give him six minutes," the Master decided.

When the time had gone the leash of the single hound was slipped. She ran around in a circle, whining eagerly, her nose to the sod, and then with a high yelp, set smartly off in a direction absolutely opposite to that taken by the fox. She was brought back and her nose held to the hot scent; again, with a fresh assurance, the bitch gave tongue, followed the trail to where it went under the fence, and turned, instead of bearing to the right, to the left. There were various exclamations. A kennel man declared, "She knows what she's about, and the fox will swing into Sibley's Cover." Someone else more sceptically asserted that the hound was a fool. Her sustained cry floated back from under the hill; and, in another minute, the pack, the hunt, was off. The horses rose gracefully in a sleek brown tide over the first fence; and then there was a division—the hounds scattered and bunched and scattered, some of the riders went to the left after the palpable course of the fox, others pounded direct for Sibley's Cover, and the remainder reined up over the hounds.

Although long association and familiarity had made such scenes a piece with Lee Randon's subconsciousness, today the hunt seemed nothing more than nonsense. He laughed, and made a remark of disparaging humor; but he found no support. Willing Spencer, kept out of the field by a broken collar bone, gazed at him with lifted eyebrows. Fanny and Lee turned to their horses, held for them by a groom at a mounting block, and went home. The rain had increased, but, not cold, Lee found it pleasant on his face. They jogged quietly over the roads bordered with gaunt sombre hedges, through the open countryside, into Eastlake.

Nothing, he realized, had been accomplished with Peyton Morris; the other was too numbed, shocked, by the incredible accident that had overtaken him to listen to reason. Lee felt that he could hardly have said more. He wondered what Claire had to show him. Still, he wasn't through with her husband; he had no intention of resting until every hope was exhausted. What particularly impressed him—he must speak of it to Peyton—was that no matter where Morris might get he would find life monotonously the same. It was very much like mountain climbing—every peak looked different, more iridescent and desirable, from the one occupied; but, gazing back, that just left appeared as engaging, as rare, as any in the distance. Every experience in the life surrounding him was the same as all the others; no real change was offered, because the same dull response permeated all living; no escape such as Peyton planned was possible.

Escape, Lee Randon continued, happened within; it was not, he repeated, a place on earth, or any possession, but a freedom, a state, of mind. Peyton Morris, while it was quite possible for him to be destroyed, was incapable of mental liberty, readjustments; he might drive himself on the rocks, on the first reef where he disregarded the clamor of warning bells and carefully charted directions, but he was no Columbus for the discovery of a magical island, a Cuba, of spices and delectable palms. Peyton had looked with a stolid indifference at the dangerously fascinating, the incomprehensible, smile of Cytherea. Yes, if the young donkey could be forced past this tempting patch of grazing, if he could only be driven a short distance farther down the highway of custom, Claire would be safe.

But she must be made to think that such a conclusion had been purely the result of Peyton's reserved strength, and not of a mere negative surrender following doubt. And, above all, there must be no appearance of Mina Raff having, after a short trial, herself discarded him. On such trivialities Claire's ultimate happiness might hang. Truth was once more wholly restrained, hidden, dissimulated; the skillful shifting of painted masks, false-faces, continued uninterrupted its progress. A new lethargy enveloped Lee: his interest, his confidence, in what he was trying to prevent waned. What did it matter who went and who stayed? In the end it was the same, unprofitable and stale. All, probably, that his thought had accomplished was to rob his ride of its glow, make flat the taste of the whiskey and charged water he prepared. However, shortly a pervading warmth—but it was of the spirits—brought back his lately unfamiliar sense of well-being.

The Morrises lived in a large remodelled brick house, pleasantly pseudo-classic, beyond the opposite boundary of Eastlake; and, leaving his car in the turn of the drive past the main door, Lee walked into the wide

31

hall which swept from front to back, and found a small dinner party at the stage of coffee and cigarettes. It was composed, he saw at once, of Peyton's friends; as he entered three young men rose punctiliously—Christian Wager, with hair growing close like a mat on a narrow skull and a long irregular nose; Gilbert Bromhead, a round figure and a face with the contours and expression, the fresh color, of a pleasant and apple-like boy; and Peyton. They had been at their university together; and, Lee Randon saw, they were making, with a characteristic masculine innocence, an effort to secure their wives in the same bond of affectionate understanding that held them.

Claire, who had smiled acknowledgingly with her eyes when Lee approached, returned to a withdrawn concentration upon the section of table-cloth immediately before her; she answered the remarks directed to her with a temporary measure of animation vanishing at once with the effort. Christian Wager, who was in London with a branch of an American banking firm, had married an English girl strikingly named Evadore. She was large, with black hair cut in a scanty bang; but beyond these unastonishing facts there was nothing in her appearance to mark or remember. However, a relative of hers, he had been told, distant but authentic, had been a lady-in-waiting to the Queen. Gilbert Bromhead's wife was southern, a small appealing compound of the essence of the superlatively feminine.

Lee Randon, in a chair drawn up for him at the table, studied the women, arbitrarily thrown together, with a secret amusement. Evadore Wager was frankly—to a degree almost Chinese—curious about the others. At short regular intervals, in a tone of unvaried timbre and inexhaustible surprise, she half exclaimed, "Fancy." Claire was metallic, turned in, with an indifference to her position that was actually rude, upon herself. But Mrs. Gilbert Bromhead made up for any silence around her in a seductive, low-pitched continuous talking. A part of this was superficially addressed to Claire and the solidly amazed Evadore; but all its underlying intention, its musical cadences and breathless suspensions for approval, were flung at the men. The impression she skillfully conveyed to Lee Randon, by an art which never for an instant lost its aspect of the artless, was that he, at least, older in experience than the rest there, alone entirely understood and engaged her.

The men—even Peyton, temporarily—resting confident on a successful bringing of their wives into the masculine simplicity of their common memories and affection, said little. With eyes puckered wisely against the cigarette smoke they made casual remarks about their present occupations and terse references to companions and deeds of the past. Only Peyton had been of any athletic importance; he had played university foot-ball; and, in view of this, there was still a tinge of respect in Bromhead's manner. A long run of Peyton's, crowned with a glorious and winning score, was recalled. But suddenly it failed to stir him. "How young we were then," he observed gloomily.

Christian Wager protested. "That isn't the right tone. We were young then, true, but Princeton was teaching us what it meant to be men. In that game, Morris, you got something invaluable to you now, hard endurance and fairness—"

"In my day," Lee interposed, "the team was told to sink a heel in any back that looked a little too good for us."

"There were instructors like that," Gilbert Bromhead assented; "and some graduate coaches are pretty cunning; but they are being discredited."

Wager largely, obliviously, passed over this interruption. "We learned decency," he proceeded, "in business and ideals and living; and to give and take evenly. In the war and in civil life we were and are behind the big issues. This new license and socialistic rant, the mental and moral bounders, must be held down, and we are the men to do it. Yes, and I believe in the church, the right church, we're all for that: I tell you the country depends on the men the best colleges turn out."

"My God, Christian, you must have made a lot of money lately," Bromhead observed. "You talk exactly like the president of a locomotive works. You have been dining with the best, too; I can tell that with certainty. Answer us this, honestly—do you mention the Royal Family in your prayers?"

Evadore laughed. "Do you know, that's really awfully good. He does put it on a bit, doesn't he?"

"If you let Christian go on," Peyton added, "he'll talk about the sacred ties of Anglo-Saxon blood and tradition, with the English and American exchange ruling the world. Gilbert, how did your artillery company get along with the Londoners?"

"All right, if we were near a brick yard."

Claire rose abruptly, and they drifted out to a reception room opening, with a wide arch, beyond the hall. Gilbert Bromhead's wife hesitated; then, confidentially, she told Lee that she adored to sit on stairs. "Very well," he assented; "these of the Morrises' are splendid." He was a step below her, and her knees and his shoulder settled together.

"I like older men so much," she admitted what she had already so adroitly conveyed; "patches of grey above the ears are so distinguished."

"Older than what?"

Apparently forgetful that her gesture included Gilbert Bromhead she indicated the rooms that now held the others. "Young men are so head over heels," she particularized; "they are always disarranging things." She laughed, a delectable sound. "I oughtn't to have said that, and I wouldn't—to them. I might almost tell you the story about the man in the department store and the drawers." Their contact was more pronounced. "Isn't that

English girl extraordinary? I didn't believe for a minute that was her own color till I was close to it. Her hair isn't dyed; but why does she wear that skimpy bang?" Again she laughed, a pure golden melody. "But you admired it, I know you did; men are so unaccountable. Could you trust her, do you think? It wasn't very nice to make fun of her husband." Adroitly, without the flutter of a ruffle, she moved to a higher step, and Claire—before Lee had any premonition of her appearance—stood below them with chocolates.

"She is rather attractive," his companion admitted, when Claire had gone. "She doesn't like me, or Mrs. Wager, though; and I must say she made it plain in her own house. I've been studying her, and there is something wrong. Is she happy with Peyton Morris? I thought he was right nice until you came." She turned for a better view, through the balustrade, of the doors beyond, and then drew her skirt close so that he could move up beside her. "It's just like a smoke-house in there," she reported. "I don't truthfully think cigarettes are nice for a woman; and I wouldn't dream of taking whiskey; in the South we never. You'd call that out of date." She bent forward, arranging the ribbon of a slipper, and her mouth met his in a long kiss.

"What made you suppose you could do that?" she demanded; "how did you know I wouldn't be cross with you? But ... somehow I didn't mind. Although you mustn't again, so publicly. I wonder why, with you, it seemed so perfectly nice, and not at all as if I had only met you?"

There was a response to that as recognized, as exact, as the bishop's move in chess; indeed, it was expected of him; she was hesitating, waiting for it; but he was unable to reassure her with the conventional sentiment. A month ago he would have commanded and developed an enticing situation; but now, for Lee Randon, it was without possibilities, hardly more than perfunctory. A shade of vexation invaded her bearing, and she moved a significant infinitesimal fraction away from him. Then she discovered a wind blowing down the stairs. "I have to take such good care of myself," she told Lee, preparing to descend. "It is because I am so delicate—I can get upset at nothing. Here you are all so strong; you have an advantage over me. Gilbert, dear," she called from the hall, her voice musical with tender reproach, "I can't see how you love me, you stay away so far."

"What did the little ass say to you?" Claire asked. Lee was standing with her by the piano, and the others were around the fireplace in the farther spaciousness. "Nothing much," he replied. "You mean that she never stopped. I'll admit she's skillful; but she needn't think I'm a fool. But you will never guess what I want to tell you. My dear Lee, that Mrs. Grove wrote me a letter. I have it here in my dress, for you to read. It's a scream." He took the sheet of note paper: it was grey with an address on East Sixty-sixth Street embossed in pale vermilion, and had an indefinable scent. The writing was decisive:

### "MY DEAR MRS. MORRIS,

"It is so difficult for me to express my disturbance at what Mina Raff has just told me, that I am asking to see you here, at my house in New York. Engagements make it difficult for me to leave at present. I hope you will not find this impertinent from an older woman, threatened very much as you in her affections by an impossible calamity—"

The signature, Savina Grove, had the crispness of a name often attached to opinions and papers of authority.

"That's rather cool," he agreed.

"Cool! The woman's demented. No, I suppose she thinks I am an honest wronged woman or something objectionable of the sort. I was going to throw it away when I kept it to amuse you."

"It does, Claire; and I'm glad to see it; impertinent as she admits it may be, you must consider. As Mrs. Grove writes, you are both caught."

"If you think I'll go see her you are madder still."

"I realize you won't; but worse things could happen. It's the only possible approach to Mina Raff; I had a chance to try Peyton, but it did no good. It seems to me this Mina ought to have some understanding."

Claire Morris said: "You can do it."

He reflected. "Well, perhaps; I'm your uncle; there are no brothers, and what other family you have is away. It might be useful. Anyhow, she would hear a thing or two about you from me."

"Seriously, Lee, you'd only get angry; I can see Mrs. Grove as though she were in the room—the utmost New York self-satisfaction. And I won't have you discussing my affairs."

"Absurd. A thousand people will be talking about them soon if this isn't managed. I have an idea I had better go to New York and try what can be done there. I got along well enough with the girl herself; and perhaps, though it's not likely, Mrs. Grove has some influence."

"Of course, I can't stop you," Claire said; her hand strayed over his, on the piano. "I'm simply enraged at myself, Lee. Why, I should let him go with cheers—except where I was sorry for him—but I can't. He is such a sweet child; and, you see, he was all mine."

"I can't leave before Thursday." He considered. "I'll have a wire sent to the Groves, say something regretful and polite about you—measles."

"Don't bother," she returned.

33

Peyton came stiffly up to them. "I happened to mention, Claire, that we had some champagne left, and it created the intensest excitement. I told them it would do no good, that you were keeping hold of it; but they insisted on a look at the bottles."

"Get them, Peyton," she replied unhesitatingly. "I was keeping it, but perhaps for now. This is a very appropriate time for you and me, and the last of the cases left over from our wedding."

An expression of pain tightened his mouth; he turned away without further speech. "We'll have it in the dining-room," Claire announced; "big glasses filled with ice." They gathered about the bare table, and Peyton Morris ranged the dark green bottles, capped in white foil, on the sideboard. He worked with a napkin at a cork: there was a restrained sibilant escaping pressure, and the liquid rose in frothing bubbles through the ice.

It was, Lee thought, a golden drink, flooded, up to a variable point, with an inimitable gaiety. In comparison whiskey was brutalizing; sherry was involved with a number of material accompanying pleasures; port was purely masculine and clarets upset him; beer was a beverage and not a delight; ale a soporific; and Rhine wines he ignored. Champagne held in solution the rhythm of old Vienna waltzes, of ball rooms with formal greenery, floating with passions as light as the tarleton skirts floating about dancing feet. But it wasn't, he insisted, a wine for indiscriminate youth—youth that couldn't distinguish between the sweet and the dry. It was for men like himself, with memories, unrealized dreams. Ugly women, and women who were old, and certainly prudes, should never be given a sip.

Peyton Morris again filled all the glasses; there was a clatter of talk, the accent of the South, about Lee; but he grew oblivious of it. Champagne always gave Fanny a headache; neither was it a drink for contented mothers, housewives. Contrarily, it was the ideal, the only, wine for seductions. It belonged most especially to masked balls, divine features vanishing under a provocative edge of black satin. He thought of little hidden tables and fantastic dresses, fragile emotion; lips and knees and garters. It all melted away before the intentness of Claire's expression. Peyton was doggedly holding to the rim of the table; Gilbert Bromhead was very close to Evadore; the black sheath of her hair had slipped and her eyes were blank; the blanched delicate hand of the South nearest Christian Wager had disappeared, Christian's hand on that side could not be seen. Peyton once more filled the glasses:

"It must all go," Claire insisted; "I won't have a drop left."

Wager's sentimentality overflowed in approved and well-established channels: Princeton was their mother, their sacred alma—alma mater. Here, under Peyton's roof, they had gathered to renew ... friendships unbroken with their wives, their true wives; oceans couldn't separate them, nor time, nor—nor silver locks among the gold. They must come to London next December: anniversary of mutual happiness and success. Take the children, the sons of old Princeton, to Christmas pantomine.

"Once," Evadore told them, "I went to a night club. Do you know what that is, over here? I don't believe I can explain it; but there are quantities of champagne and men and principally girls; but they're not girls at all, if you see what I mean, not by several accidents. It would have been splendid, but I got sick, and it turned into a ghastly mess, mostly in the cab. That was rather thick, wasn't it?"

Claire rose, and Lee Randon heard her say, under her breath, "Oh hell"; but there was another full bottle, and she had to sit again. He had promised Fanny not to stay long, and, if he were coming home, she never went to sleep until he was in the house. Lee wasn't drunk, but then, he recognized, neither was he sober. Why should he be the latter? he demanded seriously of himself. His glass was empty, the champagne was all gone. Mrs. Gilbert Bromhead was perceptibly leaning on Christian Wager, her skill blurred; Evadore's face was damply pallid, her mouth slack; she left the table, the room, hurried and unsteady, evidently about to repeat the thickness of the act that had marred her enjoyment of the night club; Claire was openly contemptuous of them all.

Outside, it had grown much colder, the ruts in the road were frozen, treacherous, but Lee Randon drove his car with a feeling of inattentive mastery. He saw some stars, an arc light, black patches of ice; and, as he increased his speed, he sang to an emphatic lifted hand of a being in the South Seas who wore leaves, plenty of leaves ... But none of the silly songs now could compare with—with the bully that, on the levees, he was going to cut down. However, in his house, he grew quiet. "Lee," his wife called sleepily from their room, "you are so late, dear. I waited the longest while for some of the addresses for our Christmas cards. You must remember to give them to me tomorrow."

Her voice, heavy with sleep and contentment and love, fell upon his hearing like the sound of a pure accusing bell. He wasn't fit to have a wife like Fanny, children as good as Helena and Gregory: he, Lee Randon, was a damned ingrate! That bloody doll—he had threatened to put it in the fire before—could now go where it belonged. But the hearth was empty, cold. Cytherea, with her disdainful gaze, evaded his wavering reach.

III

34

Fanny, where the Groves were concerned, was utterly opposed to the plan which, Lee gathered, Claire had half supported. "It's really too foolish," his wife told him; "what can Mrs. Grove and you have to say to each other? And you won't get anywhere with Mina Raff. Indeed, Lee, I think it isn't quite dignified of you."

"That won't bother me," he replied indulgently. "I was wondering—you haven't been away for so long—if you'd come with me. This other affair wouldn't take half a day: you could buy clothes and there are the theatres."

"I'd love to." She hesitated. "When did you mean to go?" But, when he said the following noon, she discovered that that didn't allow her enough time for preparations. "You don't realize how much there is to do here, getting the servants and the children satisfactorily arranged. You might telephone me after you're there; and, if you didn't come back at once, perhaps I could manage it."

Lee telegraphed Mrs. William Loyd Grove of his intention; and, with a table put up at his seat in the Pullman car for New York, he occupied himself opportunely with the reports of his varied profitable concerns. He had had a reply, sufficiently cordial, to his telegram, arranging for him to go directly to the Groves' house; but that he had declined; and when he gave the driver of a taxi-cab the address on East Sixty-sixth Street it was past four and the appropriate hour for afternoon tea.

The house, non-committal on the outside—except for the perceived elaboration of the window draperies within—was, Lee saw at once, a rich undisturbed accumulation of the decorative traditions of the eighteen-eighties. The hall was dark, with a ceiling and elaborate panels of black walnut and a high dull silver paper. The reception room into which he was shown, by a maid, was jungle-like in its hangings and deep-tufted upholstery of maroon and royal blue velvets, its lace and twisted cords with heavy tassels, and hassocks crowded on the sombrely brilliant rugs sacred in mosques. There was a mantle in colored marbles, cabinets of fretted ebony, tables of onyx and floriated ormolu, ivories and ornaments of Benares brass and olivewood.

In the close incongruity of this preserved Victorianism Mrs. William Loyd Grove, when she appeared soon after, startled Lee Randon by her complete expression of a severely modern air. She was dressed for the street in a very light brown suit, rigidly simple, with a small black three-cornered hat, a sable skin about her neck, and highly polished English brogues with gaiters. Mrs. Grove was thin—no, he corrected that impression, she was slight—her face, broad at the temples, narrowed gracefully to her chin; her eyes were a darker blue than the velvet; and her skin at once was evenly pale and had a suggestion of transparent warmth. The slender firm hand she extended, her bearing and the glimpse of a round throat, had lost none of the slender flexibility of youth.

"The first thing I must do," she told him in an unsympathetic, almost harsh, voice, "is to say that I agree with you entirely about this house. It's beyond speech. But William won't have it touched. Probably you are not familiar with the stubborn traditions of old New Yorkers. Of course, when Mrs. Simeon Grove was alive, it was hopeless; but I did think, when she died, that something could be done. You can see how wrong I was—William can't be budged."

She was, he silently continued his conclusions, past forty, but by not more than a year, or a year and a half. All that her signature suggested was true: she was more forcible, decisive, than he had expected. Money and place, with an individual authentic strength of personality, gave her voice its accent of finality, her words their abruptness, her manner an unending ease.

"Mina said she might be here," Mrs. Grove went on, from an uncomfortable Jacobean chair, "if something or other happened at the studio. But I see she is not, and I am relieved."

"Mrs. Morris regretted she couldn't come," Lee told her inanely; and his hostess replied:

"I can't at all say that I believe you—I was so upset I couldn't resist the attempt. But I hope she understood that it was absolutely impossible for me to go to Eastlake."

He nodded, a shade annoyed by the briskness of her attack.

"We are immensely concerned about Mina," Mrs. Grove went on. "You see, with our son killed in the Lafayette Escadrille early in the war, practically she has been our only child. She is a daughter of a cousin of William's. Mina, I must admit, has become very difficult; I suppose because of her genius. She is perfectly amenable about everything in the world, until her mind gets set, like concrete, and then she is out of reach. Tell me a little about Mr. and Mrs. Morris."

Lee Randon spoke sharply for a minute or two, and a frown gathered on his hearer's brow. "Why," she observed, "it is worse than I had hoped. But I should have guessed from the name—Peyton Morris. I am very sorry; you are fond of her, of Claire, that is evident."

"I should not have come here for any other reason," he admitted. "I am not much of a meddler: it is so dangerous for everyone concerned. Then it might be that this was the best for all three of them."

"What a curious, contradictory thing for you to say," she commented, studying him. "You mustn't let William hear that; he's far worse than I am."

"I don't mean we can proceed from that attitude," Lee explained, "it was a sort of digression. I want to do whatever is possible to break it up; yes, purely for Claire."

"I hope we may succeed." Her voice showed doubt. "William isn't always tactful, and I've told him again and again he's taking the wrong tone with Mina. What a pity the Morrises have turned out thoroughly nice—don't tell me your Claire didn't curse me, I know these girls—it is so much easier to deal with vulgar people. I can see now what it was in the young man that captured Mina, she'd like that type—the masculine with an air of

35

fine linen." The tea-table was rolled up to them. "If you would rather have Scotch or rye it's here," she informed him. "But even the tea, you'll notice, is in a glass with rum; positively, soon no one will look at soup unless it's served as a highball."

Lee Randon did prefer Scotch: none better, he discovered, was to be imagined; the ice was frozen into precisely the right size; and the cigars before him, a special Corona, the Shepheard's Hotel cigarettes, carried the luxury of comfort to its last perfection. Mrs. Grove smoked in an abstracted long-accustomed manner. "Well," she demanded, "what is there we can do?"

"I rather trusted you to find that."

"How can I? What hold have we on her? Mina is getting this nonsensical weekly sum; her contract runs for two years yet; and then it will be worse. Outrageous! I tell her she isn't worth it. And, now, this tiresome Morris has money, too; and you say he's as bad as Mina. Have you talked to her about Mrs. Morris? Mina is strangely sensitive, and, if you can find it, has a very tender heart."

"I might do that over here," he suggested. "In Eastlake it wasn't possible. You've discouraged me, though; I suppose I had the idea that you could lock her up on bread and water."

She laughed. "An army of Minnesota kitchen maids would break into the house; millions of people have voted Mina their favorite; when she is out with me the most odious crowds positively stop my car. I won't go with her any more where she can be recognized." Lee rose, and his expression showed his increasing sense of the uselessness of their efforts.

"You mustn't give up," she said quickly; "you never can tell about Mina. You will come here for dinner, certainly; I'll send the car to your hotel at seven-thirty, and you will bring your bag. We can't argue over that, can we? William will enjoy having you very much. Do you mind my saying he'll be relieved? He is such a Knickerbocker. I needn't add, Mr. Randon, that you shall be entirely free: whenever you want to go down town Adamson will take you." The exact moulding of her body was insolent. "Well, then, for the moment—" She gave him no chance at refusal, but, with the curtness of her hand, the apparent vanishing of all knowledge of his presence, dismissed him before he was aware of it to the adroitness of the maid in the hall putting him into his overcoat.

In a double room at his hotel, repacking the articles of toilet he had spread around the bathroom, Lee thought, but without heat, damn that Grove woman. He didn't want to go to the Grove house, it would complicate things with Fanny; and, if William did enjoy him, Lee Randon, would he enjoy William? It was questionable in the present state of his mind. Dinner, a servant at the Groves' informed him, would be at eight. His bag was swiftly and skillfully unpacked for him—this always annoyed Lee—and the water was turned into the tub. His room, richly draped and oppressive as the one downstairs, had a bed with a high carved oak headboard from which a heavy canopy, again of velvet and again crimson, reached to the floor at its foot; and by the side of the bed ran a long cushion over which he repeatedly stumbled.

His immediate necessity was to telephone Fanny; she was delighted at the sound of his voice; but, when he told her what had happened, where he was, an increasing irritation crept into her voice. "I can't understand it at all," he heard her say, so clearly that it reconstructed her, expression and probable dress and setting, completely. "You asked me to come over and shop, and go to the theatre with you; and now that I have everything arranged, even Christopher pacified, you go to the Groves'. It seems to me most peculiar."

He couldn't help it, he replied, with a slight responsive sharpening of his own speech; he had driven to the hotel, where he had secured their room, and Mrs. Grove had made it impossible for him to stay there. When he left—it would be late tomorrow or early the next day, Lee thought—she could meet him and do as they planned. But Fanny refused to agree: it would, now, be a needless expense. No, the other was what she had eagerly looked forward to. Lee, drawing her attention once more to the fact that it wasn't possible, was answered by so long a silence that he concluded she had hung up the receiver.

"Have a good time," Fanny said at last; "you will, anyhow, with the Raff woman. I suppose Mrs. Grove, who seems to get everything she wants, is fascinating as well."

"Indeed, I don't know, Fanny!" he exclaimed, his patience almost exhausted. "It hasn't occurred to me to think about her. I'm sorry you won't do what I suggest; it's not different from what we first thought of."

"Good-bye," she answered reluctantly; "the children are here and send their love. They'd like to speak to you, but probably you're in a hurry."

"I may be late for dinner now," he admitted.

The receiver in his house was abruptly, unmistakably, replaced. No one else, and for so little perceptible cause, could make him as mad as Fanny frequently did. He put on his waistcoat, changed his money from the trousers on the bed to those he was wearing, in a formless indignation. This wasn't his fault, he repeated; positively, judged by her manner, he might be doing something wrong. Fanny even managed to convey a doubt of Mrs. Grove, Mrs. William Loyd Grove. But she couldn't see how ridiculous that was.

William Grove Lee liked negatively; there was, patently, nothing in him to create an active response. His short heavy body was faultlessly clothed; his heavy face, with its moustache twisted into points, the clouded

36

purple of his cheeks contradicted by the penetration of a steadily focussed gaze, expressed nothing more than a niceness of balance between self-indulgence, tempered by exercise, games in open air, and a far from negligible administration of the resources he had inherited.

"You are a relative of the Morrises?" he asked Lee, turning from the menu set before him in a miniature silver frame. This Lee Randon admitted, and Grove's eyebrows mounted. "Can't anything be done with the young man?"

"How are you succeeding with the young woman?" Lee returned.

"Oh, women—" William Grove waved his hand; "you can't argue with women. Mina wants her Peyton—if that's his name; God knows I've heard it enough—and there's no more to that."

"It begins to look as though she'd get him," Lee observed; "I must say we haven't got far with Morris."

"Extraordinary."

It was Mrs. Grove who spoke. She was dressed in grey, a gown cut away from sheer points on her shoulders, with a girdle of small gilt roses, her hair in a binding of grey brocade and amber ornaments; and above her elbows were bands of dull intricately pierced gold.

"I wonder what it's all about?"

Lee gazed at her with a new interest. "So do I," he acknowledged; "I was thinking of that, really, before this happened: what is it all about?"

"I can answer that readily enough," Grove assured them; "anyone could with a little consideration. They saw too much of each other; they ran their heads into the noose. Trouble always follows. I don't care who they are, but if you throw two fairly young people of opposite sex together in circumstances any way out of the ordinary, you have a situation to meet. Mina has been spoiled by so much publicity; her emotions are constantly over-strung; and she thinks, if she wants it, that she can have the moon."

"You believe that, I know, William," his wife commented; "I have often heard you say so. But what is your opinion, Mr. Randon—have you reached one and is a conclusion possible?"

"I can't answer any of your questions," he admitted; "perhaps this is one of the things that must be experienced to be understood; certainly it hasn't a great deal to do with the mind." He turned to William Grove, "Your view has a lot to recommend it, even if it solves nothing. Suppose you are right—what then?"

"I don't pretend to go that far," Grove protested; "I am not answering the questions of the universe. Savina has an idea there's a mystery in it, a quality hidden from reason; and I want to knock that on the head. It's a law of nature, that's all; keep away from it if you want security. I can't imagine people of breeding—you will have to overlook this, Mr. Randon, on the account of Morris—getting so far down the slide. It belongs to another class entirely, one without traditions or practical wisdom. Yet, I suppose it is the general tone of the day: they think they can handle fire with impunity, like children with parlor matches."

"It can't, altogether, be accounted for so easily," Lee decided. "The whole affair has been so lied about, and juggled to suit different climates and people, that hardly any of the original impulse is left on view. What do you think would happen if for a while we'd lose our ideas of what was right and wrong in love?"

"Pandemonium," Grove replied promptly.

"Not if people were more responsible, William," Savina Grove added; "not for the superior. But then, all laws and order were made for the good of the mob. I don't need the policeman I see in the streets; and, really, I haven't a scrap more use for policeman-like regulations; I could regulate myself—"

"And there," he interrupted, "is where Mina fails; she can't run herself for a damn; she ought to have a nurse. Your theories contradict each other, as well—you say one thing and do quite differently."

She was silent at this, gazing at her hands, the beautifully made pointed fingers bare of rings. On their backs the veins, blue-violet, were visible; and there was a delicate tracery inside the bend of her arms. But her face, Lee reflected, was too passive, too inanimate; her lack of color was unvaried by any visible trace of emotion, life. She was, in fact, plain if not actually ugly; her mouth was too large; on the street, without the saving distinction of her dress, he wouldn't have noticed her.

But what, above the rest, engaged him was her resemblance to someone he knew but couldn't recall. What woman, seen lately, had Mrs. Grove's still, intent face, her pointed chin and long throat? She lifted her hand, and the gesture, the suspended grace of the wrist, was familiar to him. Finally Lee Randon, unable to satisfy his curiosity, exasperated at the usual vain stupidity of such comparisons, gave up the effort. William Grove informed Lee that he might accompany him to his club, stay, or go as he willed. Mrs. Grove, it developed, would be at home, where, if he chose, they might pursue the cause of Lee Randon's presence there.


There was, Lee soon grasped, very little that was useful to be said. They repeated what had been gone over before. Mrs. Grove explained again Mina Raff's unpredictable qualities, and he spoke of Peyton and Claire Morris. Beyond the admission of their surrender, Peyton's and hers, to each other, Mina had told the Groves nothing; Savina Grove was ignorant of what they intended. That it would begin at once was evident. "William is always a little annoyed by my contradictory character," she observed, gazing down at her slippers. They were grey, slight like a glove, on slight arched feet that held his attention. The conversation about the situation before them, expanded to its farthest limits, inevitably dragged; they said the same things, in hardly varied words, a third and even a fourth time; and then Lee's interest in it wholly deserted him—he could excite himself about Mina no longer.

This left him confronted with himself and Mrs. Grove. A clock on the stairway struck ten. Her face hadn't a vestige of cordiality, and he wondered if she were fatigued, merely polite in remaining in the room with him? She needn't inconvenience herself on his account! It was pleasant enough at the Groves'; without doubt—in her own world—she was a woman of consequence, but he wasn't carried away by the privilege of studying her indifferent silences. Then she completely surprised him:

"I suppose you have been to all the cafés and revues you ever want to see; but I almost never get to them; and it occurred to me that, if you didn't too much mind, we might go. What do you think—is it utterly foolish?"

On the contrary, he assured her, it would amuse him immensely. Lee Randon said this so convincingly that she rose at once. To be with Mrs. William Loyd Grove at Malmaison—that, of all the places possible, presented itself at once—would furnish him with an uncommon evening. Consequently, driving smoothly over Fifth Avenue, a strange black river of solidified asphalt strung with fixed moons, in answer to her query, he proposed Malmaison, and the directions were transmitted into the ivory mouth-piece beside her. At the moment when the day was most threatened it had shown a new and most promising development. Over the grey dress Mrs. Grove wore a cloak with a subdued gold shimmer, her hat was hardly more than the spread wing of a bird across the pallor of her face, and the deep folds of the gloves on her wrists emphasized the slender charm of her arms. No young—younger woman, he decided, could compete with her in the worldly, the sophisticated, attractiveness she commanded: on the plane of absolute civilization she was supreme. In the semi-gloom of the closed car, sunken in her voluminous wrap of dull gold, with a high-bridged nose visible, a hand in its dead-white covering pressed into the cushion, she satisfied his every aesthetic requirement. Women, he reflected, should be primarily a show on a stage carefully set for the purpose of their loveliness. Not many men, and scarcely more women—so few were lovely—would agree with him there. Argument would confront him with the moral and natural beauty of maternity; very well, in such instincts, he thought with a resignation quite cheerful, he was lacking. Birth, self-oblivion, was no longer the end of his dream-like existence. Lee Randon wanted to find the justification, preserve the integrity, of his personality, and not lose it. Yes, if nature, as it seemed fully reasonable, had intended the other, something incalculable had upset its plans; for what now stirred Lee had nothing to do with breeding. Long-continued thought, instead of making his questioning clearer, endlessly complicated it. There was always a possibility, which he was willing to consider, that he was lacking in sheer normality; and that, therefore, his doubts, no more than neurasthenic, were without any value.

He was ready to face this, but unable, finally, to accept it, to dismiss himself so cheaply. Whatever it was, troubling his imagination, was too perceptible at the hearts of other men. It wasn't new, singular, in him; nor had he borrowed it from any book or philosophy: it had so happened that he had never read a paragraph, satisfactory to him in the slightest, about the emotional sum of a man and a woman. What he read he couldn't believe; it was a paste of moralistic lies; either that or the writer had no greater power of explication than he. But, while he might deny a fundamental irregularity, the majority of men, secretly delivered to one thing, would preach virtuously at him the other. He recalled how universal were the traces of dissatisfaction he had noticed; an uneasiness of the masculine world that resembled a harborful of ships which, lying long and placidly at anchor, began in a rising wind to stir and pull at their hawser chains.

Lee didn't mean that this restlessness was confined to men; simply he was intent on his own problem. The automobile turned into a cross-town street; they met, entered, a mass of cars held at Broadway, advanced a few feet, stopped, went on, and, twisting through the traffic, reached Malmaison. He left his outer things at the door, but Mrs. Grove kept her cloak, and they mounted in an elevator to the café floor. The place was crowded with brightly filled tables surrounding the rectangular open dancing space, and Lee signalled for a captain. That experienced individual, with a covert glance at Lee Randon's companion, a hand folded about a sum of money that would have paid the butcher for a week at Eastlake, found, however, exactly what they wanted; and Mrs. Grove's dominating slimness emerged by degrees, like a rare flower from leaves of quiet gold.

They sat facing each other. At a table on Lee's left, on a floor a foot higher, sat a woman, Spanish in color, with a face like a crumpled petunia. The girls of a larger party, beyond Savina Grove, were young, with the vigorous nakedness of their shoulders and backs traced by black cobwebs of lace. The music began, and they left to dance; the deserted tables bore their drinks undisturbed while the floor was choked by slowly revolving figures distilling from the rhythm frank gratification. There was an honesty of intention, the admission that life and nights were short, lacking in the fever at the Eastlake dancing; here, rather than unsettled restraint, was the determination to spend every excited nerve on sensation, to obtain the last drop from glasses the contents and odors of which uniquely resembled the drinks of pre-prohibition. These girls, consciously animating their shapely bodies with the allurement if not the ends of creation, prostitutes of both temperament and fact, were, Lee Randon decided, calmer—yes, safer—in mind and purpose than were his most admirable friends.

Certainly they were better defined, more logically placed than, for example, Mrs. William Loyd Grove—her dress, her powdering and perfume, the warm metal clasped about the softness of her arms, and the indicated purpose about them, were not worlds apart. But the latter met its announced intention; it was dissipated—normally—in satiety. But, where Mrs. Grove was concerned ... Lee speculated. She was evidently highly engaged, not a shade repelled, by what she saw; in a cool manner she drew his gaze to a specially scarlet and effective dress:

"With her figure it's very successful," she commented.

What struck him immediately was that the proportions she had pointed out and her own were identical; and Lee had a vision of Mrs. Grove in the dress they were studying. The same thing, it appeared, was in her mind. "Well," she challenged him, "I could, you know." This he admitted discreetly, and asked her if she cared to dance.

"Why not?"

In his arms she was at once light and perceivable; everything a part of her was exquisitely finished; he discovered more and more surely that she was flesh and blood, and not, as he had regarded her, an insulated social mechanism. Leaving the dancing floor, she was careless, in the manner everywhere evident, in the disposition of her skirt. Lee had come prepared for the pleasure to be had from on-looking; but he had become the most oblivious of all the active participants. After a second brief understanding with the captain, another quickly-disposed currency note, there was the familiar smothered uncorking of champagne by his ear. To Lee Randon's lavishness Mrs. Grove gave no attention, and he was obliged to banish a petty chagrin by the knowledge that he had fully met the obligations of her presence. The propping of her elbows on the table, her casual gazing over the lifted rim of her glass, her silences, all admitted him to her own unremarked, her exclusive and inalienable, privilege.

She still, however, retained her personal remoteness from him; what she gave belonged to him, in their situation, conventionally; it had no greater significance; and, forming nearly all of the duty of life, her life, she discharged her responsibility beautifully. She wasn't, certainly, gay in the sense most familiar to him—Anette, in the same circumstances, would have radiated a bubbling sensual pleasure, indulged in a surface impropriety; any girl around them would have given more than Mrs. Grove; everything, probably. But he preferred the penetrating judgments, the superior mental freedom, of his companion. If she were interested in a prostitute, she didn't, with a laborious self-consciousness, avoid that term; she was neither obviously aware of those fragile vessels of pleasure nor ignorant of them; indeed, Lee told himself, she was more a part of their world, however continent she might remain, than she was of Fanny's.

Fanny, here, would have been equally fascinated and shocked; but, essentially, she'd be hurt; and, at the same time, rebellious with the innate resentment of the pure, the contained, for the free. She would never have agreed to the champagne, either; they would have ordered lemonades or claret cup; and, by midnight, gone back to the hotel. It was now past two o'clock. There was no lessening in the vigor of the dancing, the laughter, or in the stream of laden trays; no trace of fatigue in Mrs. Grove. She had the determined resilience of a woman approaching, perhaps, the decline, but not yet in it; of one who had danced into innumerable sun-rises from the night before, destroying many dozens of pairs of satin slippers.

When it occurred to her to gather up the petal-like folds of her cloak, get her hands into the gloves rolled back on her wrists, it was nearer three than two. A hollow voice on the street called the number of the Grove automobile, the door closed smoothly on them, and again she was absorbed into the cushions and her wrap. But there was a change in his feeling for her, an indefinable but potent boundary had been crossed: they had looked together, informally, at life, at passion, and the resulting sympathy had, finally, put aside the merely casual. Lee lighted a cigarette, and, without speech, she took it from him, transferred it to her own lips.

Eastlake and Fanny, Helena and Gregory, seemed very remote; a quality of his being suppressed at home here possessed him completely: in a black silk evening waistcoat, with no responsibilities, no thought of time or work, he was, lightly and wholly, an idler in a polite sphere. The orchids in their glass holder, dimly visible before him, were a symbol of his purely decorative engagement with life. Now Lee couldn't reconcile himself to the knowledge that this was no more than an interlude—with music—in his other, married existence. It was as unsubstantial as an evening's performance, in temporary finery, of a high comedy of manners.

Savina Grove said, "It has been surprisingly nice."

"Hasn't it," he agreed; "and, when you spoke, I was trying to realize that it will be so soon over."

Immediately after he cursed himself for a blunder, a stupid error in emphasis, from which she drew perceptibly away. She extinguished the cigarette, his cigarette, and that, as well, added to the distance between them.

"I should go back to Eastlake tomorrow afternoon," he observed, in a manner which he made entirely detached. To that she objected that he would not see Mina Raff, nothing would be accomplished. "She might have dinner with you tomorrow night," she thought; "Mina gets back to the Plaza a little before seven. But we can call the studio."

In view of what he had already done, Mrs. Grove's proposal seemed unavoidably reasonable. He would telephone Fanny again in the morning and explain. Fanny, his wife! Well, he continued, as though he were angrily retorting to a criticism from without, no man ever better realized the splendid qualities of his wife. That was beyond contradiction; and he sharply added that not Fanny, but the role of a wife, a housewife, was under observation. Mrs. Grove was married, but that didn't keep her from the Malmaison, at what Eastlake disapprovingly called all hours of the night. She had no aspect of a servitude which, while it promised the most unlimited future rewards, took the present grace, the charm, from women. That—the consequent loss or gain—was open to question; but the fact remained: for the majority of women marriage was fatal to their persons. Only the rich, the fortunate and the unamenable escaped.

"In a very few minutes now," Mrs. Grove said, "you will be able to sleep."

"I've never been wider awake," he protested; "I was thinking of how marriage submerged most women while you escaped."

She laughed quietly, incomprehensibly.

"Well," he insisted, aggrieved, "haven't you?"

She leaned toward him; almost, he told himself, there was a flash of animation on her immobile face. "Escape, what do you mean by that?" she demanded. "Does anyone escape—will young Morris and Mina? And you?"

"Oh, not I," he replied, thrown off his mental balance by the rapid attack of her questioning; "I am tied in a thousand ways. But you surprise me."

"I could," she remarked, coldly, returning to her corner. "Your self-satisfaction makes me rage, How do you dare, knowing nothing, to decide what I am and what I can do? You're like William, everyone I meet—so sure for others."

"No, I'm not," he contradicted her with a rude energy; "and, after all, I didn't accuse you of much that was serious. I only said you were apparently above the circumstances that spoil so many women."

"It isn't necessary to repeat yourself," she reminded him disagreeably; "I have a trace of memory."

"And with it," he answered, "a very unpleasant temper."

"Quite so," she agreed, once more calm; "you seem fated to tell me about myself. I don't mind, and it gives you such a feeling of wisdom." The car stopped before the Grove house and, within, her good-night was indifferent even for her. What, he wondered, what the devil, had upset her? He had never encountered a more incomprehensible display of the arrogantly feminine.

In his room, however, re-establishing his sense of comfort, he found, on a low table by the bed, a choice of whiskies, charged water, cigarettes, nectarines, orange-brown mangoes, and black Belgian grapes, Attached to an electric plug was a small coffee percolator; for the morning, Lee gathered. His pajamas, his dressing gown and slippers, were conveniently laid at his hand. He was, in fact, so comfortable that he had no desire to get into bed; and he sat smoking, over a tall drink, speculating about his hostess. Perhaps she had difficulties with the obdurate correctness of William; but Mrs. Grove would have been too well-steeled there to show any resentment to a virtual stranger; no, whatever it was lay within herself. He gave it up, since, he proclaimed aloud, it didn't touch him.

The opened windows admitted the vast unsubdued clamor of New York; the immeasurable force of the city seemed to press in upon the room, upon his thoughts. How different it was from the open countryside, the quiet scene, of his home in Eastlake. There the lowing of a chance cow robbed of her calf, her udder aching, the diminishing barking of dogs and the birds—sparrows in winter and robins in the spring—were the only sounds that disturbed the dark. In the morning the farmer above Lee rolled the milk down the road, past his window, on a carrier, and the milk cans made a sudden rattle and ringing. Then Christopher washed the porches. Fanny, no matter how late she had been up the night before, was dressed by eight o'clock, and put fresh flowers in the vase. He hazarded the guess that Mrs. Grove was often in bed until past noon; here servants renewed the great hot-house roses with long stems, the elaborate flowers on the dining-table.

In the morning, as he had foreseen, the percolator was connected, cream and sugar placed beside it; and before his shaving was over, he had a cup of coffee with a cigarette casting up its fragrant smoke from the saucer. His shoes might have been lacquered from the heighth of the lustre rubbed into them; a voice the perfection of trained sympathetic concern inquired for the exacted details of the suspended preparation of his eggs.


His dinner engagement with Mina Raff, arranged through her secretary, was for fifteen minutes past seven; and, meanwhile, as Mrs. Grove had offered, Adamson drove Lee down-town. The afternoon had nearly gone before he returned to East Sixty-sixth Street; but the maid at the door told him that there was tea up in the library. This he found to be a long gloomy room finished in a style which, he decided, might be massively Babylonian. A ponderous table for the support of weightless trifles filled the middle of the rug; there were deep chairs of roan leather, with an immense sofa like the lounge of a club or steamer; low bookcases with leaded glass; and windows the upper panes of which were stained in peacock colors and geometrical design.

The tea things were on a wagon beside the center table; there were a number of used cups and crumpled napkins, and whiskey glasses, in evidence, but Mrs. Grove was alone. She had been about to have them removed, she told him, when he rang. "No, I am not in a hurry; and it's such a disagreeable day you ought to have a highball."

She was in black, a dress that he found unbecoming, with a collar high about her throat and wide sleeves heavily embroidered in carmine. "You will hate that one," she said of the chair he selected; "I can't think why chairs have to be so very uncomfortable—these either swallow you whole or, like a toboggan slide, drop you on the floor." Lee drew up a tabourette for his glass and ash tray. The banal idea struck him that, although he had met Mrs. Grove only yesterday, he knew her well; rather he had a sense of ease, of the familiar, with her. The sole evidence she gave of an agreement in his feeling was that she almost totally neglected to talk. She smoked, absorbed in a frowning abstraction. A floor lamp behind them was lighted, and there was an illumination at the mantel, but the depths of the library were wrapped in obscurity: its sombreness had increased, the air was heavy with the dust of leather, a vague funereal oppressiveness.

Lee's sense of familiarity increased, but his ease left him, driven away by the strength of a feeling not exactly of being at home but of returning to an old powerful influence. Mrs. Grove's head was in shadow. There was a stir at the door, and William Grove entered. He was, he told Lee civilly, glad that Adamson had been of use. "I walk whenever it's possible," he proceeded; "but that way you wouldn't have reached Beaver Street yet. Nothing to drink, thanks, Savina, but a cigarette—" Lee Randon reached forward with the silver box and, inadvertently, he pressed into Mrs. Grove's knee. He heard a thin clatter, there was a minute hot splash on his hand, and he realized that she had dropped her spoon. She sat rigidly, half turned toward the light, with a face that shocked him: it was not merely pale, but white, drawn and harsh, and her eyes, losing every vestige of ordinary expression, stared at him in a set black intensity.

"I'm sorry," Lee Randon said mechanically, and he offered the cigarette box to the other man; but, internally, he was consumed with anger. The woman positively was a fool to mistake his awkwardness; he hadn't supposed that anyone could be so super-sensitive and suspicious; and it damaged his pride that, clearly, she should consider him capable of such a juvenile proceeding. Lee rose and excused himself stiffly, explaining that it was time for him to dress; and, in his room, telephoning Fanny, he determined to leave New York, the Groves, as early as possible in the morning.

Fanny responded from Eastlake in a tone of unending patience; nothing he could do, her voice intimated, would exhaust her first consideration of him; she wouldn't—how could she?—question the wisdom of his decisions, even when they seemed, but, of course, only to her faulty understanding, incomprehensible.

"You make it sound as though I were over here on an errand of my own," he protested cheerfully; "I'd rather be in Eastlake."

Helena, she told him, had been bad again; there was a recognized opinion between them that, while Gregory was like his mother, Helena surprisingly resembled Lee Randon. "Well, don't be too severe," he said. Someone had to be, the reply came, faint and indistinct. "Is there anything else?" he asked. Of course, how stupid, she was keeping him; the sound was now open and colored with self-reproach. She was so sorry. "Damn!" Lee exclaimed, leaving the telephone with the feeling that Fanny had repelled his affection. Women were beyond him.

In this mood he was unprepared for the appearance of Mina Raff, immediately after his name was sent up to her rooms, on the minute arranged. What, next, about her occurred to him was the evidence of her weariness. A short and extremely romantic veil hung from the close brim of her hat—with her head bent forward she gazed at him seriously through the ornamental filaments; her chin raised, the intent regard of her celebrated eyes was unhampered. She didn't care where they went, she replied to his question, except that she preferred a quiet place, where they could talk.

The St. Regis, he thought, would best answer this requirement; and he had started toward the taxi-cab stand when she informed him that she had kept her car. It was larger and more elaborately fitted than the Grove limousine; in its deep upholstery, its silk curtains and velvet carpet and gold mounted vanities, Mina Raff was remarkably child-like, small; her face, brightening at intervals in the rapidly passing lights outside, was touched by pathos; she seemed crushed by the size, the swiftness and complexity, of her automobile, and by the gathering imperious weight of her fame. She was still, however, appealingly simple; no matter what she might do it would be invested with the aspect of innocence which, admirable for her art, never for an instant deserted her personality.

Lee Randon, who liked her better with each accumulating minute, wondered why he was completely outside the disturbance of her charm. As a young man, he concluded, he would have been lost in a passionate devotion to her. Mina realized to the last possible indefinite grace the ideal, always a silver abstraction, of youth; the old worn simile of an April moon, distinguished in her case by the qualification, wistful, was the most complete description of her he possessed. Young men—Peyton Morris—were worshippers of the moon, the unattainable; and when they happily attained a reality they hid it in iridescent fancy.

What now formed Lee's vision had, together with no less a mystery, a greater warmth and implied reality from him. Cytherea and Mina Raff shared nothing; somehow the latter lacked the magnetism essential to the stirring of his desire. This, perhaps, was inevitable to his age, to the swift passage of that young idealism: after forty, the nebulous became a need for sensuous reality. Certain phases of Mina, as well, were utterly those of a child—she had the eluding sweetness, the flower-like indifference, of Helena, of a temperamental virginity so absolute that it was incapable of understanding or communicating an emotional fever. But, in the degree of her

41

genius, she was above, superior to, experience; it was not, for her, necessary; she was not changed by it, but changed it into herself, into the validity of whatever she intrinsically was.

His thoughts returned to the unfortunate occurrence in the library at the Groves'; his indignation at Mrs. Grove was complicated, puzzled, by the whole loss of the detached self-possession which, he had thought, was her most persistent characteristic. Her expression, in memory, specially baffled him; under other, accountable, circumstances he should have said that it was a look of suffering, of drawn pain. He couldn't recall the appearance of a shade of anger; yet the spoon had fallen as if from a hand numb with—with resentment. No other deduction was possible. He wished it were permissible to speak to her again about what—but obviously— had been no more than an accident; he objected to leaving such a ridiculous misconception of himself lodged permanently in her mind. But he couldn't bring it up again; and, after all, it mattered very little. Mrs. Grove was welcome to whatever flattering of her seductiveness her pride demanded. When he had dispatched, with Mina Raff, his duty to Claire, succeeded or failed—the latter, he added, was of course inevitable—he'd return to Eastlake and the Groves would go out of his life.

The curtain of what he had thought of as a play, an interlude, would fall heavily, conclusively, and the music end.

At the St. Regis he chose the more informal dining-room with panellings and high columns of wood, and medallions in white marble. It was neither full nor empty, and they were conducted to a table set for two. Lee was conscious of heads turning, and of a faint running whisper—Mina Raff had been recognized. However, without any exhibited consciousness of this, she addressed herself to him with a pretty exclusion; and, pausing to explain her indifference to food, she left the selection of everything but the salad to Lee; she had, she admitted, a preference for alligator pears cut into small cubes with a French dressing. That disposed of, he turned to her:

"I noticed, at the Plaza, that you are hard at it."

"Indeed, yes," she replied; "but we are still only rehearsing; not a scene has been shot. You see, that makes it all so expensive; I want to do as well as possible for the men who have money and confidence in me."

This, from her manner, her deceptive look of fragility everywhere drooping with regret, was patent. What she said, thought, felt, was magnificently reflected, given visibility, by her fluid being. "But you haven't come over here to talk to me about that," she said directly; "you want me to give up Peyton."

He nodded, relieved that she had made the introduction of his purpose so easy.

"I ought to tell you, before we begin," she warned him, "that I can't. Nothing can convince me that we are wrong. We didn't try to have this happen, we did all we could—but it was too late—to prevent it," Mina Raff repeated Peyton's own assurance to him. "Things were taken out of our hands. Why I went to Eastlake I don't know, it was dreadfully inconvenient, and my director did what he could to keep me working. But, as you know, I persisted. Why?" She stopped and regarded him imploringly, through the romantic veil. "I haven't the smallest idea," she continued. "Peyton had seen me again in New York; I knew then that I meant a lot to him; but it couldn't have happened if I hadn't stayed with Anette."

Her voice, her wonderment, he thought, were colored by superstition. Evidently, up to a certain point, she had resisted, and then—how charming it must have been for Morris—she collapsed. She had convinced herself that they were intended for each other. Lee asked, "How well do you know Peyton?"

"Not at all in the way you do," she admitted candidly; "I understand him only with my heart. But isn't that everything? I know that he is very pure, and doesn't ordinarily care for women—usually I have no feeling about men—and that he played football at Princeton and is very strong. You have no idea, Mr. Randon, how different he is from the men I am thrown with! There are some actors, of course, who are very fine, wonderful to work with; but the ones not quite so finished.... It's natural, for many reasons, in a woman to act; but there is something, well—something about men acting, as a rule; don't you agree?"

Lee did, and told her so with a growing pleasure in the rightness of her perceptions. "Peyton is altogether different from the men of the stage," he developed her observation; "and it is a capital thing he did play football; for, in the next year or so, until he grows used to your life, he'll have a collection of men to knock down. I'd like to tell you whatever I have discovered about him, for your own consideration, and Peyton is a snob. That isn't necessarily a term of contempt; with him it simply means that he is impatient, doubtful, at what he doesn't know. And first under that head come the arts; they have no existence for him or his friends. A play or a book pleases him or it doesn't, he approves of its limiting conventional morals, or violently condemns what he thinks is looseness, and that's the extent of his interest."

Mina Raff gazed at him blankly, this time from under the scallops of the veil. "That is hard to believe," she objected; "he talks to me beautifully about my pictures and a future on the stage. He says that I am going to revolutionize moving pictures—"

"I don't question that," he put in; "but did Peyton show you how it would be done?"

She hesitated, gracefully lowering her potent gaze.

"Probably," Lee Randon added keenly, "it was to happen because you were so excessively beautiful." There was no reply to this. "I don't need to tell you," he admitted, "that I did my best to discourage him; and I pointed out that the time must come when you would fancy, no, need, someone else."

"Oh, that was cruel!" she cried softly; "and it isn't, it won't be true. Do you think, just because I happen to be an actress, that I can't be faithful?"

"It is all a question of degree," he instructed her, "of talent or genius. Talent may be faithful to a number of things—a man or a country or even an ideal; but the only fidelity of genius is to itself."

"I hadn't thought of that," she reflected, sadly.

"Why should you?" he demanded; "you are being natural; I am the disturbance, the conventional voice sentimentally reading from the call book. But you don't have those in moving pictures: it would be a sentimentally stupid director. You must believe me: your acting will always be incomprehensible to Peyton: he will approve of the results and raise hell—for the comparatively short time he will last—with the means. Tell me this: together with his conviction that you'd carry the stage up into heaven, didn't he speak of your retiring?"

The faint smile about her lips was a sufficient answer. That smile, he recognized, pensive and unlingering, served a wide and practical variety of purposes. "In the end," he insisted, "Peyton will want to take you to a home in a correct suburb; that conception he'll never get away from." She answered:

"And what if I liked that, wanted it? You mustn't think my life is entirely joyful."

"I don't," he as promptly assured her; "but you will never get away from it; you will never sit contentedly through long afternoons playing bridge; you're cursed, if you want to call it that."

"I saw Peyton's child," she said at a tangent. "He had hold of the nurse's apron in such a funny decided fist. I wanted to hug him, but I remembered that it wasn't the thing to do. She has that," a shade of defiance darkened her voice at her reference to Claire.

"Babies are no longer overwhelmingly important," Lee retorted; "not in the face of emotion itself; they have become a sort of unavoidable, almost an undesirable by-product."

"They won't be with me," Mina Raff promised.

It was evident to him that she saw herself in the role of a mother; her face had a tender maternal glamour, her eyes were misted with sentiment; a superb actress. "A baby of my own," she whispered; "a baby and a house and Peyton."

"Nothing duller could be imagined." Momentarily he lost his self-restraint. "You have something inimitable, supremely valuable, and you are dreaming like a rabbit. If you must be a mother, be that one on the screen, for the thrilling of millions of limited minds."

"He seemed to like me." She had paid no attention to him, back again in the thought of the Morrises' son.

"If he did," Lee dryly added; "he will very soon get over it; Ira won't love you conspicuously."

"Why—why that never entered my head," Mina was startled; "but, yes, how could he? And I can't bear to have anyone, the most insignificant person alive, hate me. It makes me too wretched to sleep. They will have to understand, be generous; I'll explain so it is entirely clear to them." Her voice bore an actual note of fear, her delicate lips trembled uncontrollably.

"You can't blame them, Ira and his mother, if they refuse to listen. Eastlake as a town will dispense with you; and Claire's family—it is really quite notable—will have their say wherever they live, in Charleston and London and Spain. When Ira is grown up and, in his turn, has children, they will be very bitter about your memory. However, publicly, I suppose it will do you more good than harm. The public loves such scandal; but, with that advertisement, the other will continue. It isn't logical, I'll admit; except for Claire I should support you. That is where, and only where, I am dragged into your privacy. And, too, for your sake, it would have been better if you had hit on a different sort of man, one without the background of such stubborn traditions. You will have to fight them both in him—where they, too, may come to blame you—and about you. There is a strain of narrow intolerance through all that blood."

Mina Raff's eyes fluttered like two clear brown butterflies which, preparing to settle, had been rudely disturbed. Then her mouth was compressed, it grew firm and firmer, obdurate; as though an internal struggle, evident in her tense immobility, had been decided against what was being powerfully urged upon her. A conviction that here, too, finally, he had failed, was in possession of Lee Randon, when he saw the determination drain from her face: it assumed a child's expression of unreasoning primitive dread. She drew a hand across her forehead.

"I shall have to think," she told him; "I am very much upset. It makes me cold, what you said. Why did you come to New York and talk to me like this? Oh, I wish Peyton were here; he'd answer you; he isn't a coward like me."

"Since you are so tired, and I've been so very objectionable, I think perhaps you had better go back to your hotel," Lee proposed. "It's after ten." She rose immediately, but had to remain until the waiter was summoned with their account. In her limousine she seemed smaller, more lost in her fate and money, than before. She resembled a crushed and lovely flower; and Lee reflected that it was a shame no one was there to

43

revive her. Mina Raff, at the Plaza, insisted, holding his hand in a mingled thoughtfulness and pictorial misery, on sending him to the Groves'; and his last glimpse of her, over his shoulder, was of a slight figure hurled into upper expensive mansions by an express elevator.

A car not the Groves' was outside their house; and, as Lee was passing the drawing-room doors, William Grove called him in. He found there a Dr. Davencott and his wife, obviously on terms of close intimacy with the house. The physician was a thickly-built man with an abrupt manner continually employed in sallies of a vigorous but not unkindly humor. Lee gathered that his practice was large and select; and he quickly saw the reason, the explanation, of this: Dr. Davencott had carried the tonic impatience of earlier years among inconsequential people into a sphere where bullying was a novelty with a direct traceable salutary effect. But whatever harshness was visible in him was tempered by his wife, who was New England, Boston itself, at its best. She had a grave charm, a wit, rather than humor, which irradiated her seriousness, and gave even her tentative remarks an air of valuable finality.

To this Mrs. Grove contributed little. She practically avoided speaking to Lee Randon; and he was certain that she was, cheaply and inexcusably, offended at him. Then, in moving, her gaze caught his, their eyes held fixed; and, as he looked, the expression he had seen on her face that afternoon in the library, drawn and white with staring black eyes, came upon her. It amazed him so much that he, too, sat regarding her in an intentness which took no account of the others. One of Mrs. Grove's hands, half hidden in green tulle, was clenched. She breathed in an audible sigh and, with what appeared to be a wrenching effort, turned from him to the general conversation.

Lee Randon, losing his first impression of her attitude, was totally unable to comprehend the more difficult state that had its place. A possible explanation he dismissed before it had crystallized into thought. At the same time, the restlessness which had left him for the past twenty-four hours returned, more insistent than ever. He felt that it would be impossible to remain seated, calmly talking, for another minute. The conversation of the Davencotts that had so engaged him now only sounded like a senseless clatter of words and unendurable laughter. He wished they would go; that all of them except Savina Grove would vanish; but why he wanted her to stay, why he wished to be alone with her, and what, in such a circumstance, he would say, were all mysteries. Lee determined to rise and make his bow, to escape; he was aware of an indefinable oppression, like that he had often experienced during a heavy electric storm; he had the absurd illusion that a bolt of lightning.... Lee Randon didn't stir: he sat listening with a set smile, automatic small speech, and a heart with an unsteady rising pound.

The Doctor's stories, he thought, went on unsupportably; his wife was wise, correct, just, to a hair's breadth. Good God, when would they go? Now—there was a break in the conversation—he would rise and say good-night. Probably they wanted to discuss things more personal than his presence allowed and were waiting for just that. He was aware that Mrs. Grove's gaze, as though against her resolute effort, was moving toward him; but, quite desperately, he avoided it; he gazed up at a chandelier of glittering and coruscating glass and down at a smooth carpet with Chinese ideographs on a light background. He heard the flexible vibration of the pleasure traffic on Fifth Avenue; and, perhaps because it was so different, it reminded him of the ringing milk cans in the early morning by his house.

Lee Randon made a sharp effort to rouse himself from what threatened to be a stupor faintly lurid with conceptions of insanity; and the result of this mental drawing himself erect was even more startling, more disconcerting, than his previous condition. It came from the realization that what animated Mrs. Grove was passion. This was incredible, but it was true; he had never before seen, nor imagined, such an instant sultry storm of emotions held precariously in check. Beyond measure it surprised and baffled and agitated him. He understood now that sense of impending lightning; and, at the same time, he had a sense that a peremptory brass gong had been struck beside him, and that he was deafened by the reverberations. Mrs. Grove's still pallid face, her contained, almost precise, manner, took on a new meaning—he saw them, fantastically, as a volcanic crust that, under observation, had hardened against the fire within. Then he was at a loss to grasp why he, Lee Randon, was permitted to see so much.

His thoughts returned to himself—the voices of the Davencotts, of William Loyd Grove, echoed from a distance on his hearing—and he tried to re-arrange his bearing toward his unsought discovery: this was of enormous importance. He must at once regulate his approach to Mrs. Grove, get himself firmly in hand; the situation, for him particularly, had far-reaching unpredictable possibilities. For all her exactness, Savina Grove had a very exclusive and definite attractiveness; and, faced by such a dilemma, Lee had the best of reasons for doubting the ultimate regularity of his response.

But he was, he thought, mentally halting, racing absurdly to unjustified conclusions; nothing, naturally, disturbing would arise; but that assurance, the heights of reason, soon faded. There could be no doubt of the cause of Mrs. Grove's blanched staring: just as there was no evasion of the danger created by no more than his scant recognition. Passion discovered was a thousand diameters increased; mutually admitted, it swept aside all opposition. Lee Randon, however, had no intention of involving himself there while, ironically, he was engaged in securing for Claire Morris her husband; he didn't propose to compromise his ease of mind with William Grove's wife. There was, as well, the chance that she was a little unbalanced; progressing, he might involve himself in a regrettable, a tragic, fix. He would not progress, that was all there was to that! Lee felt better, freer already, at this resolution; he wasn't, he protested inwardly, a seducer of women; the end itself, the consummation, of seduction, was without tyrannical power over him. Lee wasn't materially, patiently, sensual in that uncomplicated manner. No, his restlessness was more mysterious, situated deeper, than that; it wasn't so readily satisfied, drugged, dismissed. The fact struck him that it had little or no animal urgency; and in this, it might be, he was less lucky than unlucky.

Mrs. Davencott rose and resumed her wrap, retained with her on the back of the chair. Lee met the pleasant decisiveness of her capable hand, the doctor grasped his fingers with a robust witticism; and he was replying to the Davencotts' geniality when he had a glimpse of Mrs. Grove's face turned slightly from him: the curve of her cheek met the pointed chin and the graceful contour of her exposed long throat; there was the shadow of a tormenting smile on the pale vermilion of her lips, in her half closed eyes; her hair, in that light, was black. A sensation of coldness, a spiritual shiver, went through Lee Randon; the resemblance that had eluded him was mercilessly clear—it was to the doll, to Cytherea.


When Dr. Davencott and his wife had gone Lee sank back into his chair, more disorganized by his culminating discovery than by any of the extraordinary conditions that had preceded it. Its quality of the unexpected, however, wasn't enough to account for the profound effect on him; that was buried in the secret of instinctive recognitions. "Well, the thing for me to do is to go to bed," he said aloud, but it was no more than an unconvinced mutter, addressed to the indeterminate region of his feet. Savina Grove was standing by the door, in the place, the position, in which she had said good-bye to the Davencotts. Her flamboyant tulle skirt, contrasted with the tightly-fitting upper part of her dress, gave her, now, in the sombre crowded furnishings, the rich draped brocades, of the room, an aspect of mid-Victorian unreality.

"It is for me, as well," she agreed, but so long after he had spoken that the connection between their remarks was almost lost. However, neither of them made a movement to leave the drawing-room, Savina Grove returned slowly to her chair. "No one, I think, has ever found it out like that." Her remark was without intelligible preliminary, but he grasped her meaning at once. "How you happened to stir it in me I have no idea—" she stopped and looked at him intently. "A terrible accident! I would have done anything, gone any distance, to avoid it. I am unable, with you, to pretend—that's curious—and that in itself gives me a feeling of helplessness. All sorts of impossible things are coming into my head to say to you. I mustn't." Her voice was brittle.

"There is no need for you to say what would make you miserable," he replied. "I am not in a position to question you; at the same time I can't pretend—perhaps the safest thing of all—not to understand what, entirely against your will, I've seen. I am very much, very naturally, disturbed by it; but you have nothing to worry about."

"You say that because you don't know, you can't possibly think, what goes on here," she pressed a hand to her breast. "Why," her words were blurred in a mounting panic, "I have lost my sense of shame with you. It's gone." She gazed despairingly around as if she expected to see that restraining quality embodied and recoverable in the propriety of the room. "I'm frightened," she gasped. Lee rose instinctively, and moved toward her with a gesture of reassurance, but she cried, "Don't! don't! don't!" three times with an increasing dread. He went back to his chair.

"Now I have to—I want to—tell you about it," she went on rapidly; "it has always been in me as long as I can remember, when I was hardly more than a child sitting alone; and I have always been afraid and ashamed. The nicest thing to call it is feeling; but in such an insane degree; at night it comes over me in waves, like a warm sea. I wanted and wanted love. But not in the little amounts that satisfied the others—the men and girls together. I couldn't do any of the small things they did with safety: this—this feeling would sweep up over me and I'd think I was going to die.

"All that I had inherited and been told made me sure that I was horridly immodest; I wouldn't, if it could be helped at all, let anyone see inside me; I couldn't have men touch me; and whenever I began to like one I ran. It was disgusting, I was brought up to believe; I thought there was something wrong with me, that I was a bad girl; and I struggled, oh, for days on end, to keep it hidden."

It was strange, Lee told himself, that marriage, the birth of her son, hadn't made her more happily normal; and, as if she had perceived his thoughts, she added, "Even from William. It would have shocked him, sickened him, really, more than the rest. He had to dominate me, be masculine, and I had to be modest, pursued—when I could have killed him." Her emotion swept her to her feet. "But I was, he thought, proper; although it tore and beat and pounded me till I was more often ill than not. Young William nearly grew up and, because of him, I was sure I had controlled it; but he was killed. Still, in five or six years it would be over; and now you, I—"

"Nothing has happened," he heavily reiterated; "nothing has or can happen. We are neither of us completely young; and, as you say, in a few years all will be over, solved. We are both, it seems, happily married." She interrupted him to cry, "Is anyone happily married? Don't we fool ourselves and doesn't life fool us?"

"It's the best course in a bad affair."

45

"Bah!" She was infuriated at him. "You are like the others—worms in chestnuts. It is bad because you are contented. I hate life as much as you do, far more; but I am not satisfied; how could anyone be?"

He, too, had risen, and stood close before her. "Don't make a mistake about me," he warned her; "there are a great many men whom it would be safer to tell this to. If I haven't had such a sharp struggle as you, I've been wondering—yes, when I should have been happiest—about the uselessness of most of living. I'm not safe at all."

"I don't want to be safe," she whispered.

With an involuntary and brutal movement he took her in his arms and kissed her with a flame-like and intolerable passion. She made no effort to avoid him, but met his embrace with an intensity that rivalled his own. When he released her she wavered and half fell on a chair across the low back of which her arm hung supinely. The lightning, he thought, had struck him. Winding in and through his surging, tempestuous emotion was an objective realization of what was happening to him: this wasn't a comfortable, superficially sensual affair such as he had had with Anette. He had seen, in steel mills, great shops with perspectives of tremendous irresistible machines, and now he had the sensation of having been thrown, whirling, among them.

Savina's head went so far back that her throat was strained in a white bow. He kissed her again, with his hands crushing the cool metallic filaments of the artificial flowers on her shoulders. She exclaimed, "Oh!" in a small startled unfamiliar voice. This would not do, he told himself deliberately, with a separate emphasis on each word. William Grove might conceivably come in at any moment; and there was no hope, no possibility, of his wife quickly regaining her balance; she was as shattered, as limply weak, as though she were in a faint. "Savina," he said, using for the first time that name, "you must get yourself together; I can't have you exposed like this to accident."

She smiled wanly, in response, and then sat upright moving her body, her arms, with an air of insuperable weariness. Her expression was dazed; but, instinctively, she rearranged her slightly disordered hair.

"We must find out what has happened to us," he went on, speaking with difficulty out of the turmoil of his being. "We are not young," he repeated stupidly; "and not foolish. We won't let ourselves be carried away beyond—beyond return."

"You are so wise," she assented, with an entire honesty of intention; but her phrase mocked him ferociously.

The tide of his own emotion was gathering around him with the force of a sea like that of which she had already, vividly, spoken. There was damned little of what could be recognized as admissible wisdom in him. Instead of that he was being inundated by a recklessness of desire that reached Savina's desperate indifference to what, however threatening, might overtake her. He couldn't, he hadn't the inclination to, do less. Reaching up, she drew her fingers down his sleeves until they rested in his gripping hands. Her palms clung to his, and then she broke away from him:

"I want to be outraged!" Her low ringing cry seemed suppressed, deadened, as though the damask and florid gilt and rosewood, now inexpressibly shocked, had combined to muffle the expression, the agony, of her body. Even Lee Randon was appalled before the nakedness left by the tearing away of everything imposed upon her. She should have said that, he realized, unutterably sad, long ago, to William Grove. But, instead, she had told him; and, whatever the consequences might be, he must meet them. He had searched for this, for the potency in which lay the meaning of Cytherea, and he had found it. He had looked for trouble, and it was his in the realization alone that he could not, now, go home tomorrow morning.


In his room the tropical fruits and whiskey and cigarettes were by his bed, the percolator ready for morning; and, stopping in his preparations for the night, he mixed himself a drink and sat moodily over it. What had happened downstairs seemed, more than anything else, astounding; Mrs. Grove, Savina, had bewildered him with the power, the bitterness, of her feeling. At the thought of her shaken with passionate emotion his own nerves responded and the racing of his blood was audible in his head. What had happened he didn't regret; dwelling on it, the memory was almost as sharply pleasant as the reality; yet he wasn't concerned with the present, but of the future—tomorrow.

He should, probably, get home late in the afternoon or in the evening; and what he told himself was that he wouldn't come back to the Groves, to Savina. The risk, the folly, was too great. Recalling his conclusions about the attachments of men of his age, he had no illusion about the possibly ideal character of an intimacy with William Grove's wife; she, as well, had illuminated that beyond any obscurity of motive or ultimate result. Lee's mind shifted to a speculation about the cause of their—their accident. No conscious act, no desire, of his had brought it on them; and it was evident that no conscious wish of hers had materialized their unrestrainable kisses. Savina's life, beyond question, must have been largely spent in hiding, combatting, her secret—the fact that her emotion was too great for life.

However, Lee Randon didn't try to tell himself that no other man had shared his discovery; indeed, Savina, too, had wisely avoided that challenge to his experience and wisdom. Like her he deliberately turned away from the past; and, in the natural chemistry of that act, the provision for his masculine egotism, it was dissolved into nothingness. He was concentrated on the incident in the library: dancing with her, he had held her in a far greater, a prolonged, intimacy of contact; something in the moment, a surprising of her defences, a slight weariness in a struggle which must then seem to her unendurable, had betrayed her. Nothing, then, than what had occurred, could have been farther from his mind; he had never connected Mrs. Grove with such a possibility; she hadn't, the truth was, at first attracted him in that way. Now he thought that he had been blind to have missed her resemblance to Cytherea. She was Cytherea! This, in a measure, accounted for him, since, with so much to consider, he badly needed an accounting. It wasn't simply, here, that he had kissed a married woman; there was nothing revolutionary or specially threatening in that; it was the sensation of danger, of lightning, the recognition of that profoundly disturbing countenance, which filled him with gravity and a determined plan of restraint.

He recalled the fact that both Peyton Morris and Mina had insisted that they had not been responsible for what had overtaken them; at the time he had not credited this, he was certain that some significant preliminaries had been indulged in; but positively Savina and he had been swept off their feet. A sense of helplessness, of the extreme danger of existence, permeated and weakened his opposing determination—he had no choice, no freedom of will; nothing august, in him or outside, had come to his assistance. In addition to this, he was—as in maturity he had always been—without a convenient recognition of right and wrong. What he principally felt about Savina was a helpless sense of tragedy, that and a hatred for the world, for the tepid society, which had no use for high passion.

To have kissed her, under the circumstances, appeared to him not only natural, but inevitable; and he was suffering from no feeling of guilt; neither toward William Grove, in whose house he was a guest, nor to Fanny—those widely heralded attitudes were largely a part of a public hypocrisy which had no place in the attempted honesty of his thoughts. Lee was merely mapping out a course in the direction of worldly wisdom. Then, inconsistently leaving that promise of security, he reviewed every moment, every thrilling breath, with Savina Grove after the Davencotts had gone: he felt, in exact warm similitude, her body pressed against his, her parted lips; he heard the little escaping "Ah!" of her fervor.

He put his glass down abruptly and tramped from wall to wall, his unbuttoned silk waistcoat swinging about his arms. Lee Randon now cursed himself, he cursed Savina, but most of all he cursed William Grove, sleeping in complacent ignorance beside his wife. His imagination, aroused and then defrauded, became violent, wilfully obscene, and his profanity emerged from thought to rasping sound. His forehead, he discovered, was wet, and he dropped once more into the chair by the laden tray, took a deep drink from a fresh concoction. "This won't do," he said; "it's crazy." And he resumed the comforting relief that tomorrow would be different: he'd say good-bye to the Groves together and, in four hours, he'd be back in Eastlake. The children, if he took a late train, would be in bed, and Fanny, with her feet on the stool, engaged with her fancy work.

Then his revolving thoughts took him back to the unanswered mystery of what, actually, had happened to Savina and him. He lost her for Cytherea, he lost Cytherea in her; the two, the immobile doll and the woman torn with vitality, merged to confound him. In the consideration of Savina and himself, he discovered that they, too, were alike; yet, while he had looked for a beauty, a quality, without a name, a substance, Savina wanted a reality every particle of which she had experienced and achingly knew. He, more or less, was troubled by a vision, but her necessity was recognizable in flesh. There, it might be again, she was more fortunate, stronger, superior. It didn't matter.

No inclination to sleep drugged the activity of his mind or promised him the release, the medicine, of a temporary oblivion. He had a recurrence of the rebellious spirit, in which he wondered if Grove did sleep in the same room with Savina. And then increasingly he got what he called a hold on himself. All that troubled him seemed to lift, to melt into a state where the hopeless was irradiated with tender memories. His mood changed to a pervasive melancholy in which he recalled the lost possibilities of his early ambitions, the ambitions that, without form or encouragement, had gone down before definite developments. When he spoke of these, tentatively, to Fanny, she always replied serenely that she was thankful for him as he was, she would not have liked him to be anything queer.

But if he had met Savina first, and married her, his career would have been something else entirely; now, probably—so fiercely their combined flame would have burned—it would be over. However, during its course—he drew in a long audible breath. It was no good thinking of that! He completed his preparations for the night; but he still lingered, some of the drink remained. Lee was glad that he had grown quieter, reflective, middle-aged; it was absurd, undignified, for him to imitate the transports of the young. It pleased him, though, to realize that he wasn't done, extinguished, yet; he might play court tennis—it wasn't as violent as racquets or squash—and get back a little of his lapsed agility; better still, he'd ride more, take three days a week, he could well afford to, instead of only Saturday and holidays in the country.

It was a mistake to disparage continually the life, the pleasures and friends, he had—the friends he had gathered through long arduous years of effort. He must grow more familiar with Helena and Gregory, too; no one had handsomer or finer children. And there was Fanny—for one friend of his she had ten; she was universally liked and admired. Lee was, at last, in bed; but sleep continued to evade him. He didn't fall asleep, but sank into a waking dose; his mind was clear, but not governed by his conscious will; it seemed to him that there was no Savina Grove, but only Cytherea; her smile, her fascination, everywhere followed him. A damned funny business, life! At times its secret, the meaning of love, was almost clear, and then, about to be freed by knowledge, his thoughts would break, grow confused, and leave him still baffled.

Lee Randon was startled to find the brightness of morning penetrating his eyes; ready for his bath, with the percolator choking and bubbling in the next room, he rehearsed, reaffirmed, all that he had decided the night before. No one was with him at the breakfast table elaborate with repousse silver and embroidered linen and iced fruit; but, returning upstairs, he saw Savina in her biscuit-colored suit in the library. "William had to go to Washington," she told him; "he left his regrets." She was, Lee perceived, almost haggard, with restless hands; but she didn't avoid his gaze. She stood by the table, one hand, gloved, slightly behind her on it. Bending forward he kissed her more intently, more passionately, more wholly, than ever before.

"I hadn't meant to do that," he said; but his speech was only mechanical, as though, when he had once made it up, it discharged itself, in a condition where it was no longer valid, in spite of him. Savina replied with a silent smile. Her drawn appearance had gone; she was animated, sparkling, with vitality; even her body seemed fuller.

"We shall have a long unbroken day together," she told him; "I have to go out for an hour, and then it will begin, here, I think, with lunch."

"I ought to be back in Eastlake," he confessed.

"Don't think of that till it comes. Eastlake has had you a long time, compared with a day. But there are days and days." They kissed each other. "I'll go now." She kissed Lee. "Lunch will be at two." He kissed her. He didn't leave the library until a maid announced that lunch was ready and the fact of her return. At the table they spoke but little; Lee Randon was enveloped in a luxurious feeling—where Savina was concerned—of security; there was no need to hurry; the day lengthened out into the night and an infinity of happy minutes and opportunities. They discussed, however, what to do with it.

"I'd like to go out to dinner," she decided; "and then a theatre, but nothing more serious than a spectacle: any one of the Follies. I am sick of Carnegie Hall and pianists and William's solemn box at the Opera; and afterwards we'll go back to that café and drink champagne and dance."

That, he declared, with a small inner sinking at the thought of Fanny, would be splendid. "And this afternoon—?"

"We'll be together."

They returned to the library—more secluded from servants and callers than the rooms on the lower floor—where, at one end of the massive lounge, they smoked and Savina talked. "I hardly went to sleep at all," she admitted; "I thought of you every second. Do you think your wife would like me?" She asked the vain question which no woman in her situation seemed able to avoid.

"Of course," he lied heroically.

"I want her to, although I can't, somehow, connect you with her; I can't see you married. No doubt because I don't want to; it makes me wretched." She half turned in his arms, pressed hard against him, and plunged her gaze into his.

"It often seems strange to me," he admitted, caught in the three-fold difficulty of the truth, his feeling for her, and a complete niceness in whatever touched Fanny. He attempted to explain. "Everything about my home is perfect, but, at times, and I can't make out why, it doesn't seem mine. It might, from the way I feel, belong to another man—the house and Fanny and the children. I stand in it all as though I had suddenly waked from a dream, as though what were around me had lasted somehow from the dream into life." He repeated to her the process of his thoughts, feelings, at once so familiar and inexplicable.

She wasn't, he found, deeply interested in his explanation; she was careless of anything but the immediate present. Savina never mentioned William Grove. Animated by countless tender inventive expressions of her passion, she gave the impression of listening to the inflections of his voice rather than attending, considering, its meanings. She was more fully surrendered to the situation than he. The disorganized fragments of a hundred ideas and hints poured in rapid succession, back of his dominating emotion, through Lee's brain. He lost himself only in waves—the similitude to the sea persisted—regular, obliterating, but separate. Savina was far out in a tideless deep that swept the solidity of no land.

She was plastically what he willed; blurred, drunk, with sensation, she sat clasping rigidly the edge of his coat. But his will, he discovered, was limited: the surges of physical desire, rising and inundating, saturating him, broke continually and left him with the partly-formed whirling ideas. He named, to himself, the thing that hung over them; he considered it and put it away; he deferred the finality of their emotion. In this he was inferior, he became even slightly ridiculous—they couldn't continue kissing each other with the same emphasis hour after hour, and the emphasis could not be indefinitely multiplied; rather than meet the crescendo he drew into his region of cental obscurity.

Lee had to do this, he reminded himself, in view of Savina's utter surrender: he was responsible for whatever happened. Even here his infernal queerness—that the possession of the flesh wasn't what primarily moved him—was pursuing him: a peculiarity, he came to think, dangerously approaching the abnormal. In addition to that, however, he was not ready, prepared, to involve his future; for that, with Savina Grove, was most probable to follow. Fanny was by no means absent from his mind, his wife and certain practical realities. And, as he had told himself before, he was not a seducer. What adventures he had accepted had been the minor experiments of his restlessness, and they all ended in the manner that had finished him with Anette, in dissatisfaction and a sense of waste.

Savina stirred and sighed. "I must ring for tea," she said regretfully; and, while the servant arranged the pots and decanters and pitchers, the napkins and filled dishes, Lee paced up and down, smoking. When they were again alone her fingers stole under his arm:

"I adore you for—for everything." She had evaded the purpose of her speech. He wondered, with the exasperation of his over-wrought physical suspense, if she did. His ravishment had suffered a sharp natural decline reflected in a mental gloom. For the moment he desired nothing, valued nothing. And, in this mood, he became talkative; he poured a storm of pessimistic observation over Savina; and she listened with a rapt, transported, attention. It stopped as suddenly as it had begun, in a silence coincident with dusk. The room slowly lost its sombre color and the sense of the confining walls; it became grey and apparently limitless; as monotonous, Lee Randon thought, as life. He was disturbed by a new feeling: that perversely, trivially, he had spoiled what should have been a priceless afternoon. It would never come back; what a fool he had been to waste in aimless talk any of the few hours which together they owned.

He whispered this to Savina, in his arms; but she would permit no criticism of him. It was time, she discovered, for them to dress for their party: "I don't want you to go. Why can't you be with me? But then, the servants! Lee, I am going to die when you leave. Tell me, how can I live, what am I to do, without you?" Since no satisfactory reply to that was possible, he stopped her troubled voice with a kiss. It was remarkable how many they had exchanged.

He had the feeling, the hope, that, with nothing irrevocable consummated, their parting would be easier; but he began to lose that comfortable assurance. Again in his room, in the heavy choking folds of velvet draperies, he was grave; the mere excitation of the night before had gone. What was this, he asked himself, that he had got into? What had Cytherea to do with it? Ungallantly the majority of his thoughts were engaged with the possibility, the absolute necessity, of escape. By God, he must get out of it, or rather, get it out of him! But it wasn't too late; he could even finish the day, this delight, with safety. Savina would recover—she had already thanked him for his self-control.

It was fortunate that she was a woman of distinction, of responsibilities, with a delicate habit of mind; another might have brought disaster, followed him to Eastlake. He recalled a story of George Sand tearing off her bodice before the house of a man she loved. Yet... why hadn't he gone quietly away, early in the morning, before Savina was up? He was appalled at the depths to which he had fallen, the ignominious appearance that interrogated him from the pier-glass; Lee saw himself in the light of a coward—a cheap, safe sensation-maker. Nothing was more contemptible. Damn it to hell, what was he? Where was he? Either he ought to go home or not, and the not carried the fullest possible significance. But he didn't want to do one or the other—he wanted Cytherea, or Savina, on some absurd impracticable plane, and Fanny too. Why couldn't he go home when home was uppermost in his thoughts and do something else when it wasn't? Did the fact that Fanny might happen to want him annul all his liberty in living; or, in place of that, were they, in spirit and body, one?


It was inevitable to the vacillating state of his being that, finding Savina in an exceptionally engaging black dress with floating sleeves of sheer lace and a string of rare pearls, he should forget all his doubts in the pleasure of their intimacy. Even now, in response to his gaze, her face lost its usual composure and became pinched, stricken, with feeling. Lee Randon was possessed by a recklessness that hardened him to everything but the present moment: such times were few in existence, hours of vivid living which alone made the dull weight of years supportable. This belonged to Savina and him; they were accountable only to each other. It was a sensation like the fortunate and exhilarating effect of exactly the right amount of wine. The emotion that flooded them had freed Lee from responsibility; sharpening one set of perceptions, it had obliterated the others, creating a spirit of holiday from which nothing prosaic, utilitarian, should detract.

They hadn't yet decided where to go for dinner; and, drawing aside into a small reception room to embrace and consider, they selected the Lafayette, because its Continental air assisted the illusion of their escape from all that was familiar and perfunctory. Their table, by a railing overlooking the sweep of the salle à manger, was precisely placed for their happiness. It was so narrow that the heels of Savina's slippers were sharply pressed into his insteps; when her hand fell forward it rested on his. Lee ordered a great deal, of which very little was eaten; the hors d'oeuvre appeared and vanished, followed by the soup and an entrée; a casserole spread the savory odor of its contents between them; the salad was crisply, palely green, and ignored; and, before it seemed humanly possible, he had his cigar and was stirring the French coffee.

"Shall we be late for the theatre?" he asked indifferently.

"I haven't the least interest in it," Savina assured him; "I can't imagine why we bought the seats. Why did we, Lee, when we have each other?"

"Our own private Folly." He smiled at her.

"Not that," she reproved him; "I can't bear to think of it in a small way. Why, it will be all I'll ever have—I shall never think of anyone else like this again; and you'll go back, you'll go away. But I hope you won't forget me, not at once—you must keep me in your heart for a little."

"I'll never be able to get you out," he declared.

"You want to, then, and I am—" She lost control of herself as though she had passed into a hypnosis, uniquely frozen with passion, incapable of movement, of the accommodation of her sight; her breathing was slow, almost imperceptible in its shallowness. "I am a part of you," Savina went on when she had recovered. "It would kill me if I weren't. But it does mean something." Her heel cut until he thought he was bleeding.

"What?" he asked, through the thin azure smoke of the cigar. She shook her head contentedly:

"I don't care; I have—now, anyway—what I wish, what I've always wished for—you. I didn't know it was you right away, how could I? Not even when we had tea, and talked about Mina and your young Morris, that first afternoon. It was the next day before I understood. Why wasn't it long long ago, when I was a girl, twelve years old? Yes, quite that early. Isn't it queer, Lee, how I have been troubled by love? It bothers hardly anyone else, it scarcely touches the rest. There is a lot of talk about it, but, all the while, people detest it. They are always wearing dresses and pretentions they can't afford to have mussed. It—I am still talking of love, Lee darling—breaks up their silly society and morals ... like a strong light thrown on something shabby."

Once more he had the feeling that, before the actuality of Savina's tragic necessity, his own speculations were merely visionary, immaterial; yet he tried to put them into words, to explain, so far as he was able, what it was in him that was hers. But he did this omitting, perhaps, the foundation of all that he was trying to say—he didn't speak of Cytherea. He avoided putting the doll into words because he could think of none that would make his meaning, his attachment, clear. Lee couldn't, very well, across the remnants of dinner, admit to Savina that a doll bought out of a confectioner's window on Fifth Avenue so deeply influenced him. He hadn't lost Cytherea in Savina so much as, vitalized, he had found her. And, while he had surrendered completely to the woman and emotion, at the same time the immaterial aspect of his search, if he could so concretely define it, persisted. The difference between Savina and himself was this: while she was immersed, obliterated, satisfied, in her passion, a part of him, however small, stayed aside. It didn't control him, but simply went along, like a diminutive and wondering child he had by the hand.

Cytherea, at this moment, would be softly illuminated by the shifting glow of the fire and, remote in her magical perspective, would seem at the point of moving, of beckoning for him with her lifted hand.

"What were you seeing in the smoke?" Savina asked; and he replied with an adequate truth, "You."

"Why not just look at me, then, instead of staring?"

"I see you everywhere."

"Adorable," she whispered.

No such name, no terms of endearment, occurred to him for her; why, he didn't know; but they had no place in his present situation. He had to think of Savina as removed from whatever had described and touched other special women. The words which had always been the indispensable property of such affairs were now distasteful to him. They seemed to have a smoothly false, a brassy, ring; while he was fully, even gaily, committed, he had a necessity to make his relationship with Savina Grove wholly honest. As he paid the account she asked him if he were rich.

"Your husband wouldn't think so," he replied; "yet I am doing well enough; I can afford dinner and the theatre."

"I wish you had a very great deal of money."

"Why?" He gazed at her curiously.

"It's so useful," Savina told him generally; but that, he felt, was not completely what was in her mind. "What I have," she went on, "is quite separate from William's. It is my mother's estate."

"My brother, Daniel, has done very well in Cuba," Lee commented. Savina was interested:

"I have never been there; cooler climates are supposed to suit my heart better; but I know I should love it—the close burning days and intense nights."

"Daniel tells me there's usually the trade wind at night." His voice reflected his lack of concern.

"I have a feeling," she persisted, "that I am more of Havana than I am, for example, of Islesboro. Something in the tropics and the people, the Spanish! Those dancing girls in gorgeous shawls, they haven't any clothes underneath; and that nakedness, the violence of their passions, the danger and the knives and the windows with iron bars, stir me. It's all so different from New York. I want to burn up with a red flower in my hair and not cool into stagnation."

They were in her closed automobile, where it was faintly scented by roses yellow and not crimson. She sat upright, withdrawn from him, with her hands clenched in her lap. How she opposed every quality of Mina Raff's; what a contradiction the two women, equally vital, presented. And Fanny, perhaps no less forceful, was still another individual. Lee Randon was appalled at the power lying in the fragile persons of women. It controlled the changeless and fateful elements of life; while the strength of men, it occurred to him further, was concerned with such secondary affairs as individual ambitions and a struggle eternally condemned to failure.

Savina relaxed, every instinct and nerve turned toward him, but they were at the theatre.

50

The performance had been on, an usher told them, for almost three quarters of an hour. Their seats were in the fifth row, the middle; and there was an obscured resentful stirring as they took their places. Plunged into darkness, their hands and shoulders and knees met. Savina, scarcely above her breath, said "Ah!" uncontrollably; she was so charged with emotion that her body seemed to vibrate, a bewildering warmness stole through him from her; and once more, finally, he sank into questionless depths. The brightness of the stage, at first, had no more form nor meaning than the whirling pattern of a kaleidoscope, against which the people around him were unsubstantial silhouettes, blind to the ardor that merged Savina and him into one sentient form alone in a world of shadows.

The spectacle on the stage, Russian in motive, was set in harmonized barbaric color—violent movements under a diffused light: in the background immobile peasant-like figures held tall many-branched candlesticks; there were profane gold mitres, vivid stripes and morocco leather; cambric chemises slipping from breasts and the revelation of white thighs. It floated, like a vision of men's desire realized in beautiful and morbid symbols, above the darkened audience; it took what, in the throng, was imperfect, fragmentary, and spent, but still strong, brutal, formless, and converted it into a lovely and sterile pantomime. Yet there was no sterility in what had, primarily, animated it; the change, it seemed, had been from use to ornament, from purpose to a delight with no issue beyond that. Over it there hung, for Lee Randon, the pale radiance of Cytherea.

Other visions and spectacles followed, they melted one into the next, sensations roused by the flexible plaited thongs of desire. Lee, stupefied in the heavy air of his own sensuality, saw the pictorial life on the stage as an accompaniment, the visualization, of his obsession. It was over suddenly, with a massing of form and sound; Lee and Savina Grove were pitilessly drowned in light. Crushed together in the crowded, slowly emptying aisle, her pliable body, under its wrap, followed his every movement.

On the street, getting into the automobile, she directed Adamson to drive through the park. "I don't want to go to the Malmaison," she told Lee. Her ungloved fingers worked a link from his cuff and her hand crept up his arm. The murmur of her voice was ceaseless, like a low running and running over melodious keys. Then, in a tone no louder, but changed, unexpected, she said:

"Lee, I love you."

It startled him; its effect was profound—now that it had been said he was completely delivered to his gathering sense of the inevitable. It secured, like a noose, all his intentions; he was neither glad nor sorry; what was the use? His own feeling—if this were love and what love was—eluded him. Above every other recognition, though, was a consciousness of impending event. What happened now, in the car rapidly approaching Central Park, was unimportant, without power to contain him in its moment. They turned in at the Fifty-ninth Street entrance: through the glass there was a shifting panorama of black branches, deserted walks and benches and secretive water. He saw vaguely the Belvedere, the Esplanade fountain, and the formal length of the Mall, together with—flung against the sky—the multitudinous lighted windows of Central Park West, the high rippling shimmer of the monumental lifted electric signs on Broadway. Other cars passed, swift and soundless, he saw their occupants and then they were gone: an aged man whose grey countenance might have been moulded in sand with a frigid trained nurse; a couple desperately embracing in a taxi-cab; a knot of chattering women in dinner dresses and open furs; another alone, painted, at once hard and conciliatory, hurrying to an appointment.

The tension, his suspense, increased until he thought it must burst out the windows. Between the shudders and the kissing he kept wondering when.... It was Savina, at the speaking-tube, who commanded their return. They left the Park for Fifth Avenue, Sixty-sixth Street. Lee got out, but she didn't follow. He waited expectantly. The night had grown very much colder. Why, in the name of God, didn't she come?

"In a moment" he heard her say faintly. But when she moved it was with decision; there was no hesitation in her manner of mounting the stone steps. The maid came forward as they entered, first to help Savina, and then to take Lee's hat and coat and stick. Savina turned to him, holding out her hand, speaking in a high steady voice:

"Thank you very much—wasn't it nice?—and good-night." Without another word, giving him no opportunity to speak, to reply, she turned neither hurried nor slow to the stairway.

He was dumfounded, and showed it, he was sure, in the stupidity of his fixed gesture of surprise. The emotion choked in his throat was bitter with a sense of ill-treatment. To cover his confusion, he searched obviously through his pockets for a cigarette case which he had left, he knew, in his overcoat. Then, when the servant had retired, he softly cursed. However, the bitterness, his anger, were soon lost in bewilderment; that, with the appearance of resolving itself into a further mystery, carried him up to his room. With a mixed drink on a dressing-case, he wandered aimlessly around, his brain occupied with one question, one possibility.

Piece by piece, at long intervals, he removed his clothes, found his pajamas and dressing-gown, and washed. The drink he discovered later untouched and he consumed it almost at a gulp. Lee poured out another, and a third; but they had no effect on him.

51

In spite of them he suffered a mild collapse of the nerves; his hands were without feeling, at once like marble and wet with sweat; his heart raced. A pervading weariness and discouragement followed this. He was in a hellish mess, he told himself fiercely. The bravado of the words temporarily gave him more spirit; yet there was nothing he could do but go to bed. Nothing else had been even hinted at; he turned off the lights and opened the windows. Flares of brightness continued to pass before his eyes, and, disinclined to the possibilities of sleep, he propped himself up with an extra pillow. Then, illogically, he wondered if he had locked the door; at the instant of rising to find out, he restrained himself—if, subconsciously, he had, chance and not he had worked; for or against him, what did it matter?

He looked at the illuminated dial of his watch; the hands, the numerals, greenly phosphorescent, were sharp; it was midnight. After apparently an interminable wait he looked again—six minutes past twelve. The rumble of an elevated train approached, hung about the room, and receded. Death could be no more dragging than this. Why, then, didn't he fall asleep? Lee went over and over every inflection of Savina's final words to him; in them he tried, but vainly, to find encouragement, promise, any decision or invitation. What, in the short passage from the automobile to the house, could have so wholly changed, frozen, her? Had she, at that late opportunity, remembering the struggle, the tragic unrelenting need, to keep herself aloof from passion, once more successfully fled? Was she—he was almost dozing—Cytherea, the unobtainable?

He woke, stirred, convulsively: it was after one o'clock now. The craving for a cigarette finally moved him; and, in the dark, he felt around for those, the Dimitrinos, on the tray. The cigarette at an end, he sank back on the pillows, deciding that he must take the earliest train possible toward Eastlake. He had missed a directors' meeting today, and there was another tomorrow that he must attend, at his office. Then he grew quieter; the rasping of his nerves ceased; it was as though, suddenly, they had all been loosened, the strung wires unturned. What a remarkable adventure he had been through; not a detail of it would ever fade from his memory—a secret alleviation for advancing old age, impotence. And this, the most romantic occurrence of his life, had happened when he was middle-aged, forty-seven and worse, to be exact. He looked again at his watch, but now only from a lingering uncertain curiosity. It was five minutes of two.

The present peace that settled over him seemed the most valuable thing life had to offer; it was not like the end of effort, but resembled a welcome truce, a rest with his force unimpaired, from which he would wake to the tonic winter realities of tomorrow. An early train—

In the act of dropping, half asleep, into the position of slumber, he halted sharply, propped up on an elbow. A sense invaded him of something unusual, portentous, close by. There wasn't a sound, a flicker of audible movement, a break in the curtain of dark; yet he was breathless in a strained oppressive attention. It was impossible to say whether his disturbance came from within or without, whether it was in his pounding blood or in the room around him. Then he heard a soft thick settling rustle, the sound a fur coat might make falling to the floor; and, simultaneously, a vague slender whiteness appeared on the night. A swift conviction fastened on him that here he had been overtaken by fate; by what, for so long, he had invited. Out of the insubstantiality a whispering voice spoke to him:

"Lee, where are you? It's so cold."


IV

Twice, the following day, Lee telephoned to Fanny, but neither time was she in the house; and, kept at his office, he was obliged to take an inconvenient train that made a connection for Eastlake. When Lee reached the countryside opening in the familiar hilly vistas he had, in place of the usual calm recognitions through a run of hardly more than an hour, a sense of having come a long way to a scene from which he had been absent for years. It appeared to him remarkably tranquil and self-contained—safe was the word which came to him. He was glad to be there, but at indeterminate stations rather than in Eastlake. He dreaded, for no plainly comprehended reason, his return home. The feelings that, historically, he should have owned were all absent. Had it been possible he would have cancelled the past forty-eight hours; but Lee was forced to admit to himself that he was not invaded by a very lively sense of guilt. He made a conventional effort to see his act in the light of a grave fault—whatever was attached to the charge of adultery—but it failed before the conviction that the whole thing was sad.

His sorrow was for Savina, for the suffering of her past, the ordeal of the present, and the future dreariness. There had been no suggestion of wrong in her surrender, no perceptible consciousness of shame: it was exactly as though, struggling to the limit of endurance against a powerful adverse current, she had turned and swept with it. The fact was that the entire situation was utterly different from the general social and moral conception of it; and Lee began to wonder which were stronger—the individual truth or the imposed dogmatic weight of the world. But the latter, he added, would know nothing of this. Concisely, there was to be no repetition of last night; there would be no affair.

52

Lee Randon had completely and sharply focussed the most adverse possible attitude toward that: he saw it without a redeeming feature and bare of any chance of pleasure. His need for honesty, however special, was outraged on every facet by the thought of an intrigue. Lee reconstructed it in every detail—he saw the moments, doubtful and hurried and surreptitious, snatched in William Grove's house; the servants, with their penetration of the tone of an establishment, knowing and insufferable; he lived over the increasing dissatisfaction with quick embraces in the automobile, and the final indignities of lying names and rooms of pandering and filthy debasement. The almost inevitable exposure followed, the furies and hysterical reproaches. That, indeed, would have involved them fatally: in such circumstances the world would be invincible, crushing; holding solidly its front against such dangerous assault, it would have poured over Savina and him a conviction of sin in which they would unavoidably have perished.

As it was, he had told her—with, in himself, the feeling of a considerable discovery—that they were to a marked degree superior: he could find no more remorse at his heart than Savina showed. This, exactly, was his inner conviction—that, since he had given something not in Fanny's possession, he had robbed her of nothing. It was a new idea to him and it required careful thought, a slow justification. It answered, perhaps, once and for all, his question about the essential oneness of marriage. Yes, that was a misconception; marriage in an ideal state he wasn't considering, but only his own individual position. To love but one woman through this life and into a next would be blissful ... if it were possible; there might be a great deal saved—but by someone else—in heroically supporting such an Elysian tenet; Lee Randon definitely hadn't the necessary utopianism.

Love wasn't a sacred fluid held in a single vessel of alabaster; marriage didn't conveniently create shortsightedness. Lee couldn't pretend to answer all this for women, or even in part for Savina. Her attitude, he knew, in that it never touched the abstract, was far simpler than his; she didn't regard herself as scarlet, but thought of the rest of the world as unendurably drab. The last thing she had said to him was that she was glad, glad, that it had happened. This, too, in Savina, had preserved them from the slightest suggestion of inferiority: the night assumed no resemblance to a disgraceful footnote on the page of righteousness. It was complete— and, by God, admirable!—within itself. No one, practically, would agree with him, and here, in the fact that no one ever could know, his better wisdom was shown.

About love, the thing itself, his perceptions remained dim: he had loved Fanny enormously at the time of their wedding and he loved her now, so many years after; but his feeling—as he had tried so unfortunately to tell her—wasn't the same, it had grown calm; it had become peaceful, but an old tempestuous need had returned. Yet, until he had gone to the Groves', his restlessness had been trivial, hardly more than academic, a half-smiling interest in a doll; but now, after he had left the realm of fancy for an overt act, a full realization of his implication was imperative. Without it he would be unable to preserve any satisfactory life with Fanny at all; his uneasiness must merely increase, become intolerable. Certainly there was a great, it should be an inexhaustible, amount of happiness for him in his wife, his children and his home; he would grow old and negative with them, and there die.

But a lot of mental re-adjustment, understanding, was necessary first. Suddenly the minor adventures and sensations of the past had become, even before the completeness of the affair with Savina, insuperably distasteful to him; he simply couldn't look forward to a procession of them reaching to impotence. No, no, no! That was never Cytherea's import. He didn't want to impoverish himself by the cheap flinging away of small coin from his ultimate store. He didn't, equally, wish to keep on exasperating Fanny in small ways. That pettiness was wholly to blame for what discomfort he had had. His wife's claim was still greater on him than any other's; and what, now, he couldn't give her must be made up in different ways. This conviction invested him with a fresh sense of dignity and an increasing regard for Fanny.

What a shame it was that he could not go quietly to her with all this, tell her everything. A lie was rooted, concealed, beyond removal at the base of the honesty he planned. There was, of course, this additional phase of the difficulty—what had happened concerned Savina even more than it did his wife and him. He had Savina Grove, so entirely in his hands, to guard. And the innate animosity of women toward women was incalculable. That wasn't a new thought, but it recurred to him with special force. As much as he desired it, utter frankness, absolute safety, was impossible. Fanny's standard of duty, or responsibility, was worlds apart from his.

Bitterly and without premeditation he cursed the tyranny of sex; in countless forms it dominated, dictated, every aspect of life. Men's conception of women was quite exclusively founded on it in its aspects of chastity or license. In the latter they deprecated the former, and in the first they condemned all trace of the latter. The result of this was that women, the prostitutes and the mothers alike, as well, had no other validity of judgment. The present marriage was hardly more than an exchange of the violation of innocence, or of acted innocence, for an adequate material consideration. If this were not true, why was innocence—a silly fact in itself—so insisted upon? Lee was forced to conclude however, that it was the fault of men: they turned, at an advancing age when it was possible to gather a comfortable competence, to the young. By that time their emotions were apt to be almost desperately variable.

In his case it had been different—but life was different, easier, when he had married—and his wedding most appropriate to felicity. Yet that, against every apparent reason to the contrary, had vanished, and left him this calm determining of his fate. Through his thoughts a quirk of memory ran like a tongue of flame. He felt Savina's hand under his cuff; he felt her sliding, with her arms locked about his neck, out of her furs in the automobile; a white glimmer, a whisper, she materialized in the coldness of the night. There was a long-drawn wailing blast from the locomotive—they were almost entering the train-shed at Eastlake. When Fanny expected him, and it was possible, she met him at the station; but tonight he would have to depend on one of the rattling local motor hacks. Still, he looked for her and was faintly and unreasonably disappointed at her absence. An uncontrollable nervousness, as he approached his house, invaded the preparation of a warm greeting.

Fanny was seated at dinner, and she interrupted her recognition of his arrival to order his soup brought in. "It's really awfully hard to have things nice when you come at any time," she said in the voice of restraint which usually mildly irritated him. He was apt to reply shortly, unsympathetically; but, firm in the determination to improve the tone of his relations with Fanny, he cheerfully met the evidence of her sense of injury. "Of course," she added, "we expected you yesterday up to the very last minute." When he asked her who exactly she meant by we she answered, "The Rodmans and John and Alice Luce. It was all arranged for you. Borden Rodman sent us some ducks; I remembered how you liked them, and I asked the others and cooked them myself. That's mixed, but you know what I mean. I had oysters and the thick tomato soup with crusts and Brussels sprouts; and I sent to town for the alligator pears and meringue. I suppose it can't be helped, and it's all over now, but you might have let me know."

"I am sorry, Fanny," he acknowledged; "at the last so much piled up to do. Mina Raff was very doubtful. I can't tell if I accomplished anything with her or not." Fanny seemed to have lost all interest in Peyton Morris's affair. "I had dinner with Mina and talked a long while. At bottom she is sensible enough; and very sensitive. I like sensitive women."

"You mean that you like other women to be sensitive," she corrected him; "whenever I am, you get impatient and say I'm looking for trouble."

There was, he replied, a great deal in what she said; and it must be remedied. At this she gazed at him for a speculative second. "Where did you take Mina Raff to dinner?" she asked; "and what did you do afterward?" He told her. "She was so tired that she went back to the Plaza before ten. No, I returned to the Groves'. It's no good being in New York alone. We'll have our party together there before Christmas."

"I imagined you'd see a lot of her."

"Of Mina Raff? What nonsense! She is working all day and practically never goes out. People have such wrong ideas about actresses, or else they have changed and the opinions have stood still. They are as business-like now as lawyers; you make an appointment with their secretaries. Besides that, Mina doesn't specially attract me."

"At any rate you call her Mina."

"Why so I do; I hadn't noticed; but she hasn't started to call me Lee; I must correct her."

"They played bridge afterward," Fanny said, referring, he gathered, to the occasion he had missed. "That is, the Rodmans and the Luces did, and I sat around. People are too selfish for anything!" Her voice grew sharper. "They stayed until after twelve, just because Borden was nineteen dollars back at one time. And they drank all that was left of your special Mount Vernon. It was last night that you were at the St. Regis?"

"No," he corrected her, "the night before. Last evening I had dinner with the Groves." This was so nearly true that he advanced it with satisfaction. "Afterward we went to the Greenwich Follies."

"I don't see how you had to wait, then," she observed instantly. "You were in New York on account of Claire, you stayed three nights, and only saw Mina Raff once." He told her briefly that, unexpectedly, more had turned up. "What did you do the first night?" she persisted.

"I dragged a cash girl into an opium place on Pell Street."

"That's not too funny to be borne," she returned; "and it doesn't altogether answer my question."

"We went to Malmaison."

"We?" she mimicked his earlier query.

"Oh, the Groves. I like them very much, Fanny—" To her interruption that that was evident he paid no attention. "He is an extremely nice man, a little too conscious of his pedestal, but solid and cordial. Mrs. Grove is more unusual; I should say she is a difficult woman to describe. She dresses beautifully, Paris and the rest of it; but she isn't a particle good-looking. Not a bit! It's her color, I think. She hasn't any. Women would fancy her more than men; no one could call her pleasant."

"You haven't asked about the children." She had apparently heard nothing of what had gone before.

"Of course they are all right or you'd have told me."

"Lee, you astonish me, you really do; at times I think you forget you have a family. We'll all be dead before you know it. I'm sorry, but you will have to get into the habit of staying home at least one night a week. I attend to all I can manage about the place, but there are some things you must settle. The trouble is I haven't demanded enough from you."

"That's silly," he responded, almost falling into his discarded irritation; "I practically never go out without you. Unless you are with me I won't be in New York again for weeks."

"I should have thought you'd be back at the Groves's tomorrow. It's more amusing there, I don't doubt; but, after all, you are married to me."

"Good heavens, Fanny," he protested, "what is this about? You're really cutting with the Groves—two excessively nice people who were decent to me."

"You are such an idiot," she declared, in a warmer voice. "Can't you see how disappointed I was? First I had everything laid out on the bed, my best nightgowns and lace stockings, for the trip; then I couldn't go; and I arranged the party so carefully for you, Gregory had a practice piece ready for you to hear, and—and nothing. I wonder if any other man is as selfish as you?'

"Maybe not," he returned peaceably. "What happened was unavoidable. It was a social necessity, decided for me. I couldn't just run into the house and out again. But there is no need to explain further." He left the table, for a cigar, and returned. "You have on a new dress!"

"I ought to be complimented," she admitted, "but I am not; it's only the black velvet with the fulness taken out and a new ruffle. Clothes are so expensive that I wanted to save. It isn't French, either. Perhaps you'll remember that you said the new length didn't become me. No, you're not the idiot—I am. I must stop considering and trying to please you at every turn. I should have gone in and ordered a new dress; any other woman you know would have done that; and, I have no doubt, would have told you it was old when it wasn't. I wish I didn't show that I care so much and kept you guessing. You'd be much more interested if you weren't so sure of me. That seems to me queer—loyalty and affection, and racking your brain to make your husband comfortable and happy, don't bring you anything. They don't! You'll leave at once for a night in New York or a new face with an impudent bang at the dances. I have always tried to do what I thought was right, but I'm getting discouraged."

"Don't lose patience with me," he begged gravely. "If I am worth the effort to you, Fanny, don't stop. I do the best I can. Coming out in the train I made up my mind to stop petty quarreling. No, wait—if it is my fault that makes it easy, we're done with it."

"From the way you talk," she objected, "anyone would think we did nothing but fight. And that isn't true; we have never had a bit of serious trouble." She rose, coming around to him:

"That wasn't a very nice kiss we had when you came in. I was horrid."

Lee Randon kissed her again. The cool familiarity of her lips was blurred in the remembered clinging intensity of Savina's mouth. "Lee, dear, blow out the candles; the servants forget, and those blue handmade ones cost twenty-five cents apiece." They left the dining-room with her arm about him and his hand laid on her shoulder. Lee's feeling was curious—he recognized Fanny's desirability, he loved her beyond all doubt, and yet physically she had now no perceptible influence on him. He was even a little embarrassed, awkward, at her embrace; and its calmly possessive pressure filled him with a restive wish to move away. He repressed this, forced himself to hold her still, repeated silently all that she had given him; and she turned a face brilliant with color to his gaze. Fanny made him bring her stool—how sharply Savina's heels had dug into him under the table at the Lafayette—and showed him her ankles. "You see, I put them on tonight for you." Her stockings, he assured her, were enchanting. A difficulty that, incredibly, he had not foreseen weighed upon him: the body, where Fanny was concerned, had given place to the intellect; the warmth of his feeling had been put aside for the logic of determination; and he was sick with weariness. In his customary chair, he sank into a heavy brooding lethargy, a silence, in which his hands slowly and stiffly clenched.


On the following morning, Sunday, Lee rode with Claire Morris. Fanny, disinclined to activity, stayed by the open fire, with the illustrated sections of the newspapers and her ornamental sewing. Claire was on, a tall bright bay always a little ahead of Lee, and he was constantly urging his horse forward. "Peyton went to the Green Spring Valley for a hunt party last night," she told him; "he said he'd be back." Why, then, he almost exclaimed, he, Lee, had been successful with Mina Raff. Instead he said that she would undoubtedly be glad of that. "Oh, yes! But neither of us is very much excited about it just now; he is too much like a ball on a rubber string; and if I were a man I'd hate to resemble that. I won't try to hide from you that I've lost something; still, I have him and Mina hasn't. They shouldn't have hesitated, Lee; that was what spoiled it, in the end beat them. It wasn't strong enough to carry them away and damn the consequences. There is always something to admire in that, even if you suffer from it."

The night had been warm, and the road, the footing, was treacherous with loosened stones and mud. The horses, mounting a hill, picked their way carefully; and Lee Randon gazed over his shoulder into the valley below. He saw it through a screen of bare wet maple branches—a dripping brown meadow lightly wreathed in blue mist, sedgy undergrowth along water and the further ranges of hills merged in shifting clouds. A shaft of sunlight, pale and without warmth, illuminated with its emphasis an undistinguished and barren spot. On the meadows sloping to the south there were indefinite spaces of green. Claire was heedless of their surroundings.

"What does surprise and disturb me," she continued vigorously, "is that I haven't any sympathy for him. That is gone too; I only have a feeling that he bitched it. As you may observe, Lee, I am not at all admirable this morning: a figure of inconsistency. And the reason will amaze you—I've rather come to envy what they might have had. I am afraid that if the positions of Mina and me had been reversed I wouldn't have seen you in New York. I found that out last night when I knew Peyton wasn't going. What he said over and over was that everything could be just as it was." She laughed, riding easily, subconsciously, on the snaffle rein. "Peyton's simplicity is marvelous. In a year, or maybe less, he will be quite the same as always. I had nothing to do with it; Peyton and Mina will go on as fresh as daisies; yet only I'll be damaged or, anyway, changed. What shall I do about it?" she demanded of Lee Randon, so sharply that her horse shied.

"About what?" he returned. "My senses are so dulled by your ingratitude that I can't gather what you mean."

"Well, here I am—a girl with her head turned by a glimpse at a most romantic play, by cakes and champagne cup, and then sent home to bread without jam. Since I've known of this it has taken most of the color out of everyday things, they are like a tub-full of limp rags with the dye run from them. I want Peyton, yes, I love him; but what I thought would satisfy me doesn't. I want more! I am very serious about the romantic play—it is exactly what I mean. I had read about great emotions, seen them since I was a child at the opera, and there was the Madrid affair; but that was so far away, and I never thought of the others as real; I never understood that people really had them, in Eastlake as well as Spain, until I watched Peyton miss his. And then it came over me in a flash what life could be."

"We are all in the same fix, Claire," he told her.

"But not you," she replied impatiently; "your existence with Fanny is the most perfect for miles around. Fanny is marvelous to you, and you are as sensible as you are nice."

"You think, then, that I haven't seen any of this romantic show you are talking about?"

"If you had you wouldn't let it spoil your comfort."

The pig again!

"Well, what is it here or there?" she cried. "I'll feel like this for a little and then die alive. Did you ever notice an old woman, Lee? She is like a horrid joke. There is something unconquerably vain and foolish about old men that manages to save them from entire ruin. But a woman shrivelled and blasted and twisted out of her purpose—they either look as though they had been steeped in vinegar or filled with tallow—is simply obscene. Before it is too harrowing, and in their best dresses and flowers, they ought to step into a ball-room of chloroform. But this change in me, Lee, isn't in my own imagination. The people who know me best have complained that what patience I had has gone; even Ira, I'm certain, notices it. I have no success in what used to do to get along with; my rattle of talk, my line, is gone."

"Those relations of Mina Raff's, the Groves," he said, shifting the talk to the subject of his thoughts, "are very engaging. Mrs. Grove specially. She has splendid qualities almost never found together in one person. She is, well, I suppose careful is the word, and, at the same time, not at all dull. I wonder if she is altogether well? Her paleness would spoil most women's looks and, it seems to me, she mentioned her heart."

"Good Lord, Lee, what are you rambling on about? I don't care for a description of the woman like one of those anatomical zodiacs in the Farmers' Almanac." She turned her horse, without warning, through a break in the fence; and, putting him at a smart run, jumped a stream with a high insecure bank beyond, and went with a pounding rush up a sharp incline. He followed, but more conservatively; and, at the solid fence she next took, he shouted that she'd have to continue on that gait alone.

"Don't be so careful," she answered mockingly, trotting back; "take a chance; feel the wind streaming in your face; you'll reach Fanny safely."

What, exasperated, he muttered was, "Damn Fanny!" He had jumped a fence as high and wide as respectability; and he enormously preferred Savina's sort of courage to this mad galloping over the country. What Claire and Peyton and Mina Raff talked about, longed for, Savina took. He involuntarily shut his eyes, and, rocking to the motion of his horse, heard, in the darkness, a soft settling fall, he saw an indefinite trace of whiteness which swelled into an incandescence that consumed him. They had turned toward home and, on an unavoidable reach of concrete road, were walking. The horses' hoofs made a rhythmic hollow clatter. Claire, with the prospect of losing her love, had hinted at the possibilities of an inherited recklessness; but here was a new and unexpected cause of disturbance.

Lee would never have supposed that such ideas were at the back of Claire's head. He gazed at her, in spite of the fact that she had ruffled his temper, even with an increased interest. In her direct way she had put into words many of the vague pressures floating, like water under night, through his brain. He would act differently; Claire wasn't practical—all that she indicated couldn't be followed. It was spun of nothing more substantial than the bright visions of youth; but the world, he, Lee Randon, was the poorer for that. His was the wise course. It took a marked degree of strength; no weak determination could hope for success in the conduct he had planned for himself; and that gave him material for satisfaction.

He turned to the left, at the road leading past his driveway, and Claire went up the hill into Eastlake alone. She had thought he was describing Savina for her benefit! The truth was that he had been possessed by a tyrannical necessity to talk about Savina Grove, to hear the sound of her praise if it were only on his own voice. It assisted his memory, created, like the faintly heard echo of a thrilling voice, a similitude not without its power to stir him. The secret realms of thought, of fancy and remembrance, he felt, were his to linger in, to indulge, as he chose. Lee had a doubt of the advisability of this; but his question was disposed of by the realization that he had nothing to say; his mind turned back and back to Savina.

He wondered when, or, rather, by what means, he should hear from her again; perhaps—although it required no reply—in response to the letter he had written to the Groves acknowledging their kindness and thanking them for it. To Lee, William Loyd Grove was more immaterial than a final shred of mist lifting from the sunken road across the golf course; even his appreciation of the other's good qualities had vanished, leaving nothing at all. He was confused by the ease with which the real, the solid, became the nebulous and unreal, as though the only standard of values, of weights and measures, lay absurdly in his own inconsequential attitude.

The Randons had no formal meal on Sunday night; but there were sandwiches, a bowl of salad, coffee, and what else were referred to generally as drinks; and a number of people never failed to appear. It was always an occasion of mingled conversations, bursts of popular song at the piano, and impromptu dancing through the length of the lower floor. The benches at either side of the fire-place were invariably crowded; and, from her place on the over-mantel, Cytherea's gaze rested on the vivacious or subdued current of life. Lee Randon often gazed up at her, and tonight, sunk in a corner with scarcely room to move the hand which held a cigarette, this lifted interrogation was prolonged.

Mrs. Craddock, whom he had not seen since the dinner-dance at the club, sat beside him in a vivid green dress with large black beads strung from her left shoulder. She looked very well, he reflected; that was a becoming dimple in her cheek. He had had the beginning of an interest in her—new to Eastlake, and her husband dead, she had taken a house there for the winter—but that had vanished now. He was deep in thought when she said:

"Didn't I hear that you were infatuated with that doll?"

Who, he demanded, had told her such a strange story? "But she does attract me," he admitted; "or, rather, she raises a great many questions, natural in a person named Cytherea. The pair of castanets on a nail—Claire used them in an Andalusian dance—might almost be an offering, like the crutches of Lourdes, left before her by a grateful child of the ballet."

"I can't see what you do, of course; but she reminds me of quantities of women—fascinating on the outside and nothing within. Men are always being fooled by that: they see a face or hear a voice that starts something or other going in them, and they supply a complete personality just as they prefer it, like the filling of a paté case. That is what you have done with this doll—imagined a lot of things that don't exist."

"If they do in me, that's enough, isn't it?" he demanded. "You're partly wrong, at any rate—Cytherea is the originator and I'm the paté. But where, certainly, you are right is that she is only a representation; and it is what she may represent which holds me. Cytherea, if she would, could answer the most important question of my life."

"How tragic that she can't speak."

"Yet that isn't necessary; she might be a guide, like a pointing finger-post. I met a woman lately, as charming as possible, who resembled her; and I'm sure that if I had them together—" he left the end of his sentence in air. Then he began again, "But that could not be managed; not much can, with advantage, in this world." From beyond the hall, to the accompaniment of the piano, came the words, "She might have been a mother if she hadn't looped the loop." Lee made a disdainful gesture. "That is the tone of the present—anything is acceptable if it is trivial; you may kiss wherever you like if you mean nothing by it. But if it's important, say like—like sympathy, it's made impossible for you."

"If you were someone else," Mrs. Craddock observed, "I'd think you were in love. You have a great many of the symptoms—the wandering eye and wild speech."

"I am, with Fanny," he declaimed, struggling out of the bench corner. No one should discover the memory he carried everywhere with him. The lights had been switched off in the living-room, but the piano continued, and glowing cigarettes, like red and erratically waving signals, were visible. Returning, going into the dining-room, he saw that the whiskey had been plentifully spilled over the table. In the morning the varnish would be marred by white stains. The stairs were occupied, the angle in the hall behind which a door gave to the cellar steps, was filled; a sound, not culinary, came from the kitchen pantry. Even Fanny, with her hair in disorder, was dancing an eccentric step with Borden Rodman. All this vibrating emotion created in him, sudden and piercing, a desire for Savina.

He wanted her, the touch of her magnetic hands, her clinging body, her passionate abandon, with every sense. It was unbearable that she, too, wasn't here, waiting for him in the convenient darkness. He had to have her, he muttered. At the same time he was appalled by the force of his feeling: it shook him like a chill and gripped his heart with an acute pain. His entire being was saturated with a longing that was at once a mental and physical disturbance. Nothing in his life, no throe of passion or gratification, had been like this. Lee hastily poured out a drink and swallowed it. He was burning up, he thought; it felt as though a furnace were open at his back; and he went out to the silence, the coldness, of the terrace flagging on the lawn. The lower window shades had been pulled down, but, except in the dining-room, they showed no blur of brightness. Through the walls the chords of the piano were just audible, and the volume of voices was reduced to a formless humming.

It had cleared, the sky was glittering with constellations of stars; against them Lee could trace the course of his telephone wire. But for that his house, taking an added dignity of mass from the night, might have been the reality of which it was no more than an admirable replica. There was little here, outside, to suggest or recall the passage of a century and over. In the lapse of that time, Lee thought, more had been lost than gained; the simplicity had vanished, but wisdom had not been the price of its going.

Of all the people at present in his dwelling, Fanny was the best in the sense of old solid things; he could see her, with no change, at the board of an early household. Compared to her the others seemed like figures in a fever; yet he was, unhappily, with them rather than with Fanny. God knew there was fever enough in his brain! But the winter night was cooling it—a minor image of the final office of death; the choking hunger for Savina was dwindling. He hoped that it wouldn't be repeated. He couldn't answer for himself through many such attacks. Yes, his first love, though just as imperative, had been more ecstatic; the reaching for an ideal rather than the body of a woman.

His allegiance to Cytherea, though, was in part to the former, to youth; now it seemed to him he had preserved that through all his life. But the latter, at least in its devastating power, was new. Lee recognized it as passion, but passion to a degree beyond all former experience and comprehension. Why had it been quiescent so long to overwhelm him now? Or what had he done to open himself to such an invasion? A numbing poison couldn't have been very different. Then, contrarily, he was exhilarated by the knowledge of the vitality of his emotion; Lee reconsidered it with an amazement which resembled pride.

The penny kisses here—he was letting himself into the house—were like the candies Fanny had in a crystal dish on the sideboard, flavors of cinnamon and rose and sugary chocolate. They were hardly more than the fumes of alcohol. But the party showed no signs of ending, the piano continued to be played without a break; one sentimental song had been repeated, without the omission of a line, a held note, ten times, Lee was sure. Fanny paused breathlessly, with a hand on his arm:

"They are all having such a good time; it is absolutely successful. Isn't Borden sweet to bother teaching me that heel tap. Go in and talk to Mrs. Craddock again; I thought you liked her."

In the hall the victrola had been started in opposition to the piano beyond, and the result was a pandemonium of mechanical sound and hysterical laughter. Cytherea was unmoved, enigmatic, fascinating; the gilt of her headdress shone in minute sparkles—Lee had turned on the lights by the mantel. "You always come back to her," Mrs. Craddock said. When he replied that this time he had returned to her, she shook her head sceptically. "But I suppose you have to say it." He dropped back into a corner of one of the benches; they were a jumble of skirts and reclining heads and elevated pumps. The victrola, at the end of a record and unattended, ran on with a shrill scratch. Cytherea had the appearance of floating in the restrained light; her smile was not now so mocking as it was satirical; from her detached attention she might have been regarding an extraordinary and unpredictable spectacle which she had indifferently brought about. It was evident that among what virtues she might possess charity was not present.


After the last automobile leaving—shifted through the diminishing clamor of its gears—had carried its illumination into the farther obscurity of the road, Fanny, uncomfortable in the presence of disorder, quickly obliterated the remaining traces of their party: she emptied the widely scattered ash trays into a brass bowl, gathered the tall whiskey glasses and the glasses with fragile stems and brilliantly enamelled belligerent roosters, the empty charged water bottles, on the dresser in the pantry, and returned chairs and flowers to their recognized places, while Lee locked up the decanters of whiskey. Fanny was tired but enthusiastic, and, as she went deftly about, rearranging her house with an unfailing surety of touch, she hummed fragments of the evening's songs.

Lee Randon was weary without any qualification; the past day, tomorrow—but it was already today— offered him no more than a burden, so many heavy hours, to be supported. The last particle of interest had silently gone from his existence. His condition was entirely different from the mental disquiet of a month ago; no philosophical considerations nor abstract ideas absorbed him now—it was a weariness not of the mind but of the spirit, a complete sterility of imagination and incentive, as though an announced and coveted prize had been arbitrarily withdrawn during the struggle it was to have rewarded. There was no reason Lee could think of for keeping up his diverse efforts. He sat laxly in his customary corner of the living room—Fanny, he felt, had disposed of him there as she had the other surrounding objects—his legs thrust out before him, too negative to smoke.

His wife leaned over and kissed him; she was, she had suddenly discovered, dead with fatigue. The kiss was no more than the contact of her lips on his. The clear realization of this startled him; now not an emotion, not even tenderness, responded to her gestures of love. His indifference had been absolute! There had been periods of short duration when, exasperated with Fanny, he had lost the consciousness of his affection for her;

but then he had been filled with other stirred emotions; and now he was coldly empty of feeling. It was this vacancy that specially disturbed him: it had an appearance, new to all his processes, of permanence.

Outside his will the fact was pronounced for him that—for a long or short period—he had ceased to love his wife. There was something so intimately and conventionally discourteous in his realization that he avoided it even in his thoughts. But it would not be ignored; it was too robust a truth to be suppressed by weakened instincts. He didn't love Fanny and Fanny did love him ... a condition, he felt indignantly, which should be automatically provided against; none of the ethics of decency or conduct provided for that. It wasn't for a second, without the single, the familiar and ancient, cause, allowed. Fanny, least of any imaginable woman, had given him a pretext for complaint. Yet, with everyone acknowledging her to be the perfect wife, and he at the fore of such praise, he had incontestably stopped caring for her. It was a detestable situation.

In the whole body of preconceived thought and action there wasn't a word, a possible movement, left for him. He was, simply, a hyena; that description, not innocent of humor, was still strikingly close to what he would generally hear if the state of his mind were known. It was paralyzing, but absolutely no provision had been made for men, decent enough, who had stopped loving decent wives. Lee was not, here, considering the part of his life involved with Savina Grove: Savina had nothing to do with his attitude toward Fanny. This didn't hang on the affection he might have for one at the superficial expense of the other: Savina—while it was undeniable that she had done exactly this in the vulgar physical sense—hadn't essentially taken him away from Fanny. He had gone self-directed, or, rather, in the blind manner of an object obeying the law of gravity. He couldn't argue that he had been swept away.

It wasn't, either, that he overwhelmingly wanted to go to Savina Grove, he overwhelmingly didn't; and the strangling emotion, the desire, that had possessed him earlier in the evening had been sufficiently unwelcome. His only reaction to that was the vigorous hope that it wouldn't come back. No, he had, mentally, settled the affair with Savina in the best possible manner; now he was strictly concerned with the bond between his wife and himself. The most reliable advice, self-administered or obtained from without, he could hope for would demand that he devote the rest of his life, delicately considerate, to Fanny. She must never know the truth. This was the crown of a present conception of necessity and unassailable conduct, of nobility. But, against this, Lee Randon was obliged to admit that he was not a particle noble; he wasn't certain that he wanted to be; he suspected it. Putting aside, for the moment, the doubtfulness of his being able to maintain successfully, through years, such an imposition, there was something dark, equally dubious, in its performance. He might manage it publicly, even superficially in private, and as a father; but marriage wasn't primarily a superficial relationship. It was very much the reverse. Its fundamental condition was the profoundest instinct that controlled living; there no merely admirable conduct could manage to be more than a false and degrading, a temporary, lie. How could he with a pandering smugness meet Fanny's purity of feeling? Yet, it seemed, exactly this was being done by countless other applauded men. But, probably, the difference between them and himself was that they had no objective consciousness of their course; happily they never stopped to think. It was thought, he began to see, and not feeling that created nearly all his difficulties.

In a flash of perception he grasped that formal thought, in its aspect of right conduct, was utterly opposed to feeling. While the former condemned the surrender of Savina and himself to passion, the latter, making it imperative, had brushed aside the barriers of recognized morals. It had been a tragic, it might well be a fatal, error to oppose religion—as it affected both this world and the impossible next—to nature.

Yet men could no longer exist as animals; he saw that plainly. They had surrendered the natural in favor of an artificial purity. In a land where sea shells were the standard of value, rubies and soft gold were worthless. Lee was opposed to his entire world; he had nothing but his questioning, his infinitesimal entity, for his assistance. Literally there wasn't a man to whom he could turn whose answer and advice weren't as predictable as useless. There was nothing for him but to accept his position and, discharging it where he was able, fail where he must.

There was, however, no need for that failure to be absolute; and the underlying responsibility he had fully considered, subject to its own attained code, would have to do service as best it could. Here he paused to realize that the improved manners he had determined on were no more than the expression of his growing, his grown, indifference. It should be easy to be restrained in a situation that had small meaning or importance. What struck him again was the fact that his connection with Fanny was of far greater moment than that with Helena and Gregory. His responsibility to them was a minor affair compared to the weight increasingly laid upon their elders. Somehow, they didn't seem to need him as sharply as Fanny did. Materially they were all three more than sufficiently provided for, and spiritually, as he had so often reflected, he had little or no part in his children's well-being. Perhaps this, he had told himself, could be changed; certainly he was solely to blame if he had stood aside from their education.

He would see more of them—four days a week were now plenty for the conducting of his successful enterprises in the city—and give them what benefits his affection and experience held. In this he mustn't contradict the influence of their mother; that, so late, would only be followed by chaos; he'd merely be more with them. Helena was old enough for a small tractable horse and Gregory must have a pony. All four, Fanny and he and the children, would jog out in the spring together. From that mental picture he got a measure of reassurance; a condition resembling peace of mind again returned. As much as possible, against the elements of danger, was in his favor. He might have had a wife who, on the prevalent tide of gin and orange juice, of inordinate luxuriousness, degraded him with small betrayals. Or he might have been any one of a hundred unfortunate things. He took life too seriously, that was evident; a larger degree of mental irresponsibility would be followed by a more responsible accomplishment of the realities which bore no more heavily on him than on other men; and in this the cocktails had their office.

Lee agreed readily, therefore, when, on Friday afternoon, Fanny asked him to bring Helena and Gregory from dancing-school. This was held in the Armory; and, past five o'clock, mounting the wide stone steps in the early gloom and going through the bare echoing hall, he joined the complacent mothers ranged in chairs pushed against the wall in a spirit of interested attention. The Armory, following the general literal interpretation of the sternness of military usage, was gaunt, with a wide yellow floor and walls of unconcealed brick. In a far corner, on a temporary and unpainted platform, the pianist sat with her hands raised, her wrists rigid, preparatory to the next demand upon her strongly accentuated playing. Lee was surprised at the large number of children ranged in an irregular ring about the erect brittle presence and insistent voice of the instructor.

What scant hair he possessed, carefully disposed to cover its meagreness, was grey, and its color permeated, suggested, the tone of his thin face. Surrounded by the cruel exuberance of the children, he seemed incalculably worn, permanently weary, although he was surprisingly sharp-eyed and adequate. It was, Lee thought unsympathetically, a curiously negative occupation for a man; the small graces of the dancing teacher, the bows gravely exchanged with childish bows, the bent dancing with diminutive slips, the occasional fretful tone of his voice, further alienated Lee Randon. But the children were a source of entertainment and speculation.

He saw Gregory at once, short and sturdy-legged, in a belted jacket and white breeches; his son was standing peaceably, attentive, clasping the hand of a girl smaller than himself with obstinate bobbed hair. This, the high pointed voice in the center of the floor continued, was an Irish folk dance; they would try it again; and the reiterated details were followed by the sounding of a whistle and music. Lee had no idea of the exact number of children engaged, but he was certain that there were just as many totally different executions of the steps before them. Not one had grasped an essential of the carefully illustrated instruction; he could see nowhere an evidence of grace or rhythm. But, with a few notable exceptions, all boys, there was an entire solemnity of effort; the swinging of bare short legs, the rapid awkward bobs, were undertaken with a deep sense of their importance.

The Irish folk dance was attempted for a third time, and then relinquished in favor of a waltz. Miniature couples circled and staggered, the girls again prim, the boys stolid or with working mouths, or as smooth and vacuous as chestnuts, little sailors and apparitions in white, obviously enjoying their employment. During this not a word was exchanged; except for the shuffling feet, the piano, an occasional phrase of encouragement from the instructor, himself gliding with a dab of fat in exaggerated ribbons, there wasn't a sound. To Lee it had the appearance of the negation of pleasure; it was, in its way, as bad as the determined dancing of adults; it had the look of a travesty of that. Helena conducted a restive partner, trying vainly to create the impression that he was leading, wherever she considered it advantageous for him to go. The thick flood of her gold hair shimmered about her uncompromising shoulders, her embroidered skirt fluttered over the firmness of her body.

She was as personable a little girl as any present; and, while she hadn't Gregory's earnestness in what he attempted, she got on smoothly enough. Seeing Lee, she smiled and waved a hand almost negligently; but Gregory, at his presence, grew visibly embarrassed; he almost stopped. Lee Randon nodded for him to go ahead. There were various minor cataclysms—Helena flatly refused to dance with a boy who pursued her with an urging hand. At this conspicuous reverse he sat on a chair until the teacher brought him forcibly out and precipitated him into the willing arms of a girl larger and, if possible, more inelastic than the others. The ring was again assembled, and the complicated process of alternating a boy with a girl was accomplished.

"Never mind what he does," the instructor directed sharply; "always be sure you are right." A shift was made further around in the line, and the elder wisdom was vindicated. "Now, the chain." The whistle blew. "Left and right, left and right." In spite of this there was an equal engagement of rights with lefts. The assumption of gravity acutely bothered Lee Randon: they had no business, he thought, to be already such social animals. Their training in set forms, mechanical gestures and ideas, was too soon hardening their mobility and instinctive independence. Yes, they were a caricature of what they were to become. He hadn't more sympathy with what he had resolved to encourage, applaud, but less. The task of making any headway against that schooling was beyond him.

The dancing reached a pause, and, with it, the silence: a confusion of clear undiversified voices rose: the face of an infant with long belled trousers and solidified hair took on a gleam of impish humor; older and more robust boys scuffled together with half-subdued hails and large pretentions; groups of girls settled their skirts and brushed, with instinctive pats, their braids into order; and there was a murmur of exchanged approbation from the supporting, white-gloved mothers. Gregory appeared at Lee's side; his cheeks were crimson with health, his serious eyes glowed:

"Well, do you like it?"

60

"Yes," Gregory answered shyly. He lingered while Lee Randon tried to think of something else appropriate to say, and then he ran abruptly off. His children were affectionate enough, but they took him absolutely for granted; they regarded him very much as they did their cat; except for the conventional obeisance they made him, not so voluntary as it was trained into them, they were far more involved with Martha, their black nurse. Everywhere, Lee felt, they repelled him. Was he, then, lacking in the qualities, the warmth, of paternity? Again, as he was helpless where Fanny lately was concerned, he was unable to be other.

It was increasingly evident that he had not been absorbed, obliterated, in marriage; an institution which, from the beginning, had tried—like religion—to hold within its narrow walls the unconfinable instincts of creation. It hadn't, among other things, considered the fascination of Cytherea; a name, a tag, as intelligible as any for all his dissent. But cases like his were growing more prevalent; however, usually, in women. Men were the last stronghold of sentimentality. His thoughts were interrupted by a dramatic rift in the discipline of the class: a boy, stubbornly seated, swollen, crimson, with wrath and heroically withheld tears, was being vainly argued with by the dancing master. He wouldn't stir, he wouldn't dance. The man, grasping a shoulder, shook him in a short violence, and then issued a final uncompromising order.

The boy rose and, marching with an increasing rapidity toward the entrance, he struck aside a placid and justifiably injured child, dragged open the door, and slammed it after him with a prodigious and long echoing report. His contempt, holding its proportion in the reduced propriety of the occasion, was like a clap of communistic thunder in an ultra-conservative assembly. For a moment, together with all the others, Lee Randon was outraged; then, with a suppression of his unorderly amusement, he had a far different conception—he saw himself, for no easily established reason, in the person of the rebel who had left behind him the loud announcement of his angry dissent. Helena sought Lee immediately.

"That's his mother," she said in a penetrating whisper, indicating a woman with a resolutely abstracted expression and constrained hands. The children were gathered finally and formed into a line which, to the drumming piano, moved and halted, divided and subdivided. Led by the instructor it was involved in an apparently issueless tangle and then straightened smoothly out. The dancing class at an end, Helena and Gregory, wedged into the seat with Lee in the car, swept into an eager chatter, a rush of questions, that he was unable to follow. A Sara Lane was announced by Helena to be the object of Gregory's affection, and Gregory smugly admitted this to be true. He was going to marry her, he declared further.

"Perhaps," Lee suggested, "you'll change your mind."

"Why, Gregory has four girls," Helena instructed him.

"Well," Gregory retorted, "I can marry them all."

But what, under this reflected chatter, was his son like? What would he be? And Helena! They eluded him like bright and featureless bits of glass. His effort to draw closer to them was proving a failure; what could he give them safer than their attachment to the imponderable body of public opinion and approval? He had nothing but doubts, unanswerable questions; and a mental, a moral, isolation. It was easier to remain in the dancing class than to be sent out in an agony of revolt and strangling shame.


Often, during his conversations with Fanny, she returned to the subject of his late New York trip and stay with the Groves. She asked small interested questions, commented on the lavish running of the Grove house; she couldn't, she explained, get nectarines and Belgian grapes in Eastlake; but when she was in the city again she'd bring some out. "Mina Raff's limousine sounds luxurious," she acknowledged. But Fanny wasn't curious about Mina; after the first queries she accepted her placidly; now that she had withdrawn from the Morrises' lives, Fanny regarded her in the light of a past episode that cast them all together on a romantic screen. What mostly she asked touched upon Savina Grove. "Did they seem happy?" she inquired about the Groves. He replied:

"Very. William Grove was quite affectionate when he left for Washington."

A momentary and ominous suspense followed a sudden stopping of his voice.

"You didn't say anything about that before," she observed carefully. "When did he go, how long was he away?" She put aside what she was doing, waiting.

"He left unexpectedly; just when I forget; but during the last day I was there."

"Lee, why didn't you say that Mr. Grove had gone to Washington? It seems very peculiar."

"I told you it had slipped my mind," he retorted, striving, in a level tone, to hide his chagrin and an increasing irritation at her persistence.

"When did he come back?"

"I don't know." Suddenly he gave way to a complete frankness. "He may not be back yet."

"Then you had dinner at the restaurant and went to the theatre alone with her."

"If it's possible to be alone with anyone, you are correct. What, in the name of heaven, are you getting at?"

"Only this—that, for some reason I can't gather, you lied to me. I have had the most uncomfortable impression about her all along. Why?" Her demand had a quality of unsteady emotion. "I have been so close to

61

you, Lee, we have had each other so completely, that I have feelings I can't account for. I always know when—when you've been a little silly; there is something in your eyes; but I have never felt like this before. Lee," she leaned suddenly forward, her hands clasping the sides of her chair, "you must be absolutely truthful with me, it's the only way I can live. I love you so much; you're all I have; I don't care for anyone else now. You have taken me away from my family; you are my family. Ours isn't an ordinary marriage, like the Lucians', but worlds deeper."

Yet, he told himself, in spite of her assurances the truth would ruin them; besides, as he had recognized, it didn't belong exclusively to him; it was, as well, Savina's truth. At any cost he had to protect her. Lee replied by saying that it was useless to tell her facts in her present unreasonable humor. "Why didn't you tell me he had gone to Washington?" she repeated; her tone had a sharper edge. "Was there anything you needed to hide?" Just what, he demanded, did she suspect? Fanny didn't know.

"Only I have had this worrying feeling. Did you go straight back from the theatre or take a drive?" He was amazed at her searching prescient questions; but his manner was admirable.

"New Yorkers are not very apt to drive around their Park at night. They are rather familiar with it. There's the afternoon for that, and the morning for the bridle paths. I won't go on, though, in such a senseless and positively insulting conversation."

"You are not yourself since you returned," she observed acutely. "Sunday night you were too queer for words. You couldn't talk to Mrs. Craddock for more than a minute at a time. Did you call her Savina?" Mrs. Craddock's name, he responded in a nicely interrogating manner, he had thought to be Laura. She paid no attention to his avoidance of her demand. "Did you?"

"No." His self-restraint was fast vanishing.

"I can't believe a word you say."

"Hell, don't ask me then."

"You must not curse where the servants can hear you, and I won't listen to such talk, I'll leave the table. I wish you'd look in the mirror and see how red and confused you are. It is too bad that I cannot depend on you after so long, and with the children. You were sitting close to that woman, and—and your arms; you were kissing."

"I have her garter on my bureau."

"Stop." Her anger now raised her above petty sallies. "I have stood a great deal from you, but there is more I simply won't. Do you understand? I've always done my duty and I'll make you do yours. I never have looked at another man, nor been kissed, except that horrid one last July at the Golf Club." While she paused, breathless, he put in that it might do her good. "Oh, I see," she spoke slowly: "you think that would give you an excuse. If I did it it couldn't complain about your nasty affairs. How cheap and easy I must seem. You ought to be ashamed to try to trick me."

"If you are going to fly at conclusions you can sit in the tree alone," he protested. "It's amazing where you have arrived from nothing. Let me tell you that I won't be ragged like this; if you think so much of our life why do you make it hideous with these degrading quarrels? You would never learn that way if there was the slightest, the slightest, cause for your bitterness. You have all you want, haven't you? The house and grounds are planted with your flowers, you are bringing up the children to be like yourself. I don't specially care for this," he made a comprehensive gesture; "building an elaborate place to die in doesn't appeal to me. What is so valuable, so necessary, to you, I never think of. You are so full of your life that you don't consider mine, except where it is tied up with your interests."

"Lee Randon," she cried, "I've given you everything, it's all planned for you, here. Nothing comes on the table that you dislike—we haven't had beefsteak for months; when you are busy with your papers I keep it like a grave; and if the house seems cold, and I can't find Christopher, I don't bother you, but slip down to the furnace myself."

"Make me uncomfortable, then," he retorted; "I think that's what I'm sick of—your eternal gabbling about comfort and dinner. Let the God damn furnace go out! Or burn up."

"That's all I have, Lee," she said helplessly; "it is my life. I tried, the last month, to be different, after watching you with gayer women; but it only made me miserable; I kept wondering if Gregory was covered up and if the car would start when you wanted to go home. But I won't be sorry for it." Her head was up, her cheeks blazing. "I know, and so ought you, what being good is. And if you forget it you will have a dreadful misfortune. God is like that: He'll punish you."

"You don't need help," he commented brutally.

Detached tears rolled over her cheeks. "I won't cry," she contradicted the visible act; "I won't. You take such a cowardly advantage of me."

The advantage, he reflected, was entirely on her side. Within, he was hard, he had no feeling of sympathy for her; the division between them was absolute. With an angry movement she brushed the tears from her cheeks. "I hate her," she said viciously; "she is a rotten detestable woman."

"On the contrary," he replied, "Mrs. Grove, if you happen to mean her, is singularly attractive. There is no smallness about her."

"Hell," she mocked him, "it is really too touching. When shall you see her again?"

"Never." At once he saw that he had made a second mistake.

"How sad—never; I can't bear it. You both must have been wretched at that long hopeless parting. And she agreed to let you go—back to your wife and children." Fanny's voice was a triumph of contempt. "I ought to thank her; or be magnanimous and send you back."

"This is all built on a ridiculous assumption," Lee reminded her; "I even forget how we started. Suppose we talk about something else; Mrs. Grove, as a topic, is pretty well exhausted." Fanny, narrow-eyed, relapsed into an intent silence. She faded from his mind, her place taken by Savina. Immediately he was conscious of a quickening of his blood, the disturbed throb of his heart; the memory of delirious hours enveloped him in a feverish mist more real than his wife sitting before him with a drawn brow.


Usually after such scenes Fanny had flowered in a tender remorse for their bitter remarks, the wasted opportunity of happiness; but again she left him coldly, unmelted. He was glad—a show of affection would have been unsupportable. But his marriage was becoming precarious; Lee seemed to be without power to execute his firm intentions; a conviction of insecurity settled over him. The sense of a familiar difficulty returned; there was nothing for him to do but order his life on a common pattern and face an unrelieved futility of years. He remembered, with a grim amusement, the excellent advice he had given Peyton Morris, Peyton at the verge of falling from the approved heights into the unpredictable. If he had come to him now in that quandary, what would he, Lee, have said? Yet all that he had told Peyton he still believed—the variety of life lay on the circular moving horizon, there was none at hand. But now he comprehended the unmeasurable longing that had, for the time, banished every other consideration from the younger man. It had upset his heredity, his violent prejudices, and his not negligible religion.

Peyton, too, had fallen under the charm of Cytherea; but chance—was it fortunate?—had restrained him. Lee had seen Morris the evening before, at a dinner with Claire, and he had been silent, abstracted. He had scarcely acknowledged Lee Randon's presence. The Morrises had avoided him. Still, that was inevitable, since, for them, he was charged with unpleasant memories.

He collected in thought all the married people who, he knew, were unhappy or dissatisfied: eleven of the eighteen Lee called to mind. "What is the matter with it?" he demanded savagely, aloud, in his room. He considered marriage—isolated for that purpose—as a social contract, the best possible solving of a number of interrelated needs and instincts; and, practical and grey, it recommended itself to his reason; it successfully disposed of the difficulties of property, the birth and education of children, and of society. It was a sane, dignified, way to live with a woman; and it secured so much. Undoubtedly, on that count, marriage couldn't be bettered. As it was, it satisfied the vast majority of men and women: against the bulk of human life Fanny and he, with their friends, were inconsiderable. But the number of men who struggled above the common level was hardly greater; and he and his opinions were of that preferable minority. The freedom of money, the opportunities of leisure, always led directly away from what were called the indispensable virtues.

Men—he returned to the Eastlake streets on Saturday night—except those lost in the monomania of a dream, didn't want to work, they didn't even wish to be virtuous. They turned continually to the bypaths of pleasure, that self-delusion and forgetfulness of drink. Yes, released from the tyrannies of poverty, they flung themselves into a swift spending. The poor were more securely married than the rich, the dull than the imaginative—married, he meant, in the sense of a forged bond, a stockade. This latter condition had been the result of allowing the church to interfere unwarrantedly in what was not its affair. Religion had calmly usurped this, the most potent of the motives of humanity; or, rather, it had fastened to it the ludicrous train of ritual. That laughable idea that God had a separate scrutinizing eye, like the eye of a parrot, on every human atom!

Lee changed his position, physically and mentally—he was lying in bed—and regarded religion in itself. It was, in the hunger for a perpetual identity, almost as strong a force as the other passion. But were they conspicuously other? They had many resemblances. He didn't, by religion, refer to Christianity which, he thought, was but a segregated and weakened form of worship. It was, for example, against the Christian influence that he was struggling. He meant the sense of profound mystery, the revolt against utter causelessness, which had tormented to no clearness so many generations of minds. He accepted the fact that a formless longing was all that he could ever experience; for him, uncritically, that seemed enough; he had willingly relinquished any hope of an eternity like a white frosted cake set with twinkling candles. But viewed as a tangible force operating here and now, identical—to return to his main preoccupation—with love, it demanded some settled intelligence of comprehension.

What he wanted, he was drawn bolt upright as if by an inner shout, was an assurance that could be depended on, that wouldn't break and break and leave him nothing but a feeling of inscrutable mockery. He wanted to understand himself, and, in that, Fanny and the children ... and Savina. Obviously they were all bound together in one destiny, by a single cause. Why had he stopped loving Fanny and had no regret—but a sharp gladness—in his adultery with Savina? He discarded the qualifying word as soon as it had occurred to him: there was no adultery, adulteration, in his act with Savina; it had filled him with an energy, a mental and nervous vigor, long denied to the sanctified bed of marriage. He wanted not even to be justified, but only an explanation of what he was; and he waited, his hands pressed into the softness of the mattress on either side of him, as if the salvation of some reply might come into his aching brain. Nothing, of course, broke the deep reasonable stillness of the night. He slipped back on his pillow weary and baffled.

There, to defraud his misery, he deliberately summoned the memory of Savina, and of delirious hours. She came swiftly, with convulsive shoulders, fingers drawn down over his body; he heard her little cry, "Ah!" How changed her voice had been when she said, "I love you." It had had no apparent connection with the moment, their actual passion. It had disturbed him with the suggestion of a false, a forced, note. In a situation of the utmost accomplishable reality it had been vague, meaningless. I love you. It was a strange phrase, at once empty and burdened with illimitable possibilities. He had said it times without number to Fanny, but first—how seductively virginal she had been—on a veranda at night. Then, though not quite for the first time, he had kissed her. And suddenly her reserve, her protecting chastity, had gone out of her forever.

When had the other, all that eventually led to Savina, begun; when had he lost his love? A long process of turning from precisely the orderly details which, he had decided, should make marriage safe. He was back where he had started—the realization of how men deserted utility for visions, at the enigmatic smile of Cytherea. A sterile circle. Some men called it heaven, others found hell. His mental searching, surrounded, met, by nullity, he regarded as his supreme effort in the direction of sheer duty. If whoever had it in command chose to run the world blindly, unintelligibly, in a manner that would soon wreck the strongest concern, he wasn't going to keep on annoying himself with doubts and the dictates of a senseless conscience. What, as soon as possible, he'd do was fall asleep.

The crowing of a rooster pierced the thinning night, a second answered the first, and they maintained a long self-glorifying, separated duet. The wind which had been flowing in at the north window changed to the south-west.

The difficulties of his living with Fanny increased the next morning: it was one of the week-days when he didn't go into town after breakfast. He was dressed for riding, his horse was at the door, when, without previous announcement and unprepared, she decided to go with him. He could hear her hurrying upstairs—it upset her unreasonably to rush—and suddenly, with the audible fall of a boot on the floor, there was the unmistakable sound of sobbing.

Lee went up, half impatient and half comprehending, and found her seated on a bed, leaning her head in an arm on the foot-board. "Don't wait for me," she cried in a smothered voice; "it makes you so nervous. Just go; it doesn't matter what I do. You've—you've shown me that. Oh, dear, I am so miserable. Everything was right and so happy, and now it's all wrong."

"Nonsense," he replied tonically; "it will take Christopher a few minutes to get your saddle on. I'll be outside." Mounted and waiting for her, his horse stepping contrarily over the grass beyond the drive, he didn't care whether she came or stayed. When she appeared her eyes, prominent now rather than striking, were reddened, and the hastily applied paint and powder were unbecomingly streaked with some late irrepressible tears.

When they had returned, and through lunch and after, a not unfamiliar stubborn silence settled over Fanny. When she spoke it was with an armor-like sarcasm protecting and covering her feelings. He was continually surprised at the correctness of her attitude toward Savina; his wife could know nothing; she was even without the legitimate foundation of a suspicion; but her bearing had a perceptible frostiness of despair. What, he wondered moodily, would next, immediately, develop? Something, certainly—Fanny's accumulations of emotion were always sharply discharged; they grew in silence but they were expended in edged words.

In a way he was glad that he had made the error of speaking about William Grove's absence in Washington: it was a step toward a final resolution, a tranquilization, of the pressure at home. He didn't know what would bring it up, possibly a storm surpassing in violence all that had preceded it; and then ... the open prospect of old age. Fanny should not actually learn of the occurrence in New York, there must be no mistake about that; she would act on the supposition that he had been merely indulging in a more or less advanced dallying; but her patience in that, he judged, was at an end. Well, he could ultimately, in all sincerity, agree with her there. Not too soon, of course, for she was at present deeply suspicious of such protestations; he would maintain for a short while longer an appearance of annoyance, his old successful indignations at her minor charges, and then let her see that she had nothing left to combat from that quarter.

But how, in the other implications of such a scene, would he act? Until now his part in the inevitable frictions of matrimony had been conditioned by a tenderness toward Fanny and a measurable supporting belief that he was generally to blame. She had reduced him to the compounding of excuses; after her attack, drawing away, she had managed to make him follow her. Not cheaply, with the vulgarity of a gift, a price outheld, but with the repeated assertions of his endless love. Nothing less satisfied her. In this she was superior. But, even if he surrendered his life to the effort, could he keep up that pretence of a passion unimpaired? And had he, Lee asked himself over and over, the wish, the patience, for that heavy undertaking?

It was still fairly evident that he hadn't. All that he could hope for, which they both could summon, was luck and the deadening hands of time. He told himself, here, that it was more than probable that he was exaggerating the proportions of the whole situation—Fanny had been angry before; her resentment faded the sooner for its swift explosive character. But this assurance was unconvincing; his presentiment, which didn't rest on reason, was not amenable to a reasonable conclusion. Of this he was certain, that Fanny never had harbored the suspicion of what, for her, would be the very worst. Did she know? If she did, he decided, it was only in the form of an unanalyzed, unidentified, feeling. She wasn't a coward. His determination to keep smooth, by mere politeness, the further course of their marriage seemed frivolous. That might do, it was even indispensable, when the present corner was turned; but for the moment—

What, in the name of God, had got into her? He grew increasingly irritated at her arbitrary manner. Lee had kept forgetting that, where Fanny was concerned, it was causeless, or no better than a wild surmise, a chance thrust at random. He made up his mind that he wouldn't submit to a great deal of her bad humor. And, in this spirit, he ignored a query put to him bitingly:

"Where is the paper cutter?"

His gaze remained level on the page before him.

"Didn't you hear me, Lee? I want the paper cutter. If it's on your night table, get it."

"Let Amanda go up."

"She's out. I let both the girls go tonight. But I needn't explain." She sat expectantly upright. Obliterating his cigarette, he returned, without moving, to the magazine. Then he raised his head:

"You can't hope for much from that tone of voice."

"I'll always insist on your showing me some courtesy. I can't imagine what you think I am. You lie to me as though I were a school-girl and you haven't even common good manners. That trip to New York—I'll hear the truth about it. Anyone could tell it was serious by the effect it had on you. Put down your magazine, you might as well; you can't keep on behind it forever. Why did you try to hide that Mrs. Grove and you were alone?"

"To stop all this!" He dropped the magazine upon the floor. "To save my nerves and the noise of your eternal questions. I knew, if you found out, what would follow; this isn't the first time."

"You can't be completely trusted," she replied. "I have always had to worry and hold you up. If it hadn't been for me—but there is no use in going into that. You must tell me about the Grove woman."

"At one time it was Mrs. Grove," he observed; "now it is 'the Grove woman.' What will you call her next?"

"You will have to tell me that," Fanny said. "Lee Randon, what must I call her?"

"Perhaps, if you knew her, you'd try Savina."

"Not if it was to save me from dying. But I have no doubt of which you preferred. Did you?"

"Did I what?" He was aware that his speech was growing far louder than necessary.

"Call her Savina."

"Yes!" He sat glaring at her in an anger which he felt swelling his neck.

Fanny's expression was obscure. At his admission she had shivered, as though it had reached her in the form of an actually threatened violence, and then she was rigid. "I knew that, all the while." Her voice was low, with a pause between the words. "Savina"; she repeated the name experimentally. "Very pretty. Prettier to say than Fanny; yes, and newer. And, having called her that, you couldn't very well not kiss her, could you?"

However, his caution had again asserted itself over the dangers of a lost temper. "You have made so much of this up that you had better finish it yourself. Put what end you prefer on it; you don't need help."

"The end," she echoed, in a strange and smothered voice. "Is this it? But not yet."

Lee's gaze rested on the magazine lying spread half on the Eastern symbolism of a rug and half on the bare polished flooring. "Your story is far more interesting than any in that," he commented, with a gesture. "It's a pity you haven't turned your imagination to a better use." This, he recognized, could not go on indefinitely. Fanny added:

"But I was wrong—you'd kiss her before you said Savina. That, I believe, is the way it works. It is really screaming when you think what you went to New York for—to protect Claire, to keep Peyton Morris out of Mina Raff's hands. And, apparently, you succeeded but got in badly yourself. What a pair of hypocrites you were: all the while worse than the others, who were at least excused by their youngness, ever could dream of being. What was the good of your contradicting me at first? I knew all along. I felt it."

"What was it, exactly, that you felt?" he asked with an assumption of calmness.

"I don't understand," she acknowledged, for the moment at a loss. "It was inside me, like lead. But, whatever happened, it will come out; it always does; and you'll be sorry."

Did the truth, he wondered, always appear, and triumph over the false; was that precept of morality secure for those who depended on it? And, as Fanny threatened, would he be sorry? But most assuredly he would, for three reasons—Savina, Fanny, and himself; there might, even, be two more, Helena and Gregory; yes, and William Loyd Grove. What a stinking mess it was all turning out to be. Why wasn't life, why weren't women, reasonable? But he could not convince himself that anything final—a separation—threatened them. Fanny couldn't force an admission from him, nor speak of this, investigate it, anywhere else. Savina was well able to take care of herself. There was nothing to do but wait. In the process of that he once more picked up the magazine. Fanny said unexpectedly:

"I ordered your Christmas present. It took all the money I had in the Dime Savings Bank." He muttered a phrase to the effect that Christmas was a season for children. This recalled his own—they wouldn't be asleep yet—and, to escape temporarily from an impossible situation, to secure the paper knife, he went up to see them.

They greeted him vociferously: before he could turn on the light they were partly out of the covers, and the old argument about whose bed he should sit on in full progress. Helena's was by the door, so, returning her to the warmth of her blankets, he stopped beside her. The room, with the windows fully open, was cold, but he welcomed the white frozen purity of its barrenness. More than ever he was impressed by the remoteness of the children's bed-room from the passionate disturbances of living; but they, in the sense Fanny and he knew, weren't alive yet. They imitated the accents and concerns, caught at the gestures, of maturity; but, even in the grip of beginning instincts, they were hardly more sentient than the figures of a puppet show. Or, perhaps, their world was so far from his that they couldn't be said to span from one to the other. Gregory, in mind, was no more like him than a slip was like a tree bearing fruit—no matter how bitter. Helena more nearly resembled her mother; that had never occurred to him before.

It was undoubtedly true—her posturing recalled the feminine attitude in extreme miniature. In that he felt outside her sympathy, she belonged with her mother; to Gregory he was far more nearly allied. Gregory, anyhow, had the potentialities of his own dilemma; he might, in years to come, be drawn out of a present reality by the enigma, the fascination, of Cytherea. Lee Randon hoped not; he wanted to advise him, at once, resolutely to close his eyes to all visions beyond the horizon of wise practicability. Marry, have children, be faithful, die, he said; but, alas, to himself. Gregory, smiling in eager anticipation of what might ensue, was necessarily ignorant of so much. Something again lay back of that, Lee realized—his occupation in life. There he, Lee, had made his first, perhaps most serious, mistake. While the majority of men turned, indifferent, from their labor, there were a rare few—hadn't he phrased this before?—lost in an edifice of the mind, scientific or aesthetic or commercial, who were happily unconscious of the lapsing fretful years.

That was the way to cheat the sardonic gathered fates: to be deaf and blind to whatever, falsely, they seemed to offer; to get into bed heavy with weariness and rise hurried and absorbed. Over men so preoccupied, spent, Cytherea had no power. It was strange how her name had become linked with all his deepest speculations; she was involved in concerns remote from her apparent sphere and influence.

"Gracious, you're thinking a lot," Helena said.

"What are you thinking about?" Gregory added.

"A doll," he replied, turning to his daughter.

"For me," she declared.

"No, me," Gregory insisted.

Lee Randon shook his head. "Not you, in the least."

"Of course not," Helena supported him. "I should think it would make you sick, father, hearing Gregory talk like that. It does me. Why doesn't he ask for something that boys play with?"

"I don't want them, that's why," Gregory specified. "Perhaps I'd like to have a typewriter."

"You're not very modest." It was Helena again.

"It's father, isn't it? It isn't you."

"Listen," Lee broke in, "I came up here to be with two good children; but where are they?"

"I'm one." Helena, freeing herself definitely, closed her arms in a sweet warmth about his neck. "I'm one, too," Gregory called urgently. "No," his father pressed him back; "you must stay in bed. They are both here, I can see."

He wondered if, everything else forgotten, his children could constitute a sufficient engagement; but the sentimental picture, cast across his thoughts, of himself being led by a child holding each of his hands defeated it. He was turned in another direction.

Yet, tonight, they were remarkably engaging.... He had lost a great deal. For what? He couldn't—as usual—answer; but the memory of Savina, stronger than Fanny, metaphorically took Helena's arms away from his neck and blurred the image of Gregory. "Have you said your prayer?" he asked absent-mindedly making conversation. Oh, yes, he was informed, they did that with Martha. "I'll say mine again," Gregory volunteered. Again—a picture of a child, in a halo of innocence, praying at a paternal knee to a fresco of saccharine angels!

"Once is enough," he answered hurriedly. "I am sure you do it very nicely."

"Well, anyhow, better than Helena," Gregory admitted. "She hurries so." Lee instructed him to confine his observations to his own performance. Now was the time for him to deliver a small sermon on prayer to Helena. He recognized this, but he was merely incensed by it. What could he reply if they questioned him about his own devotions? Should he acknowledge that he thought prayer was no more than a pleasant form of administering to a sense of self-importance? Or, at most, a variety of self-help? Luckily they didn't ask. How outraged Fanny would be—he would be driven from the community—if he confessed the slightest of his doubts to his children. If, say at the table, when they were all together, he should drop his negative silence, his policy of nonintervention, what a horrified breathlessness would follow. His children, Lee thought, his wife, the servants in the kitchen, none knew him; he was a stranger to his own house.

If he had still, quite desperately, instinctively, looked to Helena and Gregory for assistance, he had met a final failure. Brushed with sleepiness they were slipping away from him. He was reluctant to have them go, leave him; the distance between them and himself appeared to widen immeasurably as he stood watching them settle for the night. He wanted to call them back, "Helena and Gregory, Gregory!" But he remained quiet, his head a little bent, his heart heavy. The tide of sleep, silent, mystical, recompensing! It wasn't that, exactly, he was facing.

Switching off the light he went into their playroom, scattered with bright toys, with alphabet blocks and an engine, a train of cars and some lengths of track, and a wooden steamboat on wheels gaily painted. Already these things had a look of indifferent treatment, of having been half cast aside. Gregory had wanted a typewriter; his jacket, at dancing-school, had been belted like his, Lee Randon's. They each had, in the lower hall, a bicycle on which they rode to and from school and to play. "Will he need me later?" Lee asked himself; "or will it be the same till the end?" But he had already decided that the latter was infinitely better.

He lingered on the second floor, putting off from minute to minute the unavoidable taking up of Fanny's demands. She was, he knew, waiting for his appearance to begin again energetically. In their room it struck him forcibly that he must make some mental diagram of his course, his last unshakable position. Certainly in admitting that he had called Savina Grove by her first name he had justified Fanny's contention that he had kissed her. Fanny should have asked him how many times that had occurred. "A hundred," he heard himself, in fancy, replying. By God, he would like to say just that, and have it all over, done with. Instead he must lie cunningly, imperturbably, and in a monumental patience. Why? He hadn't, pointedly, asked that before. Things here, his life, the future, must be held together.

After he had descended, he lingered in the hall: in the room where his wife was sitting not a sound was audible, there wasn't an indication of her presence. Lee turned away to the mantel-piece dominated by Cytherea. Here, he addressed himself silently to the doll, you're responsible for this. Get me out of it. I'll put it all in your hands, that hand you have raised and hold half open and empty. But his, he added, in an embittered lightness, was an affair of matrimony; it was a moral knot; and it had nothing to do with Cytherea, with the shape, the sea, the island, of Venus. She was merely disdainful.

Fanny was seated in the chair, the exact position, in which he had left her. And when he returned to the place he had deserted, she took no notice of him.

Her eyes were fixed in thought, her lips pinched. Was it only now, or had he never noticed it before, that her hands resembled her face, bony with a dry fine skin? Perhaps, heroically, she was thrusting the whole subject of Savina Grove from her mind; he couldn't tell; her exterior showed Lee Randon nothing, He waited, undecided if he'd smoke. Lee didn't, he found, want to. She shook her head, a startled look passed through her eyes, and Fanny sighed deeply. She seemed to come back from a far place. It was, of course, the past, her early aspirations; herself, young; but what, out of her remembrance, had she brought with her?

Nothing.

Her first words instantly dispelled what had many aspects of his last hope for peace. "It is surprising to me that you could go up to the children; but I suppose we must all be glad to have you pay attention to them at any time." This minor development he succeeded in avoiding. "I have been thinking hard," she continued, "and I have made up my mind about you; it is this—you just simply have to be different. I won't let you, us, stay like this. It is hideous."

"You are quite right," he admitted; "and I have already agreed that the change must principally be in me. If you'd explain it to me, what you have decided on, we'll find out, if possible, how to go about it."

"At least you needn't be sarcastic," she replied; "I am not as impossible as you make out. You will have to be different at home—"

"I thought it was outside home you objected to."

"It's one and the same," she went on; "and I won't have them, it, a minute longer. Not a minute! You have got to behave yourself."

"You haven't been very definite yet."

"Mrs. Grove—Savina," she flung back at him.

"That is a name and not a fact."

"It's a fact that you kissed her." Fanny leaned forward, flushed and tense, knocking over her stool. "And that you put your arms around her, and said—oh, I don't know what you did say. Did she mention me?"

"Only indirectly," he replied with a gleam of malice; "neither of us did."

"I am glad of that anyhow." But her vindictive tone betrayed the words. "Although I can easily guess why you didn't—you were ashamed. You did kiss her; why won't you admit it?"

"What's the good? You've done that for me. You have convinced yourself so positively that nothing I could say would be of any use."

"Did she call you Lee?"

"Hell, Fanny, what a God-forsaken lot of young nonsense!" His anger was mounting. "You can understand here as well as later that I am not going to answer any of it; and I'll not listen to a great deal more. Sometimes, lately, you have been insulting, but now you are downright pathetic, you are so ridiculous."

"You will stay exactly where you are until I get done." Her tone was perceptibly shriller. "And don't you dare call me pathetic; if you only knew—disgracing yourself in New York, with a family at home. It is too common and low and vulgar for words: like a travelling salesman. But I'll make you behave if I have to lock you up."

Lee Randon laughed at her; and, at the contempt in his mirth, she rose, no longer flushed, but white with wrath. "I won't have it!" Her voice was almost a scream, and she brought her hands down so violently on the table that, as she momentarily broke the circuit of the electric lamp, there was a flash of greenish light. It was exactly as though her fury, a generated incandescence of rage, had burned into a perceptible flare. This, he realized, was worse than he had anticipated; he saw no safe issue; it was entirely serious. Lee was aware of a vague sorrow, a wish to protect Fanny, from herself as much as anything; but he was powerless. At the same time, with the support of no affection, without interest, his patience was rapidly vanishing. He was conscious of Fanny not as his wife, nor as a being lost in infinite suffering, but as a woman with her features strangely, grotesquely, twisted and drawn.

His principal recognition was that she meant nothing to him; she wasn't even familiar; he couldn't credit the fact that they had long lived together in an entire intimacy. Dissolved by his indifference, the past vanished like a white powder in a glass of water. She might have been a woman overtaken by a mental paroxysm in the cold impersonality of a railway station. "Stop it," he commanded sharply; "you are hysterical, all kinds of a fool."

"Only one kind," she corrected him, in a voice so rasped that it might have come from a rusted throat; "and I'm not going to be it much longer. You have cured me, you and that Savina. But what—what makes me laugh is how you thought you could explain and lie and bully me. Anything would do to tell me, I'd swallow it like one of those big grapes." She was speaking in gusts, between the labored heavings of her breast; her eyes were staring and dark; and her hands opened and shut, shut and opened, continuously. Fanny's cheeks were now mottled, there were fluctuating spots of red, blue shadows, on the pallor of her skin.

"In a minute more you'll be sick," he warned her.

"Oh, God," she whispered, "that's all he knows, all he feels! In a minute, a minute, I'll be sick. Don't you see, you damned fool," her voice rose until it seemed impossible that she could hold the pitch, "can't you understand I am dying?"

"No." His terseness was calculated: that, he thought, would best control her wildness. "No one could be more alive. If I were you, though, I'd go up to bed; we've had enough of this, or I have; I can't speak for you. But, however that may be, and as I've said before, it has got to stop, now, at once."

If it didn't, he continued silently, he wouldn't be eternally responsible for himself; never a patient man, what might follow the end of his endurance was unpredictable. His feeling toward the woman before him was shifting, as well; the indifference was becoming bitterness; the bitterness glittered, like mica, with points of hatred. He felt this, like an actual substance, a jelly-like poison, in his blood, affecting his body and mind. It bred in him a refined brutality, an ingenious cruelty. "A mirror would shut you up quicker than anything else," he informed her; "you look like a woman of sixty—go somewhere and fix your face."

"It doesn't surprise me you are insulting," she replied, "but I didn't expect it quite so soon. I thought you might hide what you really were a little longer; it seemed to me you might try to keep something. But I guess it's better to have it all done with at once, and to meet the worst."

"You talk as though there were no one but you in this," he said concisely; "and that I didn't matter. You'll find that I have a little to say. Here it is: I am tired of your suspicions and questions and insinuations. You haven't any idea of marriage except as a bed-room farce. You're so pure that you imagine more indecencies in a day than I could get through with in five years. If there were one I hadn't thought of, you'd have me at it in no time. It was pleasant at the Groves' because there was none of this infernal racket. Mrs. Grove, no—Savina, is a wise woman. I was glad to be with her, to get away—"

"Go back, then!" Fanny cried. "Don't bother about me and your home and the children. You brought me here, and made me have them, all the blood and tearing; but that doesn't matter. Not to you! I won't let you touch me again."

"That needn't trouble you," he assured her.

"Not ... when you have her ... to touch." She could scarcely articulate, each word was pronounced as though it had cost a separate and strangling effort. "You vile, rotten coward!"

The flood of her hysteria burst so suddenly that, unprepared, he was overwhelmed with its storm of tears and passionate charges. "You ought to be beaten till you fell down. You wouldn't say these things to me, treat me like this, if I weren't helpless, if I could do anything. But I can't, and you are safe. I am only your wife and not some filthy woman in New York." As she moved her head the streaming tears swung out from her face. "God damn you." Her hand went out to the table and, rising, it held the heavy dull yellow paper cutter. Before he could draw back she struck him; the copper point ripped down his jaw and hit his shoulder a jarring blow.

68

In an instant of passion Lee Randon caught Fanny by the shoulders and shook her until her head rolled as though her neck were broken. Even in his transport of rage, with his fingers dug into her flesh, he stopped to see if this were true.

It wasn't. She swayed uncertainly, dazed and gasping, while her hair, shaken loose from its knot, slowly cascaded over one shoulder. Then stumbling, groping, with a hand on a chair, against the frame of the door, she went out of the room.


Lee's jaw bled thickly and persistently; the blood soaked, filled, his handkerchief; and, going to the drawer in the dining-room where the linen was kept, he secured and held against a ragged wound a napkin, He was nauseated and faint. His rage, killed, as it were, at its height, left him with a sensation of emptiness and degradation. The silence—after the last audible dragging footfall of Fanny slowly mounting the stairs—was appalling; it was as though all the noise of all the world, concentrated in his head, had been stopped at once and forever. He removed the sop from the cut, and the bleeding promptly took up its spreading over his throat and under his collar. That blow had killed a great deal: the Lee Randon married to Fanny was already dead; Fanny, too, had told him that she was dying, killed from within. It was a shame.

He was walking when it occurred to him that he had better keep quiet; if the blood didn't soon stop he should require help; he was noticeably weak. His feeling with regard to Fanny was confined to curiosity, but mainly his thoughts, his illimitable disgust, were directed at himself. His anger, returning like the night wind from a different direction, cut at himself, at the collapse of his integrity. He was, in reality, frightened at what had been no better than a relapse into a state of mania; he was shocked at the presence, however temporary, of a frenzy of madness.

Nothing had altered his attitude toward the woman who was his wife; all his active emotions for her had gone. Then his attention was drawn from his personality to his life, his surroundings; they were suffocating. Not to be borne! Nowhere could he discover a detail, an episode, that had the importance of reality. He had a sensation of being wrapped in a feather bed, the need to make a violent gesture—sending the white fluff whirling through space—and so be free to breathe. This house, the symmetrical copied walls, the harmonious rugs, symbols of public success and good opinion, the standard of a public approbation, exasperated him beyond endurance. He wanted to push the walls out, tear the rugs into rags, and scatter them contemptuously before the scandalized inertness of Eastlake. Lee had what was regarded as an admirable existence, an admirable family—the world imposed this judgment on him; and the desire, the determination, swept over him to smash to irremediable atoms what was so well applauded.

The thought fascinated him: to break his life wide open. He'd let it go, it was worthless to him, the companies and bonds and the woman and children, the jog-trotting on fenced roads, the vain pretentions of the country club, the petty grasping at the petticoats—where they were worn—of variety. Lee wished that he could do this in the presence of everyone he knew; he wanted to see their outraged faces, hear the shocked expressions, as he insulted, demolished, all that they worshipped. The blood, he found, had stopped; his hurt was relatively unimportant. The fever of rebellion, of destruction, increased in him until it was as violent, as blinding, as his earlier fury; and he went at once in search of Fanny.

She had undressed, and, in a nightgown effectively drawn with blue ribbons, she lay face down across the bottom of her bed. One shoulder, immaculately white except for the leaden bruises of his fingers, was bare, and an arm, from which her jewelled wrist watch had not been removed, was outstretched. He stood above her, but, breathing faintly, she made no sign of a consciousness of his presence.

"Fanny," he began, speaking with an effort of calmness out of his laboring being, "this is all over for me. As I told you so many times, I've had too much of it. It's yours, anyhow, and the children are yours, and you may do what you like with the whole affair. I'm done." Still she didn't move, reply. "I am going," he said more impatiently, "tonight. I want you to understand that this is final. You were too good a wife; I couldn't keep even with you; and I can't say, now, that I want to. Everyone will tell you that I am no good—you see, I haven't the shadow of a cause for leaving—and the best thing you can do is believe them. If I had what was recognized as a reason for going, I'd stay, if that has any sense; you may put your own interpretation on it."

She turned and half rose, regarding him from the edge of the bed. Her face, no longer brightly mottled, was sunken, and dull with despair. "I can't talk," she said; "the words are all hard like stones down in my heart. You'll have to go; I can't stop you; I knew you had gone yesterday, or was it last week? I saw it was a hopeless fight but I tried, I had to; I thought your memory would help."

"It wasn't Savina who did this," he informed her; "I want you to realize that fully. Whatever happens, she is not to blame. All, all the fault is mine; it would take too long to explain, you wouldn't believe me—you couldn't—and so I am deserting you. That is the word for it, the one you will use." Fanny gazed at him in a clouding perplexity.

"I can't think it's true." Her voice was dazed. "A thing like this couldn't be happening to us, to me. It's only for a little, we are both cross—"

He cut her short with the assurance that what he said he meant. Sentimental indulgence, he felt, was dangerously out of place. She slipped back, supine, on the bed; and, with short sobs, she cried, "Go! Go! Go!"

In his room he methodically and thoughtfully assembled the necessities for his bag; he was arranging mentally the details of his act. Where, primarily, it affected Fanny and the children, his lawyers could handle it best; it was the present consequences to himself, the step immediately before him, that demanded consideration. But his deliberation was lost in the knowledge that he would go to New York where, inevitably, he should see Savina. No one could predict what would determine that; it would unfold, his affair with Savina must conclude, as it had begun—in obedience to pressures beyond their control. An increasing excitement flowed over him at the thought of being with her, possessing her, again. There was no doubt of that in his mind; he knew that Savina would come to him. She was far more ruthless in brushing aside artificial barriers, prejudices, than, until now, he. The figure of William Grove occupied him for a little, but he seemed insubstantial, not so much a being as a convention to be smashed in his own house.

Lee Randon decided not to speak again, to say good-bye, to Fanny. It would only multiply the difficulties of his leaving; she might have another attack of rage, or—worse—of affection. He was amazed at his lack of feeling, a little disturbed: perhaps there was something fatally wrong, lacking, about him, and he was embarked on the first violent stage of physical and mental degradation. It couldn't be helped, he told himself, once more down stairs, in the hall. Beyond, the stool lay where Fanny had kicked it; and he bent over to pick up the copper paper cutter from the floor. Putting it on the table, he reflected that Fanny would, in all probability, destroy it. His handkerchief, stiff, black with dried blood, was in the crystal ash holder with a mahogany stand; and that, as unnecessarily unpleasant, he hid in a pocket.

The electric globe in the floor lamp was yellow; it was nearly burned out and would have to be replaced. This had been his special corner, the most comfortable in the pen. But the pig, he remembered, had been slaughtered last week; and he wondered if the parallel he had established would hold true to the end. In the main aspect, he concluded, yes. But the pig had died without experiencing what was, undoubtedly, both the fundamental duty and recompense of living. The pig, happily or unhappily, had remained in ignorance of Cytherea and the delights of love; but, perhaps, if only for the moment, he had better call that passion; it was a word of clearer, more exact, definition.

He left the house walking, carrying his bag up the hill into Eastlake: a train left for the city at eleven-fifty-eight. Lee turned, beyond his property, and saw the light burning in what had been his and Fanny's room; the rest of the house, except for the glimmer below, was dark. The winter night was encrusted with stars. A piercing regret seized him—that he was past the middle of forty and not in the early twenties. To be young and to know Savina! To be young and free. To be young ... the increasing rapidity with which he went forward had the aspect of an endeavor to waste no more precious time.

V

The brief level voice of Savina Grove arranging over the telephone an hour, very late in the afternoon, for him to call, gave Lee a comparatively long time in which to examine his feelings, particularly in connection with Savina. His state of mind, his intentions, he realized, should be clear for the moment when he saw her. In general they were; but the particulars, the details of any probable immediate action, evaded him. He should have to consult her about them. What he most firmly grasped of all was that he couldn't—what, in reality, he breathed to himself was they—remain in New York. The comparatively orderly and delayed legal arrangement projected by the Morrises and Mina Raff seemed to have no application to the impetuosity of the situation before him. However, he was advancing at a speed, to a position, for which there was no warrant. None at all. Perhaps Savina, satisfied by the one occasion which—he had been so careful to insist—must be the last, would regard him as merely importunate.

Strictly held to discretion by the fact of Fanny, Savina might have found him then—more available than when free—only the acceptable model of an indiscreet man. Yet, he reminded himself, he hadn't left Eastlake, broken wide open his home, on account of Savina. This, he again insisted, would have happened independently of her; his life in Eastlake had broken up of its own accord; its elements had been too tenuous for the withstanding any longer of the stress of existence. But, he was forced to add, the collapse had been hastened by his knowledge of Savina. And this brought him to the examination of what, at bottom, she meant to him. What was her significance, her bulk, in his life?

That could be approached only through an understanding of his feeling for her, what it was now and what it might become; not conspicuously easy of comprehension. Lee tried the old, the long inaccurately used, word, love. He asked himself the question squarely—did he love Savina? Damned if he knew! He might reply to that, he thought ruefully, if he grasped what love was, what the blasted phrase meant. As it was, it seemed to Lee, a dictionary of synonyms would be helpless to make all its varied significances distinct. He tried a simpler approach—did he want to be with Savina more than with anyone else? At last he had put a question to himself

70

that he could answer: he most assuredly preferred being with Savina to anyone else he knew. But that alone would not have taken him to her.

A simple desire on his part, naive like a daisy, could not have overthrown the structure of his being. Yet the connection between the two, the woman and the event, was undeniable, his impulse to go to her now irresistible. That last word, as fully as any, expressed what lately had happened to him. He was considering the occurrences logically while the fact was that logic hadn't been touched on, summoned, once. He had moved emotionally and not intellectually; he hadn't known, from hour to hour, in what direction he would proceed. Certainly nothing could be said in his defense on the score of common sense; that, though, didn't disturb him; at a time when he might have been said to rely on it, common sense had failed him utterly. He had thrown that over his shoulder. Nor was he searching for an exterior justification of his present anomalous position, for, briefly, an excuse; excuses were the furthest of all things from his mind. The truth was that he was decidedly exhilarated, as though he had left the hard narrow road for a gallop over the green. He was merely dwelling on, analyzing, the present as it was becoming the newly promising, the opening, future.

But he did need to understand—for an attitude, a choice of speech, if nothing else—his feeling for Savina. It consisted principally in the tyrannical desire to be with her, to sink in the immeasurable depths of her passion, and there lose all consciousness of the trivial mundane world. That, Lee felt, given the rest, the fact that he was here as he was, was sufficient; but—again still—he had had no voice in it. The passion had inundated him in the manner of an incoming tide and a low-water rock. Abruptly, after a certain misleading appearance of hesitation on the part of the waves, he had gone under. Well, it was very pleasant. In his case the celebrated maxims were wrong.

He left this, for the moment, and returned to what, actually, lay ahead of him. Would Savina go away with him, leave the correct William, the safety of their New York house in the style of eighteen-eighty? Lee considered in her two impulses, not alike—her overwhelming passion, herself generally; and her admission, no, cry, that she loved him, or the special part he had in her. It rather looked as though he'd be successful. It did for a fact. He had not been idle through all the day, but had drawn from the Harriman Bank twenty thousand dollars. So much had not been necessary; it was very bad business to segregate in idleness such a sum of money now; but he enjoyed the extravagance of it. Prudence, frugality, was no longer a factor in his affairs.

His present personal liberty, more complete than it had ever been before—than, he added lightly, it might ever be again—was astonishingly soothing. Sitting comfortably in a room in his customary hotel, there wasn't a pressure that could be brought to bear on him. It was now twenty minutes past four, he was to go to Savina at a quarter to six, and until then there was nothing, nothing, to force him this way or that: no directors' meetings, gabbling East-lake figures, responsibility, housewife or children. He hadn't realized the extent to which he had been surrounded and confined, the imponderable mass of what he had not only been indifferent to but actually disliked. He could lie down—he had been up the entire past night—and be called in an hour; he could sit as he was, in an unbuttoned waistcoat with his legs comfortably spread out; he could motor or walk on Fifth Avenue; smoke; drink—all in an inviolable security of being.

*Or, going back to that moment when he had, so mistakenly, turned aside from visionary promptings to a solid comfortable career, he might—what was it?—write. Perhaps his sharp regret at the loss of his youth was premature, youth itself comparatively unimportant. But no, that would involve him in fresh distasteful efforts, imperceptibly it would build up a whole new world of responsibilities: writing would be arduous, editors captious, and articles, stories, books, tie him back again to all that from which he had so miraculously escaped. Savina would be enough. What a beautiful body, so unexpectedly full, she had; how astounding, intoxicating, was the difference between what she seemed to be and what she was. Lee Randon thought with amused pity of the files of men who must have passed by her, with the most considerate bows, in ignorance of the inner truth. That discovery, while, naturally, it had not been entirely reserved for him, had accumulated in a supreme delight, been kept back, like the best of all presents, for the last. He was glad that it wasn't too late for him to enjoy it. Here, suddenly, intervening in the midst of a prosaic drudgery, a tepid and meaningless period, was a magnificent relief. By God, would he take advantage of it! Would he! There was a knock at the door, and the hotel valet hung a freshly pressed suit in the closet; the shoes into which he intended to change were in a perfection of readiness; laid out were a heavy blue silk shirt and a dull yellow tie. Lee got these various carefully selected articles of dress slowly, exactly, on. His pearl pin Fanny had given him! Well, it was a good pearl, selected personally by a celebrated dealer; and Lee was obliged to her, nothing more. He lighted a cigarette, collected his hat and gloves, his overcoat and stick, and descended in the elevator in a mood of unrestrained enjoyment.*

The door attendant, who knew him, whistled for a taxi-cab, commenting lightly on the visible accident to his jaw. But, in spite of it, Lee had an appearance, as he phrased it, of good luck. The world, he said, was evidently in favor of Mr. Randon. The latter agreed that it had such a look. He was positively jovial. He dismissed the cab before the familiar entrance on East Sixty-sixth Street, and was admitted immediately: the servant caught his coat, and he went into the drawing-room. There had been, he saw, a tea; the confusion lingering from a crowd was evident; the cups, on all the available surfaces, had not been removed; in a corner were the skeleton-like iron music racks of a small orchestra; ash trays were overflowing; and a sealskin muff, with a bunch of violets pinned to it, had been left.

Savina had gone upstairs, but she would be down at once. Lee was turned away from the door when she entered; she was wearing a cloth dress of dull red—hadn't he heard it called Cuba color?—with a heavy girdle of grotesque intertwined silver figures. With a single glance behind her she swept forward into Lee's arms, her mouth held up to his.

Listening closely to all that he had to say, she sat with her hands quietly folded on crossed knees. Perhaps twice she nodded, comprehendingly. "And so," he ended, "that is what has occurred. We are not to blame ourselves too much, as I've explained; the thing happened within itself, died of its own accord. But the past doesn't need our attention now. The future is the thing. What is it going to be? What," he hesitated, "can we make it? Maybe everything, or nothing."

"Are you leaving that for me to decide?" she asked.

"To a great extent I have to; I don't want to appear to take so much for granted. And then, only you can measure what I have to offer. I believe what I have done is considered serious, if not ruinous; but that I can't help thinking is exaggerated. I haven't been struck down yet. I don't, candidly, now, expect to be. You ought to come to this through your head, and not the heart, which I'd naturally prefer you to use. What, in fact, I am asking you is to go away with me, to live with me. I shall not, and you couldn't, very well, return. It's quite final, in other words. I must find out, too, if the irregularity upsets you. That need only be temporary. Grove and Fanny, I am sure, wouldn't persist in being disagreeable. But, if they did, we'd have to face that as well, the consequences of my—my impatience.

"No, don't answer so quickly. Do you know me, are you sure you'd be happy, satisfied, with me? I have some money, not a great deal for myself now; I should say fifteen thousand dollars a year. Fanny, very rightfully—for herself and the children—will get most of what I have. And then, are you wedded, if not to your individual life here, to New York? We should have to go away to some place rather vague—"

"Cuba," she broke in.

The irony of that suggestion carried him back to the many vainly projected trips there with Fanny. His brother was in Cuba, it was true; but that might turn out excellently: Daniel would be able to help them in the difficult readjustments to follow. He was intelligent, unprejudiced and calm and, Lee added, remote from the values, the ponderous authority, of a northern hypocritical society. Then he forgot that in the realization that Savina was going away with him, that she was to be his, not for a solitary stolen night, but for years ... openly, completely. He lost his self control and kissed her, heedless of the open doors. Now she was cooler than Lee, and pushed him away. "William will be in at any minute," she explained:

"When shall we leave?"

"We might take a train tonight for Washington, since we'll need passports and I have to have an income tax receipt, and we can manage all that best there. Then Key West, Havana, anywhere. We will hope to get off without trouble; but, if Grove interferes, accept the consequences as they come."

"Very well." Savina grew still quieter as the march of events became headlong. "I can live without a maid for a while. Tonight I won't dress for dinner, this will do very nicely for the train; and come as soon after as I can pack a bag. There will be literally nothing in it; my summer things are all out of reach. Washington will be convenient for me, too. Unless you want to see William again—" She rose.

"Not particularly," he acknowledged; "though I wouldn't drive around the city to avoid him. Somehow— I may be blind—I can't think that I am doing him an infamous wrong: that he lost you proves that. Why, under the circumstances, should you, anyone, stay? I don't feel a particle immoral, or even devilish. It's all so sensible and balanced and superior. No, no, let William watch out for himself; his club, he's so devoted to, won't fail him. Fanny and he will have their whole worlds to sympathize with their injury. We don't need sympathy."

Lee walked back to the hotel, the pig-skin wrapped walking stick swinging from an arm, his bearing confident and relaxed. He stopped at the desk for a conference with the porter—a basket of fruit from the restaurant, and, if procurable regularly or irregularly, a drawing-room on the Washington train. Then he went up and closed his bag: he had time for dinner and several cigars afterwards; he wasn't hungry, but the ceremony would kill the intervening two hours and more.

The porter found him later and delivered his tickets, including the check for a drawing-room, secured as irregularly as possible from the Pullman conductor. There were, it began to seem, to be no minor annoyances. At a few minutes before ten he was standing, as he had arranged with Savina, with his bag before the hotel; and, just past the hour, the cab which held her turned in to the sidewalk. She had two bags, but one was very small— her toilet things, she explained—and she was carrying a jewel case. There wasn't a tremor in her voice or bearing, the slightest indication that they were going farther than a theatre in the vicinity of Forty-fourth Street. Internally, Lee was excited, filled with the long strange sense of holiday.

"William went to the club," Savina told him with a smile edged with malice; "everything was as usual when he left, but when he gets back it will be changed. I'm sorry to miss his expression when he reads the letter I wrote; he won't show it to anyone."

"That sounds as though you really disliked him," Lee observed. Then he remembered the hatred he had felt for Fanny. Matrimony had a brutal hand for superficial relationships and conventions. He had spoken lightly but, watching her, he saw the grimness of her passion strike the animation from her face. The jewel case slid over the softness of her wrap to the floor, her hand crept under his cuff, clinging to his arm.

Going immediately to their train, they found the fruit in the drawing-room; the porter stopped to knock at the door and discover if they were in need of his attendance. They heard dimly the train's muffled boring under the river and were conscious of the swimming lights of the Jersey plain, the confused illuminated darkness of cities, the tranquility of open country, the ringing echo of bridges and the sustained wail of their locomotive. They were, again, reaching Washington, close in a taxi-cab; Savina's jewel case again fell unheeded; and again, after the shortest halt possible, they were whirling south in a drawing-room where night and day were indistinguishable one from the other.

On the rear platform of the orange-painted train moving deliberately along the Florida coast Lee was first aware of the still, saturating heat; that, in itself, was enough to release him from the winter-like grip of Eastlake. He lost all sense of time, of hurry, of the necessity of occupation as opposed to idleness, of idleness contrasted with sleep. The promise of satiation, of inevitability, steeped his being in a pleasant lethargy. It was the same to him if they moved or stopped, whether they arrived at the next destination or remained forever in a sandy monotony of tomato fields or by a slow pass of water cutting the harshness of palmettos. On the viaducts he gazed with half-closed eyes across the sapphire and emerald green and purple water; or, directly under him, he looked down incuriously into a tide so clear that it seemed no more than a breath ruffling the sand beneath.

Savina, who had discarded cloth for dull white linen—she wished, she explained, to make the transition as sharply as possible—was more alertly interested in their constantly shifting surroundings; they were significant to her as the milestones of her incredible escape. On the steamer for Havana, marking their effects deposited in a cabin with a double iron bed and unpleasantly ubiquitous basins, she explained to Lee that she never got seasick; but he might have gathered that, she pointed out, by her willingness to undertake Cuba. Admitting that he had missed this feminine subtlety, he arranged two deck chairs in an advantageous angle, and they sat enveloped in a mildness which, heavy with the odor of water-soaked wood, was untroubled by any wind. When the steamer left its pier Savina put a hand inside one of his. The harbor lights dropped, pair by pair, back into the night; the vibration of the propeller became a sub-conscious murmur; over the placid water astern a rippling phosphorescence was stirred and subsided. A motion, increasing by imperceptible degrees, affected the deck; there was a rise and fall, regular and sleep-impelling: the uneasiness of the Gulf Stream. Havana floated into their waking vision, a city of white marble set in lustrous green, profound indigo, against the rosy veil of a morning sun.


The fortunate chance that took them to the Inglaterra Hotel—the disdain of its runner was more persuasive than the clamor of all the others who had boarded the steamer—found them a room, they soon discovered, in what was at once the most desirable and the most unlikely place. They might have the chamber until Tuesday, Lee was told, in an English inflected with the tonal gravity of Spain. It was hardly past eight in the morning, an awkward hour to arrive newly at a city, he thought, as they were carried up in the elevator. The details of the floor, the hall, they crossed, engaged his interest; not alone for the height of the ceiling, which was excessive, but because of the palms, the pointed Moorish arches filled with green painted wood lattices; the totality of an effect different from anything else he had seen.

Their room, with the lift of the ceiling emphasized by the confined space, was more engaging still: tall slatted doors opened on an iron railed balcony, the bath-room was like a tunnel on end, and the floor an expanse of polished mosaic in a pattern of yellow and grey. Lee walked out on the balcony; directly below and across a narrow paved street was a floridly impressive building obviously for the purpose of varied assemblages, and on his left a park was laid in concrete walks, royal palms on towering smooth dull trunks, unfamiliar trees with a graceful dense foliage, and innumerable stacked iron chairs about the marble statue of a man with a pointing hand. These details, however, were slowly gathered from an effect the whole of which was bewilderingly white, a whiteness intolerably luminous in the dazzling bath of the sun.

It was a scene, a city, Lee recognized, more foreign to his own than any he knew in western Europe; a difference that existed mainly in the tropical heat, visible in languorous waves rising from blanched walls and streets already—so early—fervent. Savina was filled with delight; a positive color glowed in place of the customary uniform pallor of her cheeks; she opened her bags with an irresistible youthful energy. "Think what we have been missing," she called above the sound of the water running into the tub; "and what we accepted so long for living. I suppose the wonderful thing is that we escaped. Lee, do you realize that almost no one does? They never never get away, but go from one grave, from one winter, to another. Isn't it strange, when what we did is so very easy.

"I'd like to tell a hundred people in New York that they could get away too, unfreeze themselves. When we drove horses I used to be surprised that they went along so quietly in blinders; they never seemed to learn that one kick would break into splinters the thing dragging on them. People are like that, I was and you were, too—in blinders. We've torn ours off, Lee. Tell me that you are glad." He was, without reserve. Tranquilly finding his razors, he was aware of a permeating contentment in what they had done. It was exactly as Savina had said—the forces which had held them in a rigorous northern servitude had proved, upon assault, to be no more than a defense of painted prejudices, the canvas embrasures of hypocrisy.

"It is astonishing, what so many people put up with," he agreed; "but then," Lee added, in a further understanding, "it isn't so much what you knock down as what you carry away, take everywhere, inside you. When an arrangement like ours fails, that, mostly, I suspect, is the cause. It needs a special sort of fitness. Take the hundred people you spoke of—I'd be willing to bet not five of them could get away from the past, or put out of their minds what they are brought up on. Privately they would think they were wicked, damned, or some such truck; and, sure enough, that alone would finish them."

"I haven't a speck of that," Savina admitted serenely; "I am happy. And I don't even have to ignore the thought of your wife and children; they'll get along just as well, maybe better, without you. William doesn't need me; he hasn't for a number of years. But we had to have each other."

Lee Randon considered this in relation to his feeling that he had not left Eastlake, Fanny, because of Savina. He was still convinced that his life had fallen apart of itself; but he began to see that Savina had been more deeply involved in his act of liberty than he had suspected. Without her it was probable that he would have continued to the end in the negative existence of Eastlake; yet no amount of mere assurance that that was the only admirable, the only permissible, course was valid with him unless he had a corroborating belief. And all that he might once have possessed had left him at the final blow dealt by the passion of Savina and himself.

She had been stronger than the assembled forces of heredity and precept and experience; her strength was superhuman; it was incredible that her slender body could hold such an impulse, a fury really, of vitality. Women must have been like that in earlier ages of humanity; but they were no longer; their passion had been wasted, spent, or turned aside into exhausting by-paths of sensation. He had finished shaving and, when they were dressed, they went down to breakfast in a dining-room with a marble floor and walls lustrous with bronze tiling. They had tall glasses of iced orange juice; and, with the last fragrant draught of coffee, Lee lighted a long bland cigar.

"If you like," he proceeded comfortably, "you may rush around and see as much of the city as possible. There is a big omnibus at the door. Personally, I am going to do nothing of the kind. I intend to sit and smoke, and then—smoke and sit. I am done with the proper and expected thing in every one of its forms. I have always hated churches; and the spots where soldiers fell or martyrs were burned, monuments, just annoy me; and picture galleries give me colds in the head. Above all else I don't want to be improved; if I hear a fact of any sort I am going to bed for the rest of the day."

"I don't care about those, either," Savina assented; "but the stores, yes. I have to have a mantilla and a high comb right away, now; and—I warn you—if it's only in our room I'm going to wear them. If I could get you into it I'd bring back a shell jacket covered with green braid and a wide scarlet sash, or whatever an espada wears."

"A guitar and a carnation ought to do," he responded. "Count on me for nothing until the evening, when, if you care to, we'll drive along the sea, one way and then the other, and have dinner where we happen to be. I hope you will wear the most extravagant and holiday clothes—white, and very ruffled and thin, would be nice, with emeralds."

"It's a good thing I have a lot of money," she observed; "you have some, of course, but it wouldn't begin to support your ambitions."

"I don't even care which of us has it," he admitted; "so it's there. A year ago I should have looked pained and insisted that I couldn't accept, nor allow you to use, your own money. I don't exactly have to ask you for a taxi-cab fare, though, luckily; but if you did bring the emeralds I saw you wearing in New York don't throw them away on my account."

"They are here," she assured him. "William gave them to me when we were married."

"Splendid, together with Fanny's pearl," he replied placidly; "I was afraid they had been a legacy from your mother. I much prefer them to have been William's—it will give them such a Utopian sparkle."

When Savina had gone, in a long brightly-painted car summoned from the line backed at the plaza's edge, Lee Randon returned to their room. The heat of the day, approaching noon, the ceaseless noise of Havana rose diffused to the balcony where he sat until the circling sunlight forced him to move inside. What amazing comfort! A curiously impersonal admiration for Savina grew with the understanding of her exceptionally perceptive being. She was what, above all else, he would have chosen for a companion: her extraordinary feeling was sheathed, tempered, in the satin of a faultless aesthetic sense; the delicacy of her body was resembled by the fineness of her feminine mind; she was entirely, deliciously, decorative. The black brocade mules by her bed were characteristic of her—useless charming objects that had cost twenty, thirty, dollars. Their sliding tap on the glazed floor was an appreciable part of his happiness; Savina's bottles on a dressing-table were engraved crystal with gold stoppers: it was all as it should be.


When she returned she redressed her hair, drawing it back across her ears, put in at a provocative angle a fan-like carved shell comb, and twisted a shawl of flame-colored silk—it was a manton, she instructed him—

about her shoulders. The guise of Andalusia was very becoming to her. For a dinner, Savina wore the filmy white and emeralds; they went to a restaurant like a pavilion on a roof, their table, by a low masonry wall, overlooking the harbor entrance. The heat of the day, cloaked in night, was cooled by the trade wind moving softly across the sea; the water of the harbor was black, like jet shining with the reflections of the lights strung along the shore; the lighthouse at Morro Castle marked the rocky thrust of the land. The restaurant was crowded: beyond Lee were four officers of the Spanish navy in snowy linen and corded gilt; in the subdued light the faces of women, under wide flowery hats, were illusive and fascinating; everywhere the deep crimson of Castilian wines was set against the amber radiance of champagne.

Directly below, shadowy trees hid the stone margin of the bay, and an enormous tripod, such as might be used for removing the cargoes of ships, raised its primitive simplicity. "Look, Lee!" Savina laid a hand on his wrist. A steamer, incredibly large and near, was moving slowly out through the narrow channel to the sea. Rows of golden lights shone on its decks and from the port-holes, and a drift of music reached him. "Some day soon," she went on, "we'll take a boat like that, and go—where? It doesn't matter: to a far strange land. Hills scented with tea flowers. Streets with lacquered houses. Villages with silver bells hung along the eaves. Valleys of primroses under mountains of ice. We'll see them all from little windows, and then it will be night. But, principally, we will never go back—never! never! never! We will be together for years. Let's go to the hotel now; Lee. I am rather tired; it's the heat, don't you think? I am worn, and, because I am so happy, a trifle dizzy. Not much. Nothing to worry about. But I only want you, Lee; in my heart I don't care for the valleys and bells and scents."

Yet, before they reached the hotel they stopped, Savina insisted, for cocktails of Bacardi rum, fragrant with fresh limes and sweet with a crust of sugar that remained at the bottoms of the glasses. In the night—their beds were separated by the width of the balcony doors—she called for him, acute with fright. "What is it?" she cried. "Hark, Lee, that horrible sound." The air was filled with a drumming wail, a dislocated savage music, that affected him like a nightmare grown audible.

"It's coming from across the street, from the Opera House," he told her; "some kind of a dance, I'm certain." Patently it was an orchestra, but the instruments that composed it, the measures woven of frantic screaming notes and dull stale iterations, he had no means of identifying. "Bedlam in the jungle," he said soothingly. She wished it would stop. Soon he agreed with her; without pause, without variation, with an insistence which became cruel, and then unbearable, it went on. Lee Randon, after an uneasiness which culminated in an exasperated wrath, found a degree of exactness in his description: it was, undoubtedly, the jungle, Africa, debased into a peculiarly harrowing travesty of later civilized emotions. Finally he lost the impression of a meaninglessness; it assumed a potency, a naked reality, more profound than anything in his previous knowledge. It was the voice of a crazed and debased passion. To Lee, it seemed to strip him of his whiteness, his continence, his integrity, to flay him of every particle of restraint and decency, and set him, bestial and exposed, in a ball room with glass-hung chandeliers.

Incomprehensibly the fluctuating clamor—he could distinguish low pitched drums—brought him the vision, pale and remote and mysteriously smiling, of Cytherea. He thought of that torrential discord rising around her belled purple skirt, the cool yellow of her waist crossed with fragile lace, beating past her lifted slender hand, the nails stained with vermilion, to the pointed oval of her face against the black hair and streaming gold of the headdress. Nothing, it appeared, could be farther apart than the muffled furious strains escaping in bursts through the opened windows beyond and the still apparition from the tranquility of his Eastlake house. He would have said, unhesitatingly, that the formal melody of the eighteenth century, of Scarlatti and harpsichords, was the music that best accompanied Cytherea. But she dominated, haunted with her grace, the infernal dinning sound of unspeakable defilements. Savina was racked beyond endurance:

"I can't stand it any longer," she told Lee hysterically, risen with her palms pressed to her ears. "I can hear it with every nerve. It will never go out of my brain. You must stop it. Can't you understand that it is driving me mad!" Her voice grew so shrill, she trembled so violently, that he had to hold her forcibly in his arms. When, toward dawn, it ceased, Savina was exhausted; she lay limp and white on her bed; and, across the room, he could hear the shallowness of her irregular breathing. As a grey light diluted the darkness, the trade wind, the night wind, dropped, and the heat palpably increased. Instantaneously the sun-flooded morning was born, a morning that lost its freshness, its pearly iridescence, immediately. He closed the slats of the balcony doors: Savina at last was sleeping, with her countenance, utterly spent, turned to him. The sharp cries of the newsboys, the street vendors, were drowned in the full sweep of a traffic moving to the blasts of multitudinous horns. When she woke, past ten, drinking the small cup of black coffee which locally accompanied dressing, she was still shaken. "That's the most cursed racket anyone ever had to endure!" A growing irritation made harsh his voice. "You couldn't torment a worse sound out of a thousand cats." She smiled wanly. "If we were like that in the past," he added, "I'm glad we changed, even if we are worse in other ways."

"I could hear myself screaming and screaming," Savina said. In the heated room she had an uncontrollable chill. "Lee, I can't bring myself to tell you: something black and dreadful ... had me. There was no one else. It was like a woods. The hands ripping at me—" With her face buried in her embroidered pillow, half clothed in web-like garments threaded with black ribbons, she cowered in an abject and pitiful agony.

Later, he discovered that, within the scope of his possible knowledge, his conjecture had been right: a danzon, a native Cuban ball—not, the director of the Inglaterra gave him to understand, entirely respectable— had been held in the Opera House. "But there won't be another until after we leave," Lee reassured Savina; "they are rather rare except at carnival." She shuddered. It was evident that the distressing effect on her of the music lingered through the day; her energy gave way to a passive contentment hardly removed from listlessness.

They drove, at the end of afternoon, on the Malecon, following the curving sea wall from La Punta to the scattered villas of Vedado. The sea and sky were grey; or was it blue? At the horizon they met without a perceptible change; the water became the air, the air water, with a transition as gradual as the edge of dusk. The tropical evening was accomplished rapidly, as dramatically as the uprush of the sun: they were gazing into the distance over a tide like a smooth undulating mist ... and there were lights crowning the Cabanas fortress; the passing cars made the familiar geometrical patterns with the cold bars of their lamps; they were wrapped in darkness; night had come.

Savina didn't want to go back to the hotel, their room; and, after dinner at the Paris, they went to Carmelo, where they alternated northern dances with the stridor of a northern cabaret and drinks. Savina's spirits revived slowly. To Lee she seemed to have changed in appearance since she left New York—here, losing her air of a constant reserve, she looked younger, daring. Her sharp grace, exposed in the films of summer dress, had an aspect of belonging, rather than to the character she had deserted, to a woman at once conscious of its effect and not unwilling to have it measured by the appraising gaze of the masculine public. In a way, without losing her distinction, she had become evident; another woman, one less admirably balanced, would have been conspicuous. Havana was like a, stage on which Savina—with a considered bravado they had kept the Randon— tried with intoxicating success a part she had long and secretly desired.


What, Lee found, he most enjoyed was the personal liberty he had first experienced in New York, waiting to see Savina after he had definitely left Eastlake. All the aspects of his circumferential existence, island-like in the dividing indigo of a magic sea, pleased him equally. Of course, without Savina Cuba would have been an impossibility; she was the center, the motive, of the design of his emotions; but it was surprising how contented he was strolling in the outskirts, in the minor parks and glorietas and paseos, of the world of his passionate adventure. He sat placidly in the Cortina de Valdez, looking across the narrow water to the long pink wall of the Cabanas, while Savina drove and shopped and rested. Carefully avoiding the Americans at the Inglaterra, on the streets, he had no burden of empty mutual assurances, the forced stupidities of conversations, to support. His days all had the look of a period of rest after a strain of long duration.

The strain, he realized, unknown to him at the time, had existed negatively through years before he had grown openly rebellious. A quality within him, in spite of him, had risen and swept him, under the eyes of Cytherea, beyond every circumstance of his former life. The resemblance between her and Savina he caught in fleet glances which defied his efforts to summon them; and, where that similitude was concerned, he was aware of a disconcerting, almost humiliating, shifting of balance. At first, recognizing aspects of Cytherea in Savina, now in Cytherea he merely found certain qualities of the woman. The doll, it seemed, had not been absorbed in Savina; the distant inanimate object was more real than the actual straining arms about his neck, the insatiable murmur at his ear. Yet his happiness with Savina was absolute, secure; and still totally different from her attitude toward him. She often repeated, in a voice no longer varying from her other impassioned speech, that she loved him; and, while this was a phrase, a reassurance, no man in his situation could escape, he returned it in a manner not wholly ringing with conviction.

It was the old difficulty—he wasn't sure, he couldn't satisfy himself, about its meaning. He was not, for example, lost beyond knowledge or perception in his feeling for Savina; carried along in the tempestuous flood of her emotion, he yet had time to linger over and enjoy the occurrences by the way. He liked each day for itself, and she regarded it only as an insignificant detail of their unity. All her planning, her dress and ardor and moods, were directed to one never-lost-sight-of end; but he disposed his attention in a hundred channels. Lee began to be aware of the tremendous single economy of women, the constant bending back of their instincts to a single preeminent purpose.

Yet everywhere, now, women had concentrated in a denial of that: the men he knew hadn't a monopoly of restlessness. Even Fanny, in the parading of all her rings, had not been oblivious of it. But it wasn't so much that women denied their fundamental urgency as it was that they wanted it exercised under other, more rapturous, conditions. Inexplicably, and a great many at once, women had grown aware of the appalling difference between what they might demand and what they had been receiving. In consequence of this the world of masculine complacency was being dealt some rude blows. But Lee Randon couldn't hope to go into this; the problem was sufficiently complicated from his side of the fence. There were, immediately, the practical developments of his undertaking to be met. He served nothing by putting them off. He must write, but through his lawyers, to William Grove and find out what action he proposed to take, what arrangements for divorce could be facilitated. A letter—there could be no saving impersonality here—to Fanny was more difficult.

76

From Havana, his approval of Fanny was very complete; he understood her, made allowances, now better than at any time during their marriage; given what, together, they were, her conduct had been admirable. A remarkably attractive and faithful woman, he told himself; it was a pity that, in her estimation, her good qualities had come to so little. The thing for him to do was to see his brother, and move part of the burden of his decisions over to Daniel's heavy frame.

The sugar estate of which he was Administrador was in the Province of Camagüey, at Cobra; an overnight trip from Havana, Lee had learned. It was Sunday evening now, and they would have to give up their room at the Inglaterra Tuesday. Obviously there wasn't time to write Daniel and have a reply by then. The other desirable hotels were as full as the Inglaterra. He must wire, but the composition of his telegram presented an unexpected difficulty:

Lee didn't know how to explain the presence with him of Savina; he couldn't determine how much or how little to say; and it was probable that Daniel had had a cable from Eastlake. The mere putting down of the necessary words of his message, under the concerned gaze of a clerk, with a limited comprehension of English, was hazardous. The clerk, he had discovered, would read in a loud voice of misplaced linguistic confidence whatever Lee wrote, and there was a small assemblage of Americans at the counter of a steamship company across the office. What, it began to appear, they'd have to do would be to take the train for Cobra on Tuesday. Yet they couldn't quite come down on Daniel so unexpectedly; he lived, Lee recalled, on a batey, the central dominating point of a sugar estate; and—unmarried—what accommodations he might offer were problematic. Lee, from the heading of a letter, could not build the proportions of a Casa Vivienda. Well, there would be a hotel at Cobra! That answered his doubts—Savina and he would go to Cobra and there communicate with Daniel. It would be easy to talk privately with him. Lee didn't want his approval, but only his careful opinions and reasonable assistance.

He, Lee, would not produce Savina with the triumphant indication that her resistless charm explained everything. He was no such fatuous fool! But, studying her, he got a solid assurance from the superiority of her person. Daniel would see at once that this wasn't the usual flight south of an indulgence headed for paresis. Savina, his entire affair, demanded a dignified reception. They were seated in the patio of the hotel, by a pool and the heroic bronze statue of a dancing girl in a manton; on the table between them was, at that hour, the inevitable small pitcher of Daiquiri cocktails. He told Savina what had been in his thoughts, and she nodded her approval:

"I agree that we ought to see your brother, and, through him, communicate with New York. At present things are much too uncertain. If William, or your wife, were different they could have us held on a very unpleasant-sounding charge. I know you detest conventions, but I must say I am glad other people live by them; it makes it so comfortable for us. Imagine, if William were a vulgar man, the fuss! But," she admitted, "at bottom I shouldn't have cared. You are not half as disreputable as I am, Lee. You have a proper look at this minute."

"Really," he protested, "there is no reason for you to be insulting, when I deliberately led you astray."

"You do flatter yourself," Savina replied; "when it was I all the time: I broke up your home."

"You needn't boast so loudly and pain everyone about us," he protested cheerfully. She gazed contemptuously at the surrounding tables:

"The scheming presidents of concessions and their fat wives. Have you noticed the men hurrying away apologetically in the evening, Lee? The places on Sol and Gloria Streets! And, just as you meant, if they knew who, what, we were, they'd want to have us arrested. You see, I am infringing on the privileges sacred to men. It's all right for them to do this, to go out to an appointment after ten o'clock and come back at two satisfied—"

"Savina," he interrupted her, "I know all that you were going to say, I could repeat it to you in your own words. You were about to assault the double standard. Consider it done. You are right. Everyone with sense is right there. But if I hear it again I'll think I am at Aeolian Hall listening to an English author lecture. I'll put you in your car on Forty-second Street and send you home."

"You can't send me home," she reminded him; "you are too proper and have too many scruples. You'll have to stay with me now for life. I am ruined." They laughed happily.

"You are," he echoed her.

"Isn't it nice?"

"Nothing better could be invented."

She investigated the pitcher. "The last drop."

Lee Randon signalled for the waiter, but she stopped him; the strained intensity of her face, the shining darkness of her eyes, set his heart pounding.

They left for Cobra without even the formality of a telegraphed announcement to Daniel Randon. Their compartment, in the middle of the car, with the more casual open accommodations at either end, resolute in its bare varnished coolness, indicated what degree of heat they might expect in the interior. The progress of the train through the length of the island was slow and irregular: Lee had a sense of insecure tracks, of an insufficient attention to details of transportation that required an endless, untiring oversight. Naturally they slept badly; and the morning showed them a wide plain scattered with royal palms which thickened in the distance. Such vast groves, Lee thought, robbed them of the stateliness so impressive in parks and cities. The landscape, tangled with lianas or open about massive and isolated ceiba trees, was without the luxuriance of color he had expected. It was evident that there had been no rain for a long period; and the crowded growths, grey rather than green, were monotonous, oppressive. Other than Apollinaris and the conventional black coffee of the train, and oranges bought by Lee at a junction, no breakfast was possible; and they watched uninterruptedly the leisurely passing land. Marks of sugar planting multiplied, the cane, often higher than Lee's head, was cut into sections by wide lanes; and announced by a sickly odor of fermentation, he saw, with a feeling of disappointment, the high corrugated iron sides of a grinding mill. It was without any saving picturesque quality; and the noise of its machinery, a heavy crushing rumble, was perceptible on the train.

However, Savina was attracted by the high carts, on two solid wheels, and drawn by four or six oxen, hauling the cut cane. But the villages they passed, single streets of unrelieved squalor in a dusty waste, they decided were immeasurably depressing. No one who could avoid it walked; lank men in broad straw hats and coat-like shirts rode meagre horses with the sheaths of long formidable blades slapping their miserable hides. Groups of fantastically saddled horses drooped their heads tied in the vicinity of a hands-breadth of shade by general stores. "I could burst into tears," Savina declared. But he showed her pastures of rich tufted grass with herds of well-conditioned cattle. "I wish we were there," she said. But, when the train stopped at Cobra, Savina, hesitating on the step, proposed that they go on into Camagüey, hardly more than an hour distant.

Their bags, put off, the rapid incomprehensible speech of the guard, left them, with the train moving doubtfully on, at Cobra. It was, on examination, more dismal than, from the detachment of the compartment, they had realized. The usual baked ground, the dusty underbrush, the blank façades of the low buildings that faced them from either side of the tracks, had—in addition to a supreme ugliness—an indefinably threatening air. The rawness, the machetes hanging about the booted heels of soiled idlers, the presence everywhere of negroes with an unrestrained curiosity in Lee and his companion, filled him with an instinctive antagonism. "Do you think that can be the hotel?" he asked, indicating a long plaster building with a shallow upper porch supported on iron-footed wooden columns. Above its closely-shuttered windows, in letters faded and blistered by the sun, reached the description, "Hotel de Cobra."

"We can't stay there," he continued decidedly; "I'll send for Daniel at once."

Without available help he carried their bags to the entrance of the hotel, and went into a darkened room with a cement floor which had the thick dampness of an interior saturated with spilled acid wine. There he found a man, not different from those outside, who, incapable of understanding English, managed to grasp the fact that Lee wished to see Daniel Randon immediately. The proprietor assented, and urged them up a stair. "I won't have you wait out here," Lee told Savina; "it will be only for an hour or so." The room into which they were ushered had, at least, the advantage of bareness: there was a wardrobe of mahogany leaning precariously forward, a double bed deeply sagged with a grey-white covering, a wash stand and tin basin and pitcher, and some short sturdy rush-bottomed chairs.

Its principal feature, however, was the blue paint that covered the walls, a blue of a particularly insistent shade which, in the solidity of its expanse, seemed to make all the enclosed space and objects livid. The tall shutters on one side, Lee discovered, opened on the upper porch and a prospect of the tracks beyond. "If I stayed here a night I'd be raving," Savina declared. "Lee, such a color! And the place, the people—did you notice that carriageful of black women that went by us along the street? There were only three, but they were so loosely fat that they filled every inch. Their faces were drenched with powder and you could see their revolting breasts through their muslin dresses; terrible creatures reeking with unspeakable cologne. They laughed at me, cursed us, I am sure."

"We'll have to put up with it till Daniel comes," he observed philosophically; and, on the low straight chairs, they gazed around so disgustedly that they both laughed. "I suppose he is out somewhere in the cane." Savina asked what they would do if he were away. He might be in Santiago. The company had other estates. "Not now," Lee decided; "what they call the grinding season has just begun, and every hour is important. The least thing gone wrong might cost thousands of dollars." The correctness of his assumption was upheld by an announcement unintelligible except for the comforting fact that Daniel was below.

"Perhaps I had better see him first," Lee suggested diplomatically, and Savina assented.

Daniel Randon was both tall and fat, a slow impressive bulk in white linen with a smooth impassive face and considering brown eyes. "This," he said unremarkably, "is a surprise. But I am, of course, glad; particularly since Venalez reported that Fanny was with you."

"She isn't," Lee replied tersely; there had been no cable from Eastlake, he saw, and he must plunge boldly into what he had to say. "I am sorry to tell you that she is at home. But I'm here, and not by myself." A slight expression of annoyance twitched at his brother's contained mouth. "No, you are making a mistake. I have left Fanny, Daniel. I thought perhaps you would have heard."

"Our telegraph system is undependable," was all that the other, the younger, Randon answered.

"You don't know, then. A Mrs. Grove is with me; but she is that only until the divorces can be arranged; and I counted on you—"

"Divorces?" The single word was accompanied by a faint lifting of Daniel's eyebrows.

"She was married, too," Lee explained. "You will understand better when you talk to Savina. We are not young feather-heads, Daniel; this is serious, final. Really, we came to Cuba on your account, to see you. When I tried to compose a telegram from Havana, telling you something of the situation, I couldn't—all the idiotic tourists hanging about! Well, here we are, or here I am, and Savina is upstairs, most anxious to meet you."

"Certainly," Daniel Randon agreed. He was silent for a moment in the consideration of what he had been told. Then, "I can't have you on the batey," he pronounced. He lifted a silencing hand against an anger forming in instant unmeasured speech. "Not for myself," he particularized. "You could have seven mistresses, of all colors, if the place were mine. Please remember that it isn't. It's the company's. That is quite different." Daniel was making, Lee realized, what for him was a tremendous conversational effort. "Even if I were alone, except for Cubans, it would be possible; but there is Mr. Stribling, with his wife and, at present, grown daughter, from Utica; he is the Assistant Administrador. Then we have George Vincent and Katharine—the Chief Engineer with a very new bride from, I believe, Ohio. They are very particular in Ohio. And others. You must remember that I have a photograph of Fanny with the children: it is much admired, well known. I couldn't explain your Mrs.—Mrs. Grove. Who could? We haven't a sister. Altogether I am sorry." He stopped uncompromisingly; yet, Lee recognized, in all that Daniel had said there was no word of criticism or gratuitous advice. He had voiced the facts only as they related to him; to everything else he gave the effect of a massive blankness.


Argument, Lee saw, was useless. Extended to the heart of a tropical island, the virtuous indignations of a hard propriety still bound their movements. "All that I can suggest," Daniel went on, "is that you return to Havana tomorrow evening; the company has offices there, and it will be easier for me to see you. Camagüey is nearer, but gossip there would have you in the same bed no matter how far apart your rooms were. Decidedly not Camagüey."

There was no train for Havana, it developed, before tomorrow. "And, in the meanwhile," Lee inquired, "must we stay here? Savina will be miserable."

"Why not?" Daniel gazed about casually. "I lived with Venalez a month. It is good enough if you are not too strict about a travelling beauty or two who may be stopping as well." His apologies to Savina, in the room above, were faultless. There was, simply, at the Cobra sugar estancia, no satisfactory arrangement for guests; except for an occasional party of directors, or a special mission, there were no guests. At his, Daniel's central, in Santa Clara on the sea, he hoped some day to offer them the hospitality of his own house.

When he left, Lee made no revelation of what had been said downstairs; Savina accepted the situation as it had been exposed to her. "I can't allow myself to think of a night here," she told him; "it will be a horror." She opened the slats of the long window shutters, and glowing bars of white heat fell in a ladder-like order across a blue wall; the segments of sunlight were as sharp and solid as incandescent metal. In the cobalt shadow Savina was robbed of her vitality; she seemed unreal; as she passed through the vivid projected rays of midday it appeared as though they must shine uninterruptedly through her body. Lee considered the advisability of taking her for a walk—there were, he had seen from the train, no roads here for driving—but, recalling the insolent staring and remarks she had met, he was forced to drop that possibility.

Weary from the prolonged wakefulness of the night, Savina made an effort to sleep; and, waiting until she was measurably quiet, Lee went out. The heat was blinding, it walled him in, pressed upon him with a feeling of suffocation, as though—between him and the freshness, the salvation, of any air—there were miles of it packed around him like grey cotton. To the left of the hotel, the bare plaza, half hidden in scrubby bushes, there was an extended shed with a number of doors and fragments of fence, heaped rusted tins and uncovered garbage; and, lounging in the openings, the door-frames often empty, the windows without sashes, were women, scantily covered, sounding every note in a scale from black to white. Yet, Lee observed, the whitest were, essentially, black. What amazed, disturbed, him was their indolent blinking indifference, their indecent imperviousness, in the full blaze of day.

They were, to Lee, significant, because from them he drew a knowledge of Cobra. He could not, without such assistance, have arrived at the instinctive understanding that interpreted the street into which he turned. It was the street of a delirium, running, perhaps, for half a mile; an irregular deeply rutted way formed by its double row of small unsubstantial buildings of raw or gaudily painted boards and galvanized sheet iron. They were all completely open at the front, with their remarkable contents, pandemoniums of merchandise, exposed upon a precarious sidewalk of uneven parallel boards elevated two or three feet above the road. Mostly cafés, restaurants, there was still an incredible number of banks—mere shells with flat tarred roofs and high counters built from wall to wall. The receivers, the paying tellers, were many, with the mingled bloods, the heterogeneous characteristics, of China and Colonial Spain and Africa; and, back of their activity—there was a constant rush of deposited money and semi-confidential discussion—were safes so ponderous and ancient that they might have contained the treasure of a plate fleet of Peru.

Crowding in on them, challenging each other from opposite sides, the restaurants were longer and shallow, with their groups of tables ranged against walls decorated in appallingly primitive and savage designs: palms like crawling spiders of verdigris set on columns of chocolate rose from shores, from seas, of liquid bright muds in which grotesque caricatures of men, barbarously clad or, swollen headed, in travesties of civilized garb, faced women with exaggerated and obscene anatomies. They, like the banks, were crowded; companies of negroes sat over dishes of mucous consistency and drank, with thick lips, liquors of vicious dyes. The prodigious women, often paler than the men, drinking with them, gabbled in a loud and corrupt Spanish and, without hats on their sere crinkled masses of hair, were unrestrained in displays of calculated or emotionally demented excitement.

A flat wagon passed, holding, on precarious chairs, a band furiously playing an infernal jumbled music which, as it swelled, filled all the occupants of the cafés with a twitching hysteria. Subdued masculine shouts were pierced by shameless feminine cries; lust and rage and nameless intoxications quivered like the perceptible films of hot dust on the air. Negroes, Haitians with the flattened skulls, the oily skin, of the Gold Coast, and Jamaicans glowing with a subcutaneous redness, thronged the sidewalks; and sharp-jawed men, with a burned indeterminate superiority of race, riding emaciated horses, added to the steel of their machetes revolvers strapped on their long thighs.

What, mainly, occupied Lee Randon was the nakedness of the passion everywhere surcharging the surface of life. There was, in the sense familiar to him, no restraint, no cover beyond the casual screens at the backs of the restaurants; no accident to which the uncertain material of life was subject was improbable; murder rasped, like the finger of death on wire strings, at the exasperated sensibilities of organisms exposed, without preparation, to an incomprehensible state of life a million years beyond their grasp. It fascinated and disturbed Lee: it had a definite interest, a meaning, for him. Was it to this that Savina had turned? Had the world only in the adherence to the duty typified by Fanny left such a morass as he saw about him? Was he, Lee Randon, instead of advancing, falling back into a past more remote than coherent speech? Nothing, he asserted, could be further from his intention and hope. Yet, without doubt, he was surrounded by the denial of order, of disciplined feeling; and, flatly, it terrified him.

Lee insisted, hastily, that what he wanted—no, demanded—was not this destruction of responsibility, a chaos, mentally and sensually, but the removal of it as a rigid mob imposition on the higher discretion of his individuality. The thing which, with Savina, he had assaulted was, in its way, as unfortunate as the single reeking street of Cobra. Again, the scene around him wasn't hypocritical, its intention was as thickly evident as the rice powder on the black sweating faces of the prostitutes. Hypocrisy was peculiarly the vice of civilization. His necessity was an escape from either fate—the defilement of a pandering to the flesh and the waste of a negation with neither courage nor rapture. Damn it, couldn't he be freed from one without falling into the other? Lee told himself that it must be possible to leave permanently the fenced roads of Eastlake for the high hills; it wasn't necessary to go down into the bottoms, the mire.

He regarded himself curiously as, to a large extent, the result of all the ages that had multiplied since the heated tropics held the early fecundity of human life. A Haitian lunged by with out-turned palms hanging at his knees, a loose jaw dropped on a livid gullet flecked with white, and a sultry inner consciousness no more than a germinal superstition visible in fixed blood—suffused eyes. He had an odor, Lee fantastically thought, of stale mud. Well—there he was and there was Lee Randon, and the difference between them was the sum of almost countless centuries of religions and states and sacrifice and slaughter He had a feeling that the accomplishment was ludicrously out of proportion to all that had gone into it. For the only thing of value, the security of a little knowledge, was still denied him. What, so tragically long ago, Africa begged from the mystery of night, from idols painted indifferently with ochre or blood, he was demanding from a power which had lost even the advantage of visibility. His superiority was negligible. It was confined relatively to unimportant things—such as an abstract conception of a universe partly solid and partly composed of ignited gases revolving in an infinity of time and space. He was aware of sensations, flavors, champagnes, more delicate than the brutality of a rape conceived in strangling gulps of sugar cane rum. On the outside he had been bleached, deodorized, made conformable with chairs rather than allowed to retain the proportions, powers, designed for the comfortable holding to branches. But in his heart, in what he thought of as his spirit, what had he gained, where—further than being temporarily with Savina in the beastly hotel of Cobra—was he?

His thoughts had become so inappropriate to his purpose, his presence, here that he banished them and returned to Savina. She was notably more cheerful than when he had left her, and was engaged with an omelet, rough bread, Scotch preserved strawberries, and a bottle of Marquis de Riscal; most of which, she told him, had been sent, together with other pleasant things, by Daniel Randon. She was unusually seductive in appearance, with, over the sheer embroidered beauty of her underclothes, her graceful silken knees, a floating unsubstantial wrap like crushed handfuls of lilacs. "This room kills anything I might put on," she replied to the expression of his pleasure. "After all, we shall soon be gone. I got Daniel's servant to telegraph the Inglaterra we were coming back. They'll have to watch out for us. After we see your brother here, and make a beginning of our rearrangements, we will go on, I think. Do you mind? South, Guadeloupe, perhaps, because it's so difficult to get to, and then Brazil. I have an idea we won't stay there long, either, but travel on toward the East. I do like islands, and there are quantities, quarts, to see in the Pacific." She put her arms, from which the wide sleeves fell back, around his neck, drew him close to her. "It doesn't matter where I am, if it is with you. I love you, Lee, and I am happy because I know we'll always have each other. We are not so very young, you see, and there isn't a great deal of time left, not enough to grow tired, to change in.

"I wake up at night, sometimes, with that tiresome pain at my heart, as though it were too full of you, and, for a little, I'm confused—it is all so strange. I think, for a moment, that I am still with William, and I can't imagine what has happened to the room. It frightens me dreadfully, and then I remember: it isn't William and the house on Sixty-sixth Street, but you, Lee, and Cuba. We're together with nothing in the world to spoil our joy. And, when we are old, we shall sit side by side at Etretat, I am sure, and watch the sea, and the young people in love under the gay marquees, and remember. Then we'll be married and more respectable than the weather-vanes. I want that on your account; I don't care; but you would worry, I am afraid. You are serious and a conscientious man, Lee.

"But, before that, I want to spend all my feeling, I don't want a thrill left, lost; I want to empty and exhaust myself." Her emotion was so strong that it drew her away from him, erect, with her bare arms reaching to their fullest quivering length. In the blue gloom of the room shuttered against the white day, with her wrap, the color of lilacs, lightly clasping her shoulders, she seemed to be a vision in subdued paint. Lee was held motionless, outside, by the fervor of an appeal to fate rather than to him. She was, the thought recurred to him, too slender, fragile, to contain such a passion. Then, in a transition so sudden that it bewildered him, her mouth was against his, her hands straining him to her. She was ugly then, her face was unrecognizable in an expression of paralysed fury.

The heat, Lee protested, grew worse with evening; not a stir of air brought out the dry scraping rustle of the palms, a sound like the friction of thin metal plates. The balcony, if possible, was worse than their room. In his irritation Lee cursed the scruples of his brother; Savina, prostrate on the bed, said nothing. At intervals her hand moved, waving a paper fan with a printed idyl from Boucher, given her in a café at Havana. She had none of the constrained modesty, the sense of discomfort at her own person, so dominating in Fanny. Lee finally lighted a lamp: the hours, until the precipitant onrush of night, seemed stationary; gigantic moths fluttered audibly about the illumination and along the dim ceiling. When, later, he was on the bed, it was wet under his sweating body. In a passing sleep Savina gave one of the cries of her waking emotion. In a state of unconsciousness her fingers reached toward him. From the balcony beyond them drifted a woman's challenging laughter—one of the travelling beauties Daniel had mentioned—and he could hear the bursts of discordant sound on the street of Cobra, the combined efforts of rival bands hideous singly and together beyond description. What a hell of a night, what a night in hell!

The moths, defrauded in their hunger for light, blundered softly around the walls; when Lee rose to light a cigarette they would, he felt, gather at the match and beat it out with their desirous wings. Then he heard a shot, and uplifted clamoring voices; all as unreal, as withdrawn, as a simulated murder on a distant stage. He pictured the flaring restaurants, the banks with corrugated iron locked across their fronts; the faces of the negroes brought black and lurid out of the surrounding blackness. Savina, awake, demanded a drink, and he held a clay water monkey awkwardly to her lips. The faint double blast of a steam signal rose at the back of the hotel, beyond the town; he had heard it before and now connected it with Daniel's sugar mill.

His brother hadn't perceptibly changed in fifteen years. During that time Lee had seen him scarcely at all. Suddenly he was sorry for this: Daniel was what was generally known as a strong man. Men deep in the national finances of their country spoke to Lee admiringly of him; it was conceded that he was a force. Lee wasn't interested in that—in his brother's ability, it might be, to grip an industry by the throat. He envied, speculated about, the younger man's calmness, the Chinese quality of his silence, the revelations of his carefully few words. Daniel, in past years, had been often drunk, various women had been seriously or lightly associated with his name; but he appeared to have cast them, the Bacardi and the blandishments, entirely aside. He seemed as superior to the dragging and wearing of life as a figure carved in stone, a Buddha, any Eastern presentment of the aloof contempt of a serene wisdom at the mountain of its own flesh. Lee, beside his brother, resembled a whirlpool of dust temporarily formed by the wind in a road.

Daniel had never married, he had been too cunning for that fragrant trap, as well. What were his vices? But were habits, self-indulgences, held in the background, ruthlessly subordinated to primary activity, vices? Lee wished now that Daniel had seen Cytherea; he was certain that the other would have said something valuable about her. Through his long contact with the naked tropics Daniel understood many things hidden from him. He must know, for instance, about the Brujeria, the negro magic brought through Haiti from the depths of Africa. Everyone in Cuba caught rumors, hints, of ceremonials of abject horror. But of that Daniel could never be brought to speak. Lee could even visualize him taking part, in a cold perverse curiosity, in the dances about smothered fires.

He thought there was a glimmer of day at the windows, but it was only a flash across his staring eyeballs. From the plaza below came a low sibilant conversation. It went on and on, until Lee, in an irrepressible indignation, went out on the balcony and, in a voice like the clapping of a broken iron bell, cursed the talkers into silence.

Christ, it was hot!

Savina was sitting up. "Isn't it tomorrow night, or the one after that?" she asked. "This room is like a vault that I have been in a thousand thousand years. I can't tell you how it affects me; it seems as though I must stay here forever, that if I tried to get away I'd be forced back. And I dreamed that everything I owned had been turned blue—my nightgowns and nail files and travelling clock and the oranges. You wouldn't believe how depressing a blue orange could be. We will forget it as soon as possible, Lee. Do you remember how nice the room was at the Inglaterra? I wish you'd feel my head: isn't it hotter than usual?"

"Why shouldn't it be?" he asked impolitely.

"It wouldn't be possible, would it, Lee, to have the night go on forever, to have something happen to the scheme of things? Or perhaps I'm blind." Her voice was plainly terrified. "Light a match, please. Oh, thank you. What an idiot I am. Hold me closer; then I can forget, then nothing else matters. I can never get close enough; I wish I could pour myself into you."

"You'll be able to, if this keeps up," he observed, with a note of brutality. "They will find us, in the morning, in a bowl and two pitchers."

But there was no corresponding lightness in his spirit; periods like this extended into an infinity of torment beyond time. A thinning of the dark expanded through the room. A cerulean unnatural dawn crept about him: there was the muffled clatter of horses' hoofs in the dust outside; a locomotive whistled in a far universal key. Savina slowly became visible; asleep, her personality, her vividness, were gone; she was as featureless, as pallid, as a nameless marble of remote Greece. There were marks across her feet where the mules chafed her; the mules themselves were lying on the bare floor. He saw his clothes, the familiar habit of the day, with a sharp surprise.


It had been a night without rest, without the coolness and assuagement of a release from the fever of the day; and, Lee thought, he felt as haggard as Savina looked. A wind that was hardly more than an erratic stirring of super-heated dust agitated a loose slat in a shutter and deposited a fine dun film across the floor. Savina put as much as possible, so early, into her bags. Standing before a narrow mirror nailed to a wall, with her comb, she turned. "My hair is soaked," she wailed; "just putting my arms up is more than I can manage. Haven't you been thinking about all the cold things in the world?" She slipped into a chair, spent and dejected, with her hair clouding one shoulder. It would, he repeated, be over soon, and he gazed at her with a veiled inspection. Savina was so entirely unprepared for this, the least hardship so new, that he was uncertain about the temper of her resistance.

Aware of his gaze, she smiled slowly at him, and, seated, again took up her task with the comb. "I couldn't have you see me very often like this," she proceeded: "it would be fatal. I don't mean that when I'm finished I'm irresistible, but the process simply must go on in private. I don't want to be a wife, Lee—one of those creatures in a dressing sacque with hair pins in her mouth. I can't bear the thought of you and a flannel petticoat together. That is where married women make a serious mistake: they let their husbands see them while the maid is doing their hair, or when they're smeared with creams, or, maybe, with tonsilitis." She rose. "I won't be a wife," she chanted, "I won't be—"

Her voice broke suddenly. Lee thought she had tripped, he lunged forward, but she fell crumpling on the floor. "It's this hellish heat," he asserted, lifting her to the bed. Her lips were open and dry, and her eyes, without vision, stared at the ceiling. Lee wet a handkerchief, dabbling it over her face; he had never before, he realized, seen a woman faint. It was terrifying but not grave; they did it, he had heard, very often. No wonder, after such a night. She had been gone over a minute now; there must be someone in the place who would know what to do. He put off moving, however, both because of his reluctance to leave Savina alone and because of the difficulty of any explanation. He took her hand; it was cold and damp, and her forehead was glistening with minute globes of sweat. All the blood seemed to have been withdrawn from her body.

"I'll have to go for help," he said aloud, in a commonplace manner which yet struck curiously on his hearing. There was a faint quiver of her features, a scarcely perceptible sigh, and her fingers weakly closed on his grasp. "How foolish," Savina murmured. She made an effort to raise herself up from the pillow, but he restrained her; Lee commanded her to be absolutely still. "The spirits of ammonia is in the dressing-case," she whispered. He held the clouding aromatic liquid to her mouth and she took it laboriously. "Don't call anyone, Lee," she continued; "I'll be all right in a little. So much at once! You see, I haven't been used to happiness. No wonder I was dizzy. But I fainted, Lee, didn't I? That's unusual for me."

He sat beside her, at once moved and detached from her weakness, gently holding her supine hand. She mustn't worry, he told her at short intervals. "Don't worry, this is nothing."

"You'll give me time to dress for the train," she insisted. "As soon as we get away from here I shall be better. We will, won't we?"

"Get away? What nonsense! Of course. You will be up by noon, but there is no good in your stirring before you have to. If Daniel comes, you can see him here, in your bed. Or you needn't see him at all. It's just as you feel."

Even as she lay, prostrate, on the bed, he could see her collapse; the strength, animation, interest, drained away from her; it seemed to Lee that momentarily she was again in a coma. He leaned over and placed a hand on her brow. Savina's eye-lids fluttered. Under her breast her heart was scarcely discernible. Suddenly he didn't like it; abruptly an apprehension, from which he was obliged to bar a breath of panic, possessed him. Lee covered her lightly with a sheet, and went out, softly closing the door. Before the hotel he caught the proprietor by a shoulder and pointed up to his room. "Sick, sick," he repeated the term with increasing emphasis, not successful in banishing his vagueness of dismay. The proprietor smiled uncertainly, edging from under the weight of Lee's hand. Then, "Get my brother, Mr. Daniel Randon, at once," he commanded; "soon. Mr. Randon; the sugar—" Lee waved in the direction of the mill.

This other again comprehended, and Lee saw a youth swing a bare leg over a convenient horse and vanish behind the Cobra Hotel. He went back to the room: Savina hadn't moved while he had been gone. She seemed even weaker—a thing he would have declared impossible—than before. He bathed her face and throat in water, and there was a murmur of gratitude, of love, so low that, with his ear against her lips, the individual words were lost. His disturbance increased and, when the heavy firm steps of Daniel Randon had approached on the cement of the corridor without, and he had knocked and entered, Lee pointed to the bed with an unconcealed anxiety.

Daniel bent over Savina with a comprehensive unmoved regard; he touched a cheek, with a surprising delicacy, and then turned and faced Lee. The latter said sharply, "She has fainted, but it's only the heat. She'll be all right after a rest." As he spoke, more to himself than to Daniel, in an effort of private encouragement, what confidence he had dissolved before his brother's impassive negation.

"It is more serious than that," Daniel Randon told him. "There is no doctor here we can trust, but I'll send a gas rail car into Camagüey for Fancett. It will take three hours or worse." He left promptly, closing the door soundlessly; and Lee heard his voice from the plaza, not raised but intolerantly domineering, issuing orders in a Spanish at once fluent and curt.

In the long-dragging succeeding period there was no visible change in Savina; at intervals she spoke faintly, there was the dim trace, the effort, of a smile; her hand, whenever he released it, slipped away. The heat in the room thickened; the barred sunlight cut like white knives at the opposite wall; a pungent odor of cooking peppers came in under the door. Savina's bags, nearly packed, stood open on chairs; the linen suit in which she travelled, the small hat and swathing brown veil, were ready by her low darkly polished tan shoes; gloves, still in their printed tissue paper, the comb, a small gold bag with an attached chased powder box, a handkerchief with a monogram in mauve, were gathered on the chest of drawers.

Lee had heard the rail car leave for Camagüey: there had been a series of short explosions, first scattered and then blending in a regular pulsation soon lost over the vanishing tracks. The interminable clip-clip of horses, dreary staccato voices, rose and fell, advanced and retreated, outside. But, through all his attentiveness to Savina, his crowding thoughts, he listened for the return of the car with the doctor. What was his name? Foster, Faucett—no, it was Fancett. An American, evidently. "The doctor is coming," he told Savina gently. "Daniel felt that he had better see you. From Camagüey. A good man. I want to get you out of here at once, and he will give us something." Waves of rebellion passed over him, an anger at his impotence, at the arbitrary removal of Savina from the sphere of his help. His coat was off, his collar unbuttoned, and he rolled up the sleeves of his shirt, wet with sweat and the bathing of her head.

To Lee, Savina appeared sunken; her cheeks, certainly, were hollower; there was a shadow, like the dust over the floor, in each one; she had ceased to open her eyes but they had retreated. A dreadful twenty-four, thirty, hours; how brutally hard it had been on her. She hadn't complained; he had been more upset, impatient, than Savina. What a splendid companion! But that, he irritably felt, was a cold word of description for her. What a force! She was that, magnificently, above everything else. Beside her, other people—the rest of life—were flat, tepid.

There was a thin far vibration which grew into a flowing throb; Lee identified it as the rail car. Perhaps the doctor had been absent. However, Daniel would know what to do. The footfalls approaching the door were multiplied: it was his brother and an elderly wasted man with a vermilion sprig of geranium in the lapel of a white coat. He nodded to Lee, pressed his hand, and went quickly to the bed. In the stillness while Dr. Fancett took Savina's pulse Lee again caught the shallow rapidity of her breathing. Daniel Randon stood with a broad planter's hat held with the lightness of touch characteristic of him. The man at the bed turned a speculative gaze upon Lee.

"Your wife has an acute dilatation of the heart," he pronounced. The significance of his unguarded tone shocked Lee immeasurably.

"But I don't understand that," Lee protested; "she has never had any serious trouble with her heart before." He was halted by Daniel's brief peculiar scrutiny. The doctor replied that this was not organic. "It may be the result of unaccustomed and excessive heat; an accumulation of the excessive," he added concisely. "Excesses." The single word followed after a hesitation in which Fancett was plainly at a loss. His frowning gaze

83

was still bent upon Lee. "I know so little of Mrs. Randon's history," he finally said. Daniel naturally had inferred, or perhaps the doctor deduced, that Savina and he were married. They would be, in a very short while, Lee told himself stubbornly. "You have ice on the batey? Yes, at once, please. And a nurse can come from my office on the Havana train this evening." Daniel nodded once, in acknowledgment. He moved closer to Lee:

"This is serious. You can't, of course, think of going on. I will see that she is as comfortable here as she would be with me; everything shall be done."

Lee answered that he was certain of that. A feeling of helplessness fastened on him, together with the incongruous speculation about the propriety of a cable to William Grove. The absurd idea occurred to him that Savina had two husbands; each with the right, if he desired, to be at a side of her bed, each holding one of her limp hands. He dismissed the elaborated thought in a rage at the triviality of his mind. Fancett and Daniel had gone temporarily: Lee had heard the former making arrangements to stay over night at the sugar estate. Savina's fast superficial breathing now dominated the room. He was again seated beside her, leaden-hearted and blank.

It was so useless—this illness and suffering, now! The doctor had seemed to insinuate that it might be traced to him, Lee Randon. What the devil did he mean by that? It was the fault of Daniel, the immobile, as much as anyone. In an airy room, under comfortable conditions, probably it wouldn't have happened. Savina's suit, her shoes, the bags, hadn't been disturbed. There was a faint tightening of her grasp, and he bent close, but he distinguished only random words.

"—not sorry. Willing ... with you. Don't be unhappy."

It required an enormous effort, the sound was at once all but imperceptible and burdened with an agony of labor. As he watched her he saw what, he thought, was an illusion—the blueness of the room, of the walls, seemed to settle on her countenance. It increased, her face was in tone with the color that had so disturbed her, a vitreous blue too intense for realization. He was startled: like a sponge, sopping up the atmosphere, she darkened. It was so brutal, so hideous, that he spoke involuntarily:

"No one can live blue like that."

Then, with a glance instinct with dread, he saw that he was right—Savina had died.

A calm of desperation swept over him. He must tell Daniel and the doctor. But they would still need the ice. The revolting details! And what had Fancett meant? It must all come out now—his presence in Cuba with Savina—in a storm of publicity and condemnation. He regretted this, because of Savina, dead. Alive she would have smiled her contempt; but death was different. Anyone would acknowledge that. The dead should be protected from slurs and scandal and obscene comments. A confusion of small facts poured through him, and broke into trivial fragments any single dignity of emotion; no generous sorrow saved him from the petty actuality of his situation; even his sense of loss, he realized dismayed, was dull.

Savina was rapidly growing, at last, cold; her arm was stiffening in the position in which he had left it; in a necessary forcible gentleness he composed her body. But he didn't hide her—not yet—with a sheet. That would follow soon enough. The blueness was receding, leaving her pinched, but white. She had always been pale.... By God, he had forgotten to tell them. Lee, stumbling down the stairs, found Daniel, the doctor, and the proprietor of the hotel, Venalez, talking together. As he approached there was a flash of premonition on his brother's broad unstirring face. Lee said humbly:

"She is dead."

Fancett, with Daniel Randon, went up at once, but he lingered, facing the Cuban. Venalez had a long brown countenance, with a disordered moustache. His trousers were thrust into the customary dingy boots, but his shirt was confined at the waist, and he had dispensed with a machete. He grew uneasy under Lee's stare, and shuffled his feet; then, behind a soiled thin hand, he coughed. It was clear that he wished intensely to escape, but was held by his conceptions of the obligations of conduct. "The suddenness—" Lee said, and then paused with a furrowed brow; "that's what surprises me. She was as well as you, and singing, yes—singing, that she didn't want to be a wife. I thought she had tripped on the loose silk thing she wore; and then I was certain that she had fainted from your heat." He bore heavily on the word your, and then proceeded to curse the atmosphere, in a heavy manner suggesting that it were a property, a condition, under the direction of the hotel proprietor. From that he proceeded to damn Utica and the state of Ohio.

"But you can't understand me," he added, illogically angry at that, too. Daniel was again at his side, speaking. "There is nothing for you to do here, and you may as well come to the batey with me. There are some accidents that cannot be provided against. This is one of them. She will be attended to; but you must explain about the cables."

"I had better get her things," Lee replied. He couldn't leave the delicate and beautiful trifles of Savina's living in the blue vault above. "They were scattered about the room." That, as well, Daniel assured him, had not been neglected. Her effects were to go over in the wagon with them. Lee, jolting on a springless contrivance over an informal road, kept his hand on the bags beside him. They were in Holland cases which hid the sets of initials ending in G. A revolver was shoved under the leather seat at the driver's left. There were the negro women, half naked, lounging in their doorways.

Telling himself that Savina was dead, he lingered over that term, at once so definite and obscure. There had been a pain in her heart at the Dos Hermanos, while they were having dinner, after the steamer, blazing with lights and with music on the upper deck, had swept out of the harbor. And, since then, at night, she had cried out. That, he had thought, was the expression of her consuming passion. He hadn't killed her; he would correct Fancett there. The doctor's glance, almost suspicious, had been intolerable. Savina had whispered to him, at the end, that she was sorry for nothing; she had begged him to be happy.

He roused himself and asked Daniel if they had far to go, and learned that they had almost reached the batey. Where, Lee added silently, Daniel wouldn't have us. It might well have saved Savina. The same ideas persisted in his mind. He wondered if, in the hurried packing, her handkerchief had been neglected? It was one of a number that Savina had bought in Havana. He had stayed outside, in the motor, smoking; and, when she had rejoined him, after a long wait, she had displayed her purchases. Her voice had been animated with pleasure at their reasonable price. Things small and unimportant! His brain worked mechanically, like a circling toy that had been tightly wound up and must continue until its spring was expanded.

The fundamental calamity was too close for any grasp of its tragic proportions: Savina dead was far more a set of unpredictable consequences than a personality. Alive she had drawn him into herself; she had, with her body, shut out the world of reality if not of mental query. Even the fervor of Cuba had seemed to pale before her burning spirit. What, without knowing it, Dr. Fancett had meant—a thing Lee himself had foreseen—was that Savina had killed herself, she had been consumed by her own flame. But she hadn't regretted it. That assurance, bequeathed to him in the very hush of death, was of massive importance. Nothing else mattered—she had been happy with him. At last, forgetful of the ending, he had brought her freedom from a life not different from a long dreary servitude. He would need to recall this, to remind himself of it, often in the years that would leadenly follow; for he must be regarded as a murderer—the man who, betraying William Grove, had debauched and killed his wife.

That, of course, was false; but what in the world that would judge, condemn, him wasn't? He had his memories, Savina's words. A sharper sense of deprivation stabbed at him. Why, she was gone; Savina was dead. Her arms would never again go around his neck. The marks of the mules across her narrow feet! He put out a shaking hand, and Daniel Randon met it, enveloped it, in a steady grasp that braced him against the lurching of the wagon.


On the veranda of Daniel Randon's house Lee sat pondering over his brother's emphatic disconnected sentences. "This conventionality, that you have been so severe with, is exceedingly useful. It's not too much to say indispensable. Under its cover a certain limited freedom is occasionally possible. And where women are concerned—" he evidently didn't think it necessary even to find words there. "The conventions, for example, stronger in William Grove than his feelings, saved the reputation of his wife; they kept Fanny alive and, with her heroic and instinctive pride, made it possible for you to go back to Eastlake. If you choose, of course. I can't enter into that. But, if you decide to return, you won't be supported by noble memories of your affair—was it of love or honor?—no, an admirable pretence must assist you. The other, if you will forgive me, is no more than the desire for a cheap publicity, a form of self-glorification. Expensive. The proper clothes, you see—invaluable! The body and the intentions underneath are separate. It is only the thoughtless, the hasty and the possessed who get them confused."

The veranda occupied all four sides of Daniel Randon's low, wide-roofed dwelling, continuous except for the break where an open passage led to a detached kitchen. Seated in an angle which might be expected to catch the first movement of the trade winds sweeping, together with night, from the sea, practically the whole of the batey was laid out before Lee. The sun was still apparent in a rayless diffusion above a horizon obliterated in smoke, a stationary cloud-like opacity only thinning where the buildings began: the objects in the foreground were sharp; but, as the distance increased, they were blurred as though seen through a swimming of the vision. The great bulk of the sugar mill, at the left, like—on the flatness of the land—a rectangular mountain shaken by a constant rumbling, was indistinct below, but the mirador lifted against the sky, the man there on look-out, were discernible. The mill, netted in railroad tracks, was further extended by the storage house for bagasse—the dry pulpy remnant of the crushed cane—and across its front stood a file of empty cars with high skeleton sides. There was a noisy backing and shifting of locomotives among the trains which, filled with sugar cane, reached in a double row out of sight.

The cars were severally hauled to the scales shed, weighed, and then shoved upon a section of track that, after they were chained, sharply tilted and discharged the loads into a pit from which the endless belt of a cane carrier wound into the invisible roller crushers. The heavy air was charged with the smooth oiled tumult of machinery, the blast whistles of varied signals, and the harshness of escaping steam. Other houses, smaller than Daniel's but for the rest resembling it, were strung along the open—the dwellings of the Assistant Administrador, the Chief Electrician, a Superintendent, and two or three more that Lee hadn't identified. He had been, now, nearly four weeks with Daniel, and the details of La Quinta, the procedure of the sugar, were generally familiar to him.

However, he had had very little opportunity to talk to his brother: the difficulties, in Cobra and Havana, of shipping Savina's body back to New York—William Grove, persuaded that it was unnecessary, hadn't come to Cuba; a fire in one of the out-lying colonias of the La Quinta estate, that had destroyed three caballerias of ratoon; the sheer tyranny of an intricate process which, for seven months in the year, was not allowed to pause, had kept Lee from any satisfactory communication of his feelings or convictions. But, at last, returning hot and fatigued from the clearing, by fire, of a tumba, Daniel had been sitting with him for more than an hour, and he showed no signs of immediate change or activity.

"What you say is clear enough," Lee Randon admitted; "and yet—but I can't see where—there is a sophistry in it." Daniel made a gesture both curt and indifferent. "I tell you it would be better, even at the destruction of the entire present world, to establish honesty. Since you have referred to me—what we, Savina and I, did was, simply, honest; but, again as you pointed out, its effect around us, for bad or very possibly good, was brought to nothing by the way it was drawn back into the victorious conspiring of sham. Even I don't know which, commendable or fatal, it was; I haven't been able to find out; I hadn't time. But Savina preferred the two weeks we had together to an infinity of the other. Fancett may call it an acute dilatation of the heart, but it was happiness that killed her. It's possible for me to say that because, fundamentally, I didn't bring it to her. Savina found it, created it, for herself. Through that time—was it long or short? The two weeks seemed a life—she was herself, superior."

"How about you?"

"I was absolutely contented," Lee replied.

"Isn't that a pale word for an act of passion?"

"Perhaps. It may be." A troubled expression settled over Lee's eyes. "There is something I should like to explain to you, Daniel, to ask you about, but it would take a great many words?" He cast this in the tone of a query, and palpably waited for the encouragement to proceed fully; but Daniel Randon was persistently non-committal. He had no intention, he said, of urging Lee to any speech he might later regret and wish unpronounced. "It's about my attitude toward Savina," Lee proceeded; "or it may be about a doll; I don't know. No, Savina and the doll weren't as distinct as you'd suppose; they were, in the beginning and at the end, one: Savina and Cytherea. That has given me some wretched hours; because, when it was over, I didn't miss Savina, I couldn't even call her individually back to my mind; and the inhumanity of that, the sheer ingratitude, was contemptible.

"I can explain it best by saying that Cytherea had always represented something unknown that I wanted, that always disturbed me and made me dissatisfied. She was more fascinating than any living woman; and her charm, what she seemed to hint at, to promise, filled me with the need to find it and have it for my own. That desire grew until it was stronger than anything else, it came between everything else and me and blinded me to all my life—to Fanny and the children and my companies. But, before I saw Cytherea, I was ready for her:

"Because of the conventions you uphold as being necessary to—to comfort, nothing greater. My life with Fanny had fallen into a succession of small wearing falsehoods, pretences. I had made a mistake in the choice of a career; and, instead of dropping that blunder, I spent my energy and time in holding it up, supporting it, assuring myself that it was necessary. The most I would acknowledge, even privately, was that, like the majority of men, I hated work. Like so many men I was certain that my home, my wife, were absorbing as possible. Wherever I looked, other lives were built of the same labored and flimsy materials. Mine was no worse; it was, actually, far better than most. But only better in degree, not in kind. It occupied about a fifth of my existence, and the rest was made up of hours, engagements, that were a total waste.

"At one time I had enjoyed them, I couldn't have thought of more splendid things; but the spirit of that period was not the same, and it was the spirit which made them desirable. I suppose that could be called my love for Fanny. I was glad to sit and discuss the hem of her skirt with her. It was enough just to be coming home to the house where she was waiting. I tell you, Daniel, my life then was transfigured. How long did it last—four years, six, eight? I can't be exact; but if I speak of its duration you will guess that it went. It went slowly, so slowly that for a long while I was ignorant of what was happening. It left in the vanishing of the little lubrications you insist are as needful for society as for your machinery. They began as lubrications, evasions, to keep the wheels turning smoothly, and they ended as grains of sand in the bearings.

"First there was Fanny's convention of modesty—it had been put into her before birth—which amounted to the secret idea that the reality of love was disgusting. She could endure it only when feeling swept her from her essential being. When that had passed she gathered her decency around her like Susanna surprised. Positively she had the look of a temporary betrayal. So that, you see, was hidden in a cloak of hypocrisy. Then she had the impracticable conviction that I existed solely in her, that she was a prism through which every feeling and thought I had must be deflected. Fanny didn't express this openly, it had too silly a sound, but underneath, savagely, she fought and schemed and lied—more conventions—for it. And, when the children were born, she was ready for them with such a mountain of pretty gestures and ideas that I gave them up: I couldn't fight their mother and the nurses and the maids in the kitchen—the whole bloody nice world. For one thing I wasn't home enough; when I got in for dinner they were either in bed or starched for their curtesies and kisses. They are superior children, Daniel; yet what they were taught to say sounds like the infantile sentimentalities of the stage."

The capataz of the batey gang, a tall flushed Jamaican negro, passed on a cantering white pony. The American wives, the flowers of Utica and Ohio, went by in light afternoon dresses, one propelling a baby in a cart. The Field Superintendent, lank and sun-dark under a green palmetto hat, wearing a grotesquely large revolver, saluted Daniel from the open. "Trouble at the cantina barracon," he called cheerfully.

"It was then," Lee specified, "that all my loose ends were gathered up in Cytherea. I have, I think, explained her. She was a doll, but it is more useful, now, to picture her as a principle. I didn't realize that at first: I took her to be an individual, the image of a happy personal fate that, somehow, I had missed, but might still catch up with.

"The wildest kind of a dream," Lee Randon proclaimed. "But when I became aware of Savina, or rather of her passion, I was sure I had been completely justified. She was, I believed, Cytherea. They looked alike. They were the same! However, I mistook that sameness. I can understand now, very clearly; it seems incredible that I had been so blind, so fatuous, Daniel. I actually thought that there was a choice, a special graciousness, existing and reserved for me." He laughed, not bitterly, but in a wonderment that bordered on dismay. "I felt that I had found it in Savina. I did get a lot there—more than I should have hoped for—but not precisely that. At last I know." His voice was grave, and he paused that Daniel might grasp the weight of what was to follow. "I had made the mistake of thinking that I, as an individual, had any importance. In my insane belief that a heavenly beauty, a celestial chorus girl, was kept for me, I pictured myself as an object of tender universal consideration."

"Damned anthropomorfic rot!

"It was a principle all the while," he cried; "a principle that would fill the sky, as vast as space; and ignorant, careless, of me, it was moving to its own end. And that—do you see, Daniel?—had grown destructive. It had begun differently, naturally, in the healthy fertility of animals and simple lives; but the conceit of men, men like me, had opposed and antagonized it. Magnifying our sensibilities, we had come to demand the dignity of separate immortalities. Separate worms! We thought that the vitality in us was for the warming of our own hearts and the seduction of our nerves. And so I left the safety of a species, of Fanny and children, for the barrenness of Cytherea.

"That's her secret, what she's forever smiling at—her power, through men's vanity, to conquer the earth. She's the reward of all our fineness and visions and pleasure, the idol of our supreme accomplishment: the privilege of escaping from slavery into impotence, the doubtful privilege of repaying the indignities of our birth." His rigid strained face was drenched with sweat. "We made her out of our longing and discontent, an idol of silk and gilt and perverse fingers, and put her above the other, above everything. She rewarded us, oh, yes—with promises of her loveliness. Why shouldn't she be lovely eternally in the dreams of men?

"Then, finally, Savina and Cytherea were merged again. In Savina her passion, always abnormal, hadn't been spent; there she was younger than the youngest girl I knew; incomparably more dangerous. She, too, had been constrained by the artificial, by conventionality; and when the moment of reality came it broke William Grove, Fanny, Helena and Gregory—all the threads that precariously held us. She was stronger than I, Savina was the goal and I was only the seeker—that was the difference between us—and in absorbing me she was content."

"That is very ingenious," Daniel told him. "Do you notice that the smoke is thicker in the east?"

"Not more in one direction than in another," Lee answered indirectly; "in the east and south, the north and west, up above and underneath. It's a good thing for our comfort that there's so much of it we can't see the fires. If the books of physics are to be credited, the center of the earth is liquid flame; certainly it is hot enough here to suggest something of the sort."

"It is worse in Oriente," Daniel informed him.

"What I have said," Lee Randon continued, "came from my remark, the one you disagreed with, about the need of an understanding everywhere! Isolated, in a chance individual like me, it is worse than useless, fatal. It destroys the support of a common cause with a humanity only less resentful than sentimental. And this has brought me to the reason why—in spite of her splendid proposal—I can't go back to Fanny: I have grown too detached to give her effort a possibility of success, of happiness for her."

"If you are so cursed abstract, you may as well be in Eastlake as at La Quinta," his brother asserted.

"Your saying that is curious," Lee replied, "for it is exactly what I told a man, in circumstances remarkably like my own, not long ago. I explained that life was all monotonously alike; and that, therefore, it didn't really matter where he changed to. I still think that most of it is inexcusable, perhaps hopeless, but I can't subscribe to it. What Fanny wants is contrition and the return to a time forever lost. I shouldn't be able to persuade her that I hadn't been in a temporary fever which, if she were sufficiently careful, would go and leave things very much as they were. That is her strength, her necessity, and she must uphold it until farthest old age and death."

Daniel Randon rose and went to the railing of the veranda, gazing intently into the hidden east. "You are right," he said, crediting Lee with a contention he hadn't made; "that is the refuse on Jagües."

"Helena and Gregory don't need me," Lee went on and on; "or, if you prefer—I am no longer afraid of words—I don't need them. I believe, in nature, that the length of paternity is measured by the helplessness of the young. An elephant is more devoted than a crow. My obligation was soon ended."

"Bring it down to this," Daniel's brevity was explicit: "what in the devil are you going to do?"

87

"I haven't any idea beyond the realization that I can't stay here taking up your room and Juan's time. It seems to me that for a month he has done nothing but concern himself with my comfort. I did, in Havana, while Savina was living, think of writing; but I have given it up because it would involve me in so much that is disagreeable. The amazing fact is that, since I have acquired a degree of wisdom, there is nothing for me to do, nowhere to go. The truth, I have always heard, will make you free; but for what, Daniel? What is it the truth will make you free for except to live in the solitude of public hatred? When I refuse, as I certainly shall, to return to Fanny the world where I might accomplish something will be closed to me.

"I could be a farmer if it weren't for the impossibility of my sleeping through the early part of the night; my hands are too stiff to learn a trade. I don't want to learn a trade!" he exclaimed. "And as for starting more stock companies, rolling greater quantities of refuse into cigarettes or bottling harmless colored water, or controlling a news sheet in the interest of my other interests—" he could think of no term sufficiently descriptive of his remoteness from all that. "I shall have to be what a universal Eastlake will prefer to call me. I'd stay here, at La Quinta, if you could find something for me to do—like picking the limes fresh for the Daiquiri cocktails. Do you think your company would carry me on its rolls for that? I could gather them in the morning and evening, when it was cooler. Thank God, I haven't any material ambition. I like the clothes, the life, of that nigger, the capataz, who rode by, as well as most. I'd sit up on the mirador and keep—what do you call it?—the veija, for months on end."

The servant, Juan, small and dark in his white house coat, appeared with a tray on which two glasses with stems held a fragrant amber liquid.

"That is perfection," Lee murmured; "where else could it be found? Advise me, Daniel," his voice was both light and serious. "You have never been known to give advice, but certainly my case is unusual enough to warrant extraordinary pains. Shall I make a neat hole at the proper point in my skull; or, better yet, put half a grain of a drug that will occur to you on my tongue and close my mouth on further indiscretions? That has its aspects. But not so strongly after one of Juan's drinks; they are distilled illusions, vain dreams still of hope. They have all the brave ring of accomplishment without its effort. But I can see the end even of them—atrophy. Soon Cytherea will go into the attic, have her nose broken, and the rats will eat the clothes from her indifferent body. Cytherea on a pearl shell in the Ionic Sea... I was one of her train, Daniel." He leaned sharply forward—

Daniel Randon was asleep.

CPSIA information can be obtained at www.ICGtesting.com
Printed in the USA
BVOW06s0837290816

460485BV00024B/233/P